ABOUT THE AUTHOR

Ros Barber is the author of two novels including the critically acclaimed and award-winning novel *The Marlowe Papers*. A Visiting Research Fellow at the University of Sussex, she is also a lecturer in Creative and Life Writing at Goldsmiths University and Director of Research at the Shakespearean Authorship Trust. She lives in Brighton, England.

PRAISE FOR *DEVOTION*

'Provocative… her lyrical touch is felt throughout, enlivening… a meditation on loss with beauty and even humour.'

Financial Times

'An enjoyable and engaging book… Barber's prose is compelling and she brings a real sympathy to Logan's character in particular.'

Independent

'Thoughtful, intelligent.'

Literary Review

'Intelligent, poetic writing… Barber weaves together the struggles of these complex characters with taut, high-stakes encounters in episodic chapters, making this a pacy novel in spite of the weighty subject matter; and barely a word is misplaced.'

Times Literary Review

'Compelling… Animated with fascinating, troubling ideas.'

Guardian

'Barber's sensational premise delivers an unexpectedly piercing exploration of loss and different kinds of faith.'

Kirkus

PRAISE FOR *THE MARLOWE PAPERS*

'A big, clever, vividly wrought work of conspiracy fiction, filled with impeccable but lightly worn research... sharp, concise, stunningly visual.'

Sunday Times

'Rich and charmingly playful... The thrill at reimagining the events and era comes through wave after wave in Barber's blank verse.'

Sunday Telegraph

'This terrifically accomplished and enjoyable novel/play/poem, call it what you like, restores one's faith in English fiction.'

Fay Weldon

'Enthralling... a work that combines historical erudition with a sharply satisfying read.'

Independent

'Packed with the kind of upper-echelon phrase-making that one expects from a poet of Barber's standing... as excitingly plotted as any thriller.'

Literary Review

'This is effortlessly better stuff than many far more trumpeted poets can produce, even on a good day... *The Marlowe Papers* is the best read, so far, this year.'

Sunday Express

'This highly ambitious debut makes for an engrossing read... brought to life by smatterings of exquisitely poetic descriptions and turns of phrase worthy of the Bard himself, whoever he was.'

Time Out

'A magnificently original novel... this is a marvellous reconstruction of a life, told beautifully... A truly superb achievement.'

Glasgow Herald

DEVOTION

Ros Barber

ONEWORLD

A Oneworld Book

First published in North America, Great Britain and the
Commonwealth by Oneworld Publications, 2015

This paperback edition published by Oneworld Publications, 2016

Copyright © Ros Barber 2015

ISBN 978-1-78074-921-1
ISBN 978-1-78074-729-3 (eBook)

Typeset by Tetragon, London
Printed and bound in Great Britain by Clays Ltd, St Ives plc

This is a work of fiction. While, as in all fiction, the literary
perceptions and insights are based on experience, all
names, characters, places, and incidents either are products
of the author's imagination or are used fictitiously.

Oneworld Publications
10 Bloomsbury Street
London WC1B 3SR
England

For my brother Peter,
whom I am finally allowing
to slip under the ice.

CONTENTS

PROLOGUE

Atheists

Bone-houses. Flesh-renters.

*Reeling down the High Street, swear-gobbers, spit-flobbers.
Dull-eyed beggar-dodgers, toddler-smackers, gum-droppers.*

*Watch them. Oblivious breathing machines. Coke-swiggers
and chip-munchers. Spouse-slaggers and wife-borers.*

*Bus-chasers. Tube-crammers. Rattle-throwers left to cry
all the way home at the knees of strap-hangers. Gummed up
slow, or lurching too fast in their kid-scarers: nose-pickers,
horn-thumpers.*

*Night brings its own brain-wasters. Packet-rustlers and plot-
spoilers. Street-drinkers and ear-botherers. Late-bar minidress-
totterers, naked-in-winters: rape-fodder pursued or steadied by
beer-breathers, curry-spewers.*

Where is God in all this?

*God is a tame swear word. God is a lame joke. God is unfath-
omable: disaster-monger, famine-seeder. OMG, God is a teen-
texted acronym. God is for nutters. For old ladies and nutters.*

– APRIL'S JOURNAL, 12 FEBRUARY

1.

BIOLOGY

Left

This is his punishment. This is the price of blundering into love. Logan must trundle around the insensible world, grief snapped into his wallet, loss in his suit, and pretend to live. Pour coffee down his gullet as if he can taste it. Pick at a plate of food as though nourishment mattered. Have normal conversations with normal people on normal subjects. As if he cared about films, or laws, or the weather.

His daughter's conception was a thoughtless act. A few minutes of drunken wrongdoing, succumbing to an urge to complete what he should never have begun. It was over with Rachel, whose insecurity had surfaced out of the deep pool of their lust sooner than expected; some brief weeks of buttock-gripping freedom dissolving into *Where were you*s and *Who was that*s. He became the stray tom she was trying to collar; had started to hook himself free on the chance branches of women who brushed across his path at work, or the squash club.

Why had he imagined he and Rachel could keep it casual? In retrospect the signs were as well marked as a national sporting event. In her childhood: benign neglect practised by middle-class divorcees, firm believers in the resilience of children, and determinedly oblivious to the havoc wreaked on a Daddy's girl by alternate weekend access. A part-time man would never be enough. Certainly she had claimed to desire only *a bit of fun*. But no surprise if that kicked-sore heart asked of every even half-kind man, *Are you The One?*

How could he have missed the signs? Unforgivable in a psychologist, even one whose clients are criminals. Yet he had missed them utterly, creating the inevitable moment when he must add himself to her catalogue of vanishing men; men who melted away as fast as snow on the hot hearth of her need for love. True, he had been young. Who is not a fool when they're twenty? Easy to imagine you are in control of a fling; that you can keep lust and love in their separate corners. Only later had he learned that while you are imagining sexual positions, she may be planning the furniture.

An error he'd had to correct. He'd not wanted to hurt her. So he'd drunk more whisky than was wise, but insufficient to incapacitate; gone late on a Friday to Rachel's sad lilac flat, decked out in its Tibetan singing bowls and dreamcatchers, to bruise her with the words *It's over*. Had said them with a cup of her sweetened chai in his hands, afraid to insist on what they had christened Normalitea in case the shared joke bound them more tightly together. And then, within a quartered hour, reassured by the words *It's safe*, he had made their bond permanent and parental.

What was to blame for the sowing of that unbearably precious life? As he left Rachel's arms that night, cursing himself for his weakness, oblivious to the creation of a new human being, he made a list.

- Rachel's tears. Expected, obvious, braced against. Yet still he'd felt unprepared for the full stomach sickness of watching so much water spill out of this woman at his simple utterance, a two-word curse he could easily lift.
- His mother. Who had taught him how to quiet a woman's sobbing through affectionate acquiescence: *Give Mummy a hug*.
- His biology. That persistently hopeful body part nodding into life, *Yes, yes*.

Stupid of him. Now how could he say it again? He'd have to detach more gently. Give her less of himself, until she was sick of his shadow and shooed him away. *Do the right thing, Finlay Logan; extract yourself slowly*. But six weeks later the cage came down: the pink window, and her insistence she would go ahead and *have the baby, no matter what.*

Oh, he'd wanted to blame her. Had added to his list:

- Rachel's forgetfulness. If that's what it was. Too busy chanting and meditating on life to prevent its creation by orderly contraception.
- Rachel's insecurity. The urge to own him, even as she felt him slipping away, unconsciously erasing *Take pill* from her mental To Dos.

But in his heart he knew it was his fault. How in wanting to make things better, he always managed to make things worse. There she'd stood, crying, and what could he do but hold her, stroke her hair? Not considering she would respond with strokes of her own. And how could he quash that response without being unkind, without shoving her bodily off love's kerb and back into tears? A chain of affection, like a series of small explosions, detonated desire; the passion stoked by the finding of something lost. Then they are stripping, kissing, fingers fumbling on catches and zips, and she has never been more ferocious, and before he knows it he is inside her again, thinking, *One last time, then, one last time.* Which she took as resolution. Which she took as retraction. What a mess. *You, Finlay Logan, are an idiot.*

But then his daughter arrived. And since he was banned from Rachel's home until the bloody water of the birthing pool had been sluiced away, the placenta buried beneath a patio rose, he experienced his daughter not as a mess, but as a miracle.

Flora. Extraordinary, wonderful, Flora. He only has to think her name and he is lost.

Tickets?
He finds his phone without thinking. Inside pocket. Waved at the sensor; returned. He can do so much without thinking now. Has

ordered and automated his life to float over this endless carpet
of grief without putting its feet down. Yet there are moments
that knock him against it, when he feels the sting of letting
existence rattle on despite this ever-present absence, sharp as a
friction burn. Today, across the carriage, a three-year-old, full
of her me-ness, clambers into the preoccupied lap of her father,
who, irritated, lumps her off again.

Do you not know how blessed you are? Do you not know—

The thought is caustic; he switches his gaze to the periscoping
countryside. His eyes skip along power lines, blur the palisades
of fences, trees, trees, trees – *breathe*. But he has touched it. The
effervescent green of the trees is an assault.

Train journeys leave the mind rattling loose in its cage. But
driving spooks him. Autonomous cars slink into your slipstream
and maintain their perfect metre: too close, to his old-fashioned
mind. And the way they lock on to you, mirror your every
twitch: he finds himself fighting paranoia. On longer routes,
great numbers will link up behind him, until he feels like he's
driving a train. He doesn't want to drive a train. He wants to
be alone.

No one sees the quiet tear from the eye closest to the window.

What to do, except pull up the file on his tablet? Work entices
the mind out of despair: *This way, this way.* The more he feels
the urge to sling a rope over the pulley on the garage ceiling,
the harder he works. Back to the realm where it is painless to
ask questions; where you may find answers.

Not yet, though. This case is new. April Smith, nineteen.
Named by a mother skittering on the skid-pan of her life: creator
of a girl – for she is barely a woman – whose name and face now
dominate the news. An unfathomable photograph, courtesy of
the police, who care to capture only height, build and distinguishing features. Standard procedures have robbed him of access to
anything deeper. Where he would read her – those small dark

green eyes – she is walled off, defiant. Violent, even. He wonders whether it's police policy to goad suspected perpetrators into looking culpable. Or simply the unconscious result of their certainty in the suspect's guilt: the certainty that is necessary for the arrest to occur in the first place.

Across the aisle, the father of the three-year-old has caught a glimpse of the photograph and is trying to read upside-down. *Bloody idiot*. Logan means himself but unwittingly speaks aloud and the man flinches. The file is confidential; he must move to first class and pay the extra should the guard return. Although Logan is thinner these last few months, he feels heavy. Bumping even momentarily into grief, his body grows sodden and sullen: blood thickens and slows, neurones clog with resistance. Effort is required to drag himself to the more comfortable seat where he can read alone.

April is saying nothing to anyone. Not even her defence team. But he has her diary. Opened at random, it is almost poetry… if poetry were hatred. But such contained hatred. Not the page-tearing, crossed-out scribbles of the enraged, the psychotic; no capitalized words, no vicious underscoring. Just a steady, girlish hand unleashing its controlled, cursive disgust. Another random page, and she is reporting a conversation with the Almighty.

Dear God, tell me through my left hand, what can I do with my anger?

Followed by a page of scrawl he cannot read.

It's getting rare to see something written by hand. Young people don't do that any more. They're on keyboards at six, manually illiterate by twelve. Even teenaged diarists use apps. An echo of something he said to, who was it?

He can feel Flora breaking through like a radio signal, some disturbance in the airwaves, a distress call, a sudden swell of mental

violins. He is being jolted against his will into the soundtrack
of a tragedy and he won't have it. He starts to hum – quietly,
wary of being heard – one note after another. The resultant
tune feels falsely jolly, deliberately trivial, a distracting melody
you might muddle through as you committed some white-collar
crime: fiddling the books, shuffling a justified claim to the end
of the pile. Flora goes away.

Back to the page of scrawl. Though he cannot read it, there
are words there. One of them looks like *explode*. It could be a
metaphor: *I'm so angry, I could just* – Handwriting experts will
be employed; transcripts produced. In the meantime, he must
read April: immured, uncooperative April. He stares again at
those frozen eyes. She isn't there. But in the diary she is vivid.
Only the left-hand portions, the portions where she is speaking
as God, are unreadable. Fitting, he thinks, for the Great Author
of the Mysterious. Speaks in tongues, writes in scribbles. The
rest is as neatly inscribed as any bright girl's homework. Daily,
for fifteen and a half months, she has emptied the contents of
her mind onto the page to produce this incriminating document.
To quell the baying of her demons? To order her thoughts? To
empty herself of pain? Or to justify her intentions: this astonishing, mouth-gaping crime? He swipes the notepad app, types
a lucid exploration of obsessive misanthropy.

He imagines April in a student study bedroom, lying on the
duvet on her stomach, inscribing her hatred with slow delibera-
tion. The summer has dragged its residue heat into early autumn
and a window is open; there is laughter outside. April records
it with a sneer. Through the breeze-block walls of the halls of
residence, a muffled gasp marks the crescendo of somebody
masturbating. April records that too.

> *Foul cynical onanist next door at it again*, she says.
> *Name of Rick, but he's more of a Dick. Ogled my tits*

> *while I scrubbed HIS burnt porridge out of my pan in*
> *the kitchen. Now wanking. Also fits. Dawkins fanatic.*
> *Arrogant atheist wanker asked if I wanted to join their*
> *Righteous Non-Believers' Society.*
>
> *Me: No.*
> *Dick: You're not a nutter, are you?*
> *Me: Just don't think Dawkins knew what he was*
> *talking about.*
> *Dick (to three other housemates): Nutter.*
> *General hilarity.*

For the next half-page, lying on her belly with a halo of sunlight, April catalogues all the lines she failed to deliver in the communal kitchen. She is acidic. She is logical. She is devastatingly clever. But in the kitchen, she was silent.

Rick is one of the dead.

Rick has joined his idol, Richard Dawkins, in the Great Nothingness to which he and his friends in the Righteous Non-Believers Society subscribed. One of the most popular societies at April's university, it seems to have been largely an excuse for the kind of nihilistic drinking which students have a long tradition of enjoying. But there was a serious core to it. In the decade since Dawkins's death, radical atheism has only grown in popularity, especially among the young.

Without his noticing, the train has come to a halt. A brief announcement: there will be a delay due to 'passenger trespass'.

A troublesome thought scuttles across his mind – briefly visible, then hidden in shadow – and as if in response, his phone vibrates on his nipple. The opening bars of Beethoven's Fifth: his wife. The choice of tune once amusing, now true: Jules is ever the harbinger of drama.

Finlay. You've had your phone off again. I was that close to
calling the police.

It isn't actually a crime, he replies. *And it wasn't off. Must have been the signal.*

I was watching the rail network website. There's a body on the line.

It isn't mine.

Her anxiety is a strategy for keeping him alive. She imagines her worry a thread that connects them and tugs him back to his responsibilities, insurance against his falling off the end of the world.

Clearly, clever man. Listen, Tom rang the house. He's had his mobile stolen, he couldn't remember your number. You're meeting him, yes? Later?

That was the plan.

Logan holds himself still, as one holds a door to stop it swaying in a strong wind. His wife is jittery.

He told me to tell you seven o'clock in the Battle of Trafalgar. Your kind of place, he said. Just up from the station. You can't text him because—

He's had his mobile stolen. You said. You believe that?

In his own head, he is clear: the story is a convenient way for his son to avoid meeting him on campus. God knows what Tom has said to his friends in the beer-soaked confessions so common among bonding freshers. *My father abandoned me when I was two. My father is an arsehole.* Whatever Tom has said, his father's turning up in person among them is now too embarrassing to contemplate. They'd agreed he would text when this meeting with Dr Salmon was over, and Tom would reply with directions to his halls of residence, but now it was to be a quick half by the station and Dad safely back on the train with none of his new mates any the wiser.

Jules has paused long enough to let him know she has considered the matter.

Tom's flaky, Fin, but he's not a liar. Are you—?

I'm fine.

He reads her disbelief in the silence. She is better equipped than the women of his past. With Rachel, with Johanna, where the dialogue would continue, *You don't sound fine*, followed by increased irritation on both sides, Jules knows that *I'm fine* is a closed portcullis, and that attempting to storm it will only lead to his unleashing the boiling oil. Even when his carriage is empty, he can no more be drawn into personal discussions on public transport than he would run naked through Tesco's. Jules's understanding of the portcullis is the reason she's his wife.

Call me when you're close to home, she says. *I'll come and pick you up. Did you get some lunch?*

When he's done with the pleasantries Jules requires to reassure herself he will not, any time today, become the cause of major transport delays on the Southeast rail network, he opens the diary again.

More God. A great deal about God. It is not his area of expertise. He was raised in the pretence of Christianity by parents who understood the practical benefits of Sunday School. To be found in church themselves only for christenings, weddings and funerals, they nevertheless appreciated the *grounding in morality* that a general familiarity with the Bible might distil. He remembers the Reverend Holinshead once giving him a chocolate digestive. He remembers the story of the Good Samaritan, colouring a lot of pictures of bearded people, making stiff leafy crosses for Palm Sunday, little else. Religion was a web of fables decorated with a weekly dose of singing and praying. But God – whatever that is – was not something he experienced. Nothing that might inspire *awe* occurred, if you exclude (and he had tried) the unholy view of the vicar's young and miniskirted wife bending over to pick up crayons. He can only have been six, seven, but he felt stirrings. Perhaps his later sexual appetites might be blamed on that far-too-early awakening, so that all his sins might be traced back to the revelation of Abigail Holinshead's untouchable buttocks. His inability to stay with Rachel – the very seed of Flora's creation – or Johanna – the source of Tom's fury. *Ask and it shall be given you*, Mrs Holinshead had whispered as she returned crayon after crayon to his pudgy hand. So perhaps he had asked for it. Nevertheless the young woman's misjudged combination of apparel and motion had influenced him more profoundly than any nugget of religious instruction. God was simply a word, and the more copiously it was defined the more thoroughly it slipped his understanding. God the creator. God the Father, Son and Holy Ghost. God is love. What could any of it mean? The concept was nebulous, unknowable.

April's God is very real to her. She seeks His guidance and He is free with it. She issues Him instructions and He responds. They are pen pals. Every other page, *Tell me through my left hand*, and off He goes, spilling His incomprehensible guts as volubly as she spills hers on the pages in between. Logan feels a spike of jealousy. He longs for the comfort of being immersed in such a delusion. Is aware how pain might dissolve in the knowledge of an omniscient, omnipotent being who is both listening and responding, even if you have imagined that being into reality.

He will have a good chance, he thinks, of proving that this young woman's religious convictions are a form of psychosis. He told Jules as much at breakfast, in answer to one of the questions she is routinely asking him these days, attempting to break into the Work cell where he is sheltering from his feelings.

You'll be their champion, she said, jabbing a finger at the morning headline.

Surely not. People want the girl banged up for life. Properly punished. If she's declared insane—

I think they'll be rather happy about it. They're calling for religious fundamentalism to be reclassified as a form of mental illness.

Who's They? The media?

Everyone.

He sighed. *Religious leaders?*

Well, no. It doesn't say—

Mental health organizations?

Don't be pedantic, Finlay. You know what I mean.

You mean some people. You don't mean everyone.

She buttered her toast as though she were combing out a child's tangles.

There's an editorial about it. The other papers are on it too. And politicians. There were questions in the House yesterday. You can see for yourself.

One unthinking hand launched the tablet into the channel of naked oak between them. It came to rest against the buoy of the marmalade pot.

He had been unable to read the news or listen to radio bulletins since Flora. He stayed clear of the television. There was always the danger that some story would leap out and barge him, bodily, against the wall of his emotions, smacking its knuckles into his skull. Yet hovering at a station kiosk for a bitter Americano, or failing to mute the kitchen radio at the top of the hour, he could still be ambushed. *Four children have died in a house fire in Huddersfield – A toddler, battered to death by her stepfather – The police have confirmed that the body found in woods near Northampton is that of missing teenager –* On public transport, his compulsion to read any text set in front of his eyes makes the free tabloids that commuters shake into his line of sight a menace. The unavoidable front page headline: *Calls Grow to Recognize 'God-Madness' After Bus Girl Massacre.* April's was the third religiously inspired atrocity since Easter.

I don't need to see, he said.

Jules eyed him with the scrutiny of a woman used to filing emotional stability assessments.

The Minister for Justice has said there'll be an inquiry. After the trial.

That would be the time for it, he said quietly.

With her only non-buttery finger, she wheeled the tablet back towards her. Reading aloud: *We must ask whether, in our rational age, we should any longer tolerate extreme and unsupported belief in some higher force. Especially when such beliefs lead to acts of incomprehensible violence.* Prodding him for emotion as a child pokes a worm to confirm it's alive.

Not all religious fundamentalists are psychotic, he said. *And one can be psychotic without committing murder.*

She nodded, pleased with her result. *Yet it happens often enough,* she said, *that most psychotics are kept on strong pharmaceuticals and under close supervision.*

Again, not all religious fundamentalists are psychotic.

Example?

Nanna Logan.

His father's mother, who preached Hell's tortures for non-believers but was only a danger to others when she insisted on cooking after the onset of Alzheimer's.

Jules's smile said, *You lose.*

I met your Nanna Logan.

Hardly psychotic, he insisted.

His wife chewed and swallowed a mouthful of toast.

That's debatable.

The train trundles and lurches into motion. In due course, he will speak on the matter in court, in his best psychologist's voice, wearing a suit appropriate to an Expert Witness, knowing his opinion is likely to have material consequences for the growing campaign to have religious fundamentalism contained and treated. His words will spool out from the stenographer's fingers, into newspaper editorial columns and across the internet. They will send one young woman to a secure mental unit, or alternatively to be endlessly punched, kicked and spat upon in a regular prison. They may be transmuted into words on the statute books; they may become part of the reason why this or that person is prescribed (or not prescribed) this or that treatment. They could be the most powerful words he has ever uttered, more powerful even than *It's over*, which contained enough emotional force to forge the most beautiful human being he has ever known.

Something the size and texture of an unripened plum materializes in his throat.

The problem is, he's not sure he's that far from crazy himself.

If religious fundamentalism is a form of mental illness, what about grief? For surely, one as much as the other will drive a person to insensible acts. In this last week alone he has entered a toilet cubicle purely for the relief of banging his head repeatedly against the door of it. He abandoned a week's worth of shopping in its trolley and wandered into the car park in oblivious tears, because a passing shopper happened to laugh when he thought the word 'glue'.

Why? He was in the stationery section to get some wrapping paper at his wife's request and had noticed the glue; had remembered Flora's Birkenstock sandals abandoned under the sofa from her last visit because a toe-loop had broken free, thought 'glue' and was about to reach for it before he remembered that her feet were ash, the Birkenstocks binned, and the house they were left in sold. A shopper beside him burst into scornful laughter. Navigating through tears the perfunctory briskness of the checkouts, and without groceries whose absence he would have to explain, he reasoned to himself that the stationery aisle was also the magazine aisle; that the shopper had most likely been provoked by the unkind cover of a celebrity-scouring weekly zooming in on some former beauty's cellulite or plastic surgery scars. But the reason was immaterial. The seemingly random collision of thought and laugh had catapulted him into astonished pain. His daughter had died afresh, and he was profoundly, scorchingly alone. Is still alone.

Because no one can understand what he has lost. Because he cannot tell them. The words would destroy him. He needs some kind of counsel. But because he must remain professional to those in his profession, even the one he pays to listen to him, he must counsel himself. Like now, riding the tenuous curve of a viaduct, the outskirts of the town ruffling with traffic beneath him.

What was she called, your daughter?

Flora, he says to himself. She was called Flora.

What happened, then, to this daughter called Flora?

She blew away on the wind. She was very light. She was a dandelion seed.

Where did she go, this Flora-dandelion? Where did she blow to?

To the four corners. To the peaks and troughs. To the hills and the valleys, the seas and the sounds. Where she can be always here, always gone. Lodged in the crack of your heart. Tucked in the fold of your eye.

Hole

Moving to the New Forest had been his wife's idea. How could she feel useful to a man who cried silently into the butter at the breakfast table? Who, since his daughter's death, lay flat and unresponsive as a piece of cold toast in their marriage bed? Who considered work, not wife, his sole salvation? She would move him.

Not emotionally, *Lord save us from the pull of the impossible.* But physically, out of the anchored location of memories that followed him round like statically charged apparitions. Flora's favoured kitchen chair which no longer rocked onto its back legs against his irritated exhortation; the two crescent-shaped holes in the lino mirroring her grin as she ignored him. Flora floating down the stairs in a backless dress, turning, *Don't be soppy, Daddy.* Flora on the hall phone, twisting its old-fashioned umbilicus around her fingers, swaying to the music of her blood, calling her invisible boyfriend an *adorable arsehole*.

Logan was chained to these memories as a human sacrifice is chained, waiting for the dragon to devour him. Time flowed on around him, without him: he remained with the boulder. The lives of others moved on; the sense that his had stopped was palpable. It is a commonplace that time slows for a kettle's boil, worm-crawls during an anxious wait, creeps snail-like towards an execution. But when a parent loses a child, time simply breaks. Severed the moment he learned of Flora's death, his thread of time had separated from the world's. His wife, his friends, his colleagues, continued to be dragged forward into a future he could not envisage. Logan was left where he was, experiencing time only as an eddy created by other people's wakes. Clocks continued in their business without him. The moon orbited and the earth spun, and Logan stayed exactly in the second he learned of his daughter's death.

He told Jules none of this. He had no way of describing it. And as the days passed, with her in them and him outside of them, their separation grew. But Jules was a qualified social worker. She had been awarded a distinction for her dissertation on grief. And she discerned in him a growing morbidity.

So, though he barely registered the process, she attained his careless assent to a series of questions. As devoid as he was of any appetite for living, the easiest route through any day was to murmur *Yes*; she left him alone sooner, he discovered, than if he said *I don't know*. Legally speaking, he now recognized, he was *not of sound mind*. The only consequence he had desired was for Jules to stop asking him things. But from his initial assent, the questions just became more numerous and trivial. Was this house better than that house? Was this conservatory too ugly? What about the Brockenhurst house? Was he bothered by the absence of a mains gas supply?

How could any of this matter when Flora, beautiful, astonishing, Flora—

◘   ◘   ◘

An absence, a whooshing of air. Restraining straps loose, flapping in a violent draught. The cargo doors open. Whatever was here has just gone.

Whatever you think, he said. *Don't ask me any more.*

Now he found himself on Saturday mornings padding through tracks in the forest with the new dog she had also arranged because, she said, it would *get them out. Dog owners*, she said, *chat to each other. It will help us integrate.* Not acknowledging that integration was beyond him; that despite the move, perhaps partially because of the move, he was disintegrating even faster than in London. Flora's ghosts were smoking angrily on the back step, refusing to come in because it was *hers*, Jules's; they were swearing under his breath, *It's a bit fucking green, isn't it?* These were the Floras he was making up to fill her absence. He knew the real Flora was in London, disintegrating herself as the new owners stripped the staircase back to bare wood, replaced the kitchen lino with modern flagstones. Her favoured chair had been eBayed. Even now, Flora's last skin cells were being damp-clothed from windowsills.

The Floras he invented to keep him company were fractious, resentful. *There's nothing to do round here.* A six-year-old Flora: *But I want to go to our playground. The one with the rocking lion. We're miles away, Daddy, MILES AWAY.*

Work was also, dangerously, miles away. He could write reports at home but the longer journeys to his London office left his head trespassing on the shoulders of strangers, his mind accidentally boarding trains of thought that were hurtling, driverless, into the dark.

Jules was left to steer them through a pretended normality. She would pick him up from the station on a stream of chatter that gave misery no elbow room and drive him overcautiously back to the place she insisted was *home*. In his head, it was still The Brockenhurst House. London was home and he'd given his key to a stranger. The Brockenhurst House, wood inside, wood out, pine, ash and oak, smelt like a coffin. It was the place Flora wasn't, and hadn't ever been. The name of the village – had Jules not noticed: *broken, hearse?* – was the only quiet echo of his loss.

It was a family house without a family. They had a second reception and received no one. They had four bedrooms when they would only sleep in one; two if they argued. There was a bathroom each and one for the cat.

When he noticed the pulley the previous owner erected for hoisting their canoe out of the way in the garage, his ears began ringing. They rang as loudly as the TV stations of his childhood sang after shutdown; the same note, the note you'd wake to. This house could be the end of him.

When night fell, you knew it. No protective sodium glow to dim the pitiless shining of stars, the same points of light that had glittered over breathing, digesting, dinosaurs.

I am completely alone, he said to himself in bed.

His wife clicked her teeth beside him.

I am alone. As a heart is alone. As a knife in a heart is alone.

I am alone. As a tongue is alone. As a tongue on the seabed's alone.

I am alone. As a stone is alone. As a stone in the air is alone.

— APRIL'S JOURNAL, 20 MARCH

There's a pinhead of light in her eye. A deliberate nothing. A blank that she dares you to read. What is she thinking? A full stop with no words ahead of it. Or three: an ellipsis, three dots to mark the moment we can only imagine.

She entered the bus…

April. You entered the bus…

He waits, but she doesn't complete it. Her hair is folded over her right eye like a pirate's patch with the help of a frog-shaped clip. Though she is nearly twenty, half of her is twelve.

The other half is God. The Old Testament God, returning sinners to their maker to be remade. A silent God that isn't in, doesn't answer to prayer or special pleading. A God whom she operates through her left hand; her own sock-puppet deity.

April, I'm not the police. I want to help you, not prosecute you. I want to understand. I want to help.

I, she says. *I, I, I.*

Mocking him. This isn't about you, mister. This is about me. But she spoke. Only a vowel. Yet it's something.

He starts again.

When were you born?

Her eyes assault him with a violent impatience.

April, he says.

Her face mimes stupidity; the shape that says, *Duh*.

Are you Aries or Taurus? You believe in star signs?

Her eyes flick to where a window would be, were this anything other than the interview room of a secure psychiatric unit.

He doesn't believe in star signs. He knows some young people do. That especially for misfits like April, horoscopes can look like chapters from life's missing instruction manual.

You believe in God, I know that. He will continue his side of the conversation for as long as it takes. *We all know that. But I know more, April, about your relationship with God. I've read your journal.*

A flinch. Then the heart-holding stillness of a creature who has given its position away to a predator.

God talks to you, yes?

Her gaze turns in on itself. He suspects she is listening to Him now. And He is saying, in April's journal voice, *Keep shtum, April. Don't let the bastard psychologist crack your nut open.*

Logan refills his glass with water.

Your silence might be seen as incriminating. Not by me. By the police. By the Crown Prosecution Service.

She shrugs.

What did you mean, as a stone in the air is alone? How is it in the air? You mean it's falling?

She floats her eyes to the ceiling, pushes herself back, chair and all, with a violent squeak, and begins to bang her head against the wall, rhythmically, deliberately.

When he was a baby, he is told, he did this. He doesn't know why, and doesn't remember it. His parents didn't know why either, but they told him the story more than once. How they bought a piece of yellow foam rubber from a market stall and glued it onto the headboard of his cot. How, by the time he was two, he had worn a hole in it.

You can't save her, Jules said, stirring the bolognese.

He tugged his tie from his throat, draped it over a chair like road kill: flattened, finished.

You can't save her if she won't save herself. If she won't even talk. What do you have to go on? You can't prove she's insane, only uncooperative. Maybe she wants to be convicted of murder. Maybe it suits her plans.

As always, he wished he'd said nothing. He knows this is her way of trying to connect with him: follow him to the place he has retreated to, his work. But he doesn't want her there.

I'm not sure she has *plans*, he said.

You can't be sure of anything if she won't talk.

It's early days, he said. *I have a few sessions with her yet. And it's not just assessment, either. I have an idea.*

He had no intention of sharing the idea, so he laid the table. When he'd finished, Jules, who insists on making fresh spaghetti, was turning the handle of the pasta maker. Addressing herself to the unwinding worms: *I really hope this isn't about Flora.*

A surge of emotion, so wild that at first he had trouble naming it. Breathe, Logan, breathe.

How would it be about Flora? And in his head, *Please, God, don't use her name.*

She pulled the last worms out of the contraption, slid them from the bowl into boiling water.

You're the psychologist, she said.

Salmon

I've an appointment with Dr Salmon.

He shakes the rain off his coat, folds it over his arm. He is given a visitor's badge, a smile.

The receptionist is overfamiliar with faculty. She conspires with the telephone: *Gabrielle, Dr Logan is here.* As if they have been gossiping about him. He doesn't like that she is on first-name terms with Dr Salmon.

The Alterman Centre is new. It has new funding, new logos and letterheads. A new smell, mildly tainted with ammonia, as though it is a film set made freshly for his appearance and some of the fixtures are held in place with craft glue. The designer has plumped for a contemporary blandness of grey and white. The waiting-area chairs, in which Logan is strongly directed to *SIT*, are black faux leather and low to the ground. Since the angles inherent in arse-lower-than-knee prevent a person rising with any dignity, he ignores the receptionist's imperative and stands. He pretends he is doing so to read the posters – and then finds himself reading the posters, which have recently migrated from a public exhibition associated with the International Conference of Consciousness Studies.

For many years the study of consciousness was not con-sidered a respectable scientific discipline. Consciousness was a realm reserved for philosophers and mystics, and deemed outside the remit of scientific investigation. In recent years, however, scientists have begun exploring the phenomenon of human consciousness through a number of different approaches. Scientists at the Alterman Centre have been active in studying Near Death Experiences (NDEs), recollections by patients of events that occurred when they were clinically dead, and have demonstrated the inadequacy of existing psychological, physiological and pharmacological explanations. Though original theories of a 'God-spot' have proved oversimplistic, research into Religious, Spiritual and Mystical Experiences (RSMEs) has successfully reproduced them through a complex pattern of electrical stimulation to multiple areas of the brain, driven partially by subjective biofeedback. In other research, creation of holographic—

Dr Logan?

Turning round to face a beautiful woman, Logan knows he should have prepared more thoroughly. A simple internet search would have furnished him with an image and given him time to mount appropriate defences. He hadn't for a moment imagined anyone named Dr Salmon might be so generously lipped, so exquisitely cheekboned, such a confident inhabiter of eyes he is in imminent danger of falling into. Her hair is at least swept back into a bun, naturally brown (he guesses) but tinged with a deliberately exotic red tint, and a rebellious strand has broken free to frame her face. He needs a moment to reorient himself from his dowdy assumptions, a deep breath to flush out the instant fizzing in his groin.

Dr Salmon. Thank you for meeting me.

Happy to help, she says, her voice playing the melody of the words away from platitude and into an amused assessment of his surprise. *Coffee, yes?*

Coffee, yes. Bed, yes. Anything you ask, yes. He shakes himself as he follows her out of the building via a long corridor and seamlessly into another, he like a dog with a tick in his ear, attempting to dislodge his animal response and return to being Dr Finlay Logan.

She helps him, once they are ensconced with their cups at a table, with some verbal efficiency.

You've read my paper? 'Creating God in the Human Brain'?

Its full title was 'Creating God in the Human Brain: RSMEs and Pulsed Transcranial Stimulation'.

That's why I'm here.

He had read most of it, though when he crashed into mathematics two-thirds of the way through, he had skipped to the conclusion. The statistics he'd been forced to pick up for his degree had been hard learned and effortlessly forgotten; his brain now ceased to function if it encountered any kind of maths that involved Greek letters. The conclusion of her paper had been enough. He offers her a précis.

As I understand it you've used some kind of electrical stimulation of the brain to produce quasi-spiritual experiences in a number of subjects?

Her eyes drop; she seems about to have a side-conversation with the froth on her coffee.

I'm not keen on the term 'quasi-spiritual', she says, before re-engaging.

I'm fairly sure you used that term yourself. In the article.

She glances over to the door, pushed open by a sizeable student nodding to the beat of his headphones. Then back to Logan.

The editor added the quasi. Necessary to pass peer review. I find it rather sneery.

Sneery?

You don't perceive it as such? Interesting. Armed with that information, do you realize I can immediately ascertain your position on the human soul? She skewers him with her eye. Tears a packet of brown sugar as though wringing the neck of a tiny paper chicken; dumps the contents into her coffee. Or rather *onto*, since the grains make a small glittery, taupe-coloured pile on her froth.

I'm surprised to hear a scientist even using the phrase 'human soul', he says. *You* are *a scientist, aren't you?*

I'm a scientist of RSMEs, she says. *It tends to come up in our work. It's the human soul that's under the scalpel.*

Well, I'm not sure I have a position on it.

That's the position I determined. Agnostic at the minimum.

Logan has begun to think about the price of his train ticket, the hours of travelling. She is young, this Dr Salmon, and perhaps not quite as serious an academic as he had imagined.

You think you invoked actual *spiritual experiences?*

She laughs.

Do you know what an actual *spiritual experience is, Dr Logan?*

I've never had one, if that's what you're asking.

The pile of sugar grains is sinking, beyond saving. She stirs it casually into the brew.

No, that's not what I'm asking. Obviously if you'd had one you wouldn't be agnostic. I mean, from a scientific perspective, how would you tell one from the other? In brain activity terms – at least with the sensitivity levels of our current equipment – I can tell you they are indistinguishable. And as far as my subjects are concerned, in experiential terms also.

So God is an illusion conjured by a pattern of firing in our brains?

She appears to be studying him. Under her gaze he feels a little like an intelligent chimpanzee, but continues, *If you can show this conclusively, it's a triumph for atheism.*

That's only one way of reading it, she says. *I'm guessing you're not up to speed with the work that goes on at the Alterman Centre.*

Fill me in.

She looks ready to hand him a banana.

The public perception of neuroscience is that it's there to back the materialist worldview. By which I mean, the idea that through science, we will prove that consciousness is a function of brain processes and that all the complexities of human thinking, behaviour and emotion can be reduced to the firing patterns of neurones. But some of the neuroscientists who have attempted to do that over the last fifty years have concluded that our model is wrong. If you believe consciousness is an evolutionary by-product, you should know there is a significant body of empirical data that argues against that orthodoxy. The Alterman Centre is not Government funded, Dr Logan. It is funded by private individuals concerned that scientific discovery be allowed to continue free from the constraints of Dawkinsism and dogma.

You speak of science as if it were a religion.

It's the new religion, she says. *Scientism. True science is something else. Genuine enquiry. No taboos.*

She is watching him, he perceives, with an air of gentle amusement.

Your process. Have you tried it on atheists?

She sips her coffee before she answers.

The study was – unusually for us – dependent on Research Council funding. The focus was therefore on religious believers. A study of a pathology, from the current political perspective. A study of normal human tendency, from an anthropological one. The tendency to believe in a higher power is fundamental, Dr Logan. Still dominant in most cultures and most parts of the world.

But we have outgrown it. Evolved beyond it.

Or have we looked around at our miserable English lives, Dr Logan, and at the wider state of humanity, and simply despaired? She squeezes his arm disconcertingly and seems untroubled by the fact he's disconcerted. *Have we, in fact, discovered a way to directly connect with God through the use of electrical stimuli?*

Because so far I've not been able to ascertain any fundamental difference between what you call an actual *experience and one that is induced.*

Your question assumes God is real, he says.

We can't measure God. But no one's measured Love either. Or Compassion. Would you argue they're not real? Of course, there are those who don't experience love and compassion, and when questioned, will deny their existence...

You're saying God is just a feeling? An emotion? Rather than a deity?

Humans make God 'a deity'. I'm working on a different theory.

Logan contemplates this. The hum of background conversation; the sputter of the espresso machine. He anchors himself in the comfort of normality before he continues. *So your subjects, despite knowing they are taking part in a scientific experiment* (he chews the words delicately, as if they are food that may contain grit)—

Believe they have experienced God, yes. Have obtained a direct connection with the Divine.

Matter of fact, as though she could, right now, reach the Divine on the telephone.

And?

And what?

Logan takes a considered breath: tastes on his tongue the molecules of damp that the heat of the place has steamed from coats.

Dr Salmon, excuse me, you know little of my purpose here and have been generous enough to spare your time. As I said on the phone, my client is a religious young woman currently facing serious charges.

April Smith. It isn't a question. *I guessed,* she adds. *And then I googled you.*

Ah, he says. *Well, how much the papers are leaking I am not aware, but I must ask that anything that passes between us remains confidential.*

Of course. Her unruly strand of hair suggests otherwise. *I might be trustworthy and controllable*, it says. *And I might not.*

My client, he continues, wary of uttering her name in a public place, *is not speaking to anyone else but God. And if I'm to help her, to assess her and therefore help her, I need her to speak to me.*

To assess her and therefore help her? Dr Salmon repeats, her mouth twisting a little as though trying to contain a live worm. *Your assessment will help her, will it? You know this in advance?*

It is always my intention—

He knows he sounds pompous. The woman is *making* him pompous. Time to reboot.

Gabrielle – may I call you Gabrielle? She nods. *What I want to know is what happens to your religious subjects after they – to their minds, at least – experience God at the push of a button?*

Not quite the push of the button, she says, *but I understand your meaning. Under laboratory conditions.*

Invoked by you, he says. *After their God experience at your hand, are they – are they changed?*

She gazes out, through condensation, at the main campus concourse.

Yes, very much so.

In what way?

How would you put it? At peace with themselves.

And suddenly he twigs. What it is about her, Dr Salmon, that has been needling him from the outset.

You've experienced it yourself. Whatever it is that you do to create – what did you call it?

She smiles.

A direct connection with the Divine.

You've experienced it yourself, he says, allowing the repetition to harden his suspicion into fact.

She doesn't say yes. She doesn't say no.

Would you not be curious? she asks. *In my position? Seeing my subjects go in as normal, agitated, messed-up humans and come out – I don't know – like all the bad stuff is erased?*

Logan can't help thinking he likes normal, agitated, messed-up humans. The idea of any part of him being erased – even what she so unscientifically calls the bad stuff – is less than appealing. Although if she could excise his grief, just his grief; if she could cauterize that without losing one atom of the love that gave birth to it, without dulling a single memory of the moments he will never have again...

No, not possible. The grief and the love are one. He puts the personal away; returns to a more professional concern.

But how can you be objective when you have experimented on yourself?

She shakes her head, but the smile doesn't come off.

You'd be surprised how objective one can be after experiencing oneself as an aspect of infinite intelligence.

She is surely toying with him; the mobility of her lips confirms her amusement. Then they straighten out, as if she told them to behave themselves. *But in terms of the paper you read, you must understand that when I wrote it I hadn't undergone the process. It was only after publication that I –* she seeks out an appropriate word – *succumbed. I was just too curious not to.*

Embarrassed for her, he stretches for the kind of polite trope that awkward conversationalists adopt when a subject has petered out.

Have you always been religious?

She surveys him steadily.

I'm not religious now. I'm not in the slightest bit interested in religion.

But you believe you've experienced God?

She laughs the way a kind teacher might laugh when faced with the earnest seriousness of a five-year-old.

Believe me, Dr Logan, religion may have everything to do with God, but God has nothing to do with religion.

Reality

Nursing a half in the Battle of Trafalgar, Logan taps out observations on his meeting with Gabrielle Salmon. Partly to record a conversation still vivid, and partly to stave off impatience and indignation at a busy man's time squandered by one who breakfasts while others lunch and enjoys three-month holidays. Though *enjoys*, he notes as the thought takes form, is not a very Tom verb.

> *GS reports religious observance neutralized by her process. Some subjects continue attending religious services for social reasons but report previously meaningful rituals (Mass, chanting, prayer) now feel pointless. Six-month follow-up (paper in draft stage) shows 87% drop-off in religious observance. GS happy to send a copy.*

The dregs of the daytime drinkers are nearing their personal closing times. A pink-permed squawker, who might have been someone's kindly grandmother but for the men who disappointed her beyond fertility, is attempting to bicker with someone she calls *Fre-ed* at the opposite end of the bar. Perched like an unstable parrot on her bar stool, she throws verbal peanut shells in his direction. Fred, of whom little is visible but a monkish bald patch, has imploded in his tracksuit: caved inwards from the muffled explosion of some ancient booby trap, whose fuse was unwittingly lit by a spark from the squawker's flinty beak. *Your kind of place.* No surprise that Tom would choose a pub as his father's kind of place, having heard his rants against the ubiquitous noodle and sushi bars, the corporate coffee hangouts, the shot cellars and vodkaries. But this place? This slice of late twentieth-century soap opera set? Logan returns to his notes.

> *Consider possible effect on AS. Pros and cons of assisting her to disconnect from religion. Pros. Help with*

assessment as temporarily psychotic? Motivation to communicate? Cons. Danger of her re-engaging with reality, potential traumatic impact. Danger of making her 'normal' before trial. Possible difficulty of gaining consent.

He wonders if Dr Salmon might have better luck in this regard. Not only as a woman – for he senses in April a particular hostility towards men – but as one who has undergone the process herself and might tempt April with an experience he has not a hope of describing with any conviction.

Consider GS. Too left-field? Can legal team be persuaded? What about the mother?

A shaven-headed youth is feeding his universal credit to the slot machine. Suited men are supping quiet beers before boarding trains to even quieter lives in Burgess Hill and Haywards Heath. He is none of these people. He is barely the same species. Though there are superficial similarities, he is no more them than chimps – with their binocular gaze, opposable thumbs and hairless palms – are men. For there's something around Logan, an absence, a hole in the air that contains him, as though he's an astral traveller, a complex arrangement of atoms only temporarily projected there. And he realizes, not for the first time, that everything has become unreal: not just the fake horse brasses pimping the faux beams but the barman's moustache, the inscrutable symbols on the beer mats, the depiction of car-crushed limbs on a drink-drive poster, the laugh of the parrot lady, the pinstripes on a man's tie. Nothing is real. Nausea rears in his stomach, an overwhelming loss and detachment, as if nothing, nothing—

Daddy.

Flora.

Daddy. Are you feeling all right?

Not really, no.

He knows she's not real. She's not the adult Flora. She's the pigtailed nine-year-old, the one who watched him vomit pistachio ice-cream before he knew he was allergic.

She has an angel's name.

Who?

The angel Gabrielle.

It's Gabriel, Flo. Angels are men.

Don't be silly, Daddy. She giggles, jiggling her knees with excitement. *Men aren't angels.* Black patent leather party shoes, sensible white ankle socks.

No, *but angels are men.* He has to explain reality, even when neither of them is attached to it.

You mean Bible angels.

Yes.

Gabrielle's not a man.

No.

Flora squints at him.

You like her a lot, Daddy. Is she married? Mummy says you only like ladies who are married.

All his women were stolen.

Flora's mother, Rachel, he had stolen from a sappy Rogerian therapist called Larch. He and Larch met on a training course; Larch made the mistake of inviting him to dinner, along with another couple, and a lone woman called Sally with whom they were clearly hoping to pair him off. Sally was a friend from Rachel's yoga class. Like Rachel, she seemed able to tolerate the bitterness of bean sprouts and healthy teas, but unlike Rachel, she gave off no discernible pheromones, having so thoroughly cleansed her system through the regular use of crystals and Chinese herbs that she emanated only a sense of self-righteous balance and clarity. Rachel, however, was so deliciously unbalanced that three glasses of Pinot Grigio and a joke about baby seals as he helped her clear the mains was enough to allow him to brush his fingertips against her breasts in the kitchen, on the lame excuse of retrieving an invisible grain of wild rice.

He understood the subtle needs of women: to have desire sparked through gentle accident, intrigued through flirtation and stimulated through respectful withdrawal. When your hostess has followed you into an unlit cloakroom to help you find your jacket, perhaps half expecting you to attempt a drunken snog that she can rebuff, you place on her cheek a tender and open-lipped kiss that electrifies with its frisson; stands her hairs to attention. But no more. Your soft-clasped *thank you* cradles her hand for two seconds longer than the delicious pavlova deserved. But you leave.

Later, alone in the physical crescendo conducted by your imagination, your wet hands are her willing mouth. In a week or so, knowing her workplace and fathoming her hours, you manufacture a spontaneous meeting and declare it the work of Fate. Over a coffee she *needs like heroin* you allow her to unfurl her day, spreading it over your longing like a patchwork quilt over a stain, as you meet her eyes and repeat in your head, *You are beautiful*. Your eyes shine with the words, and on some level she hears them. A practical excuse you have both engineered allows her to take your number. She will call you for support when her current man fails to respond to her subtleties. And soon, soon, she will arrive at the door of your apartment in white knee-high boots and a dress fashioned for a Greek goddess, demanding you melt her with your tongue.

Stealing women had been both an art and a pleasure. And for Logan, whose face was less Hollywood and more independent art movie requiring subtitles, an enjoyable test of his psychological skills. But the chase and the conquest were all; Logan's self-loathing was rooted in the knowledge that he was a tiresome cliché in this regard. Desire: as perfumed and sensuous as bathed legs on laundered cotton, but so quickly reduced to varicose shins and greyed sheets flapping on the line beneath the threat of rain. The blame lay, he told himself, in his biological programming, which compelled him to sow his seed widely and seek variety. By the time Flora was four, Logan was urging the local GP's wife, Johanna, to have an abortion. Unfortunately Johanna had been trying for a baby for years and refused to destroy the hope of one, even if it destroyed her marriage. The results of her husband's recent fertility test ensured it did.

Thus Tom was born, red-faced and squalling his indignation at being the locus of so much anguish before he had even drawn a breath. Logan sensed that a foetus is as much bathed in its mother's brainwaves as in her amniotic fluid, for the son's fury at his infanticidal parent burned in his tiny black eyes. His fury had not lessened in the two years it took for his father to tiptoe out of the back door with a suitcase, nor in the additional six it took his mother to give up on men, and life, completely. Having no choice on Johanna's death but to move in with Logan had sealed Tom's fury into the marrow of his bones. Logan had iced the cake of resentment with plain dereliction of duty when he left his *latest conquest* to pick the boy up from the station. Yet Jules had somehow formed a bond with the boy, despite his initial resistance. She fielded his complaints with patience while Logan responded by playing more squash. Where Johanna had been drifting into a rudderless alcoholism since Tom was a toddler, Jules placed good food in front of him at regular intervals, ironed and folded his games kit.

So skilful was Jules at quietly filling the motherly role, one might imagine Logan had stolen her expressly for the purpose. But it was merely a side-effect of the innate goodness that had made her Logan's severest challenge. For not only was Jules both kind and loyal by temperament but, when they met, she had been devoted to a Truly Good Man. For three years, while Logan gently set free one tethered woman after another, Simon Merriweather was his squash partner. Cunty, as he was known to his male friends, ran a charity for fistula repair in Sierra Leone.

The difficulty in running a charity of that nature, he explained to Logan in the changing rooms after a match, *is that hardly anyone knows what a fistula is, and when they find out, they're disgusted.* Logan was loath to admit that, had he ever known what a fistula was, his brain had erased the information. Cunty, towelling himself dry after the shower, was about to save him the embarrassment of ignorance in any case. *Disgust is not the most effective fund-raising emotion. You want to provoke empathy, pity. You can send people pictures of neglected puppies and starving children and they'll set up a direct debit, fiver a month. Make the cause AIDS or torture and they'll buy tickets for charity auctions and gala dinners. But talk about girls with a catastrophic tear in the vagina wall, who leak urine and faeces 24/7, and they'll shun the cause just as the girls' communities do. To be shunned in Freetown or Kambia is a fast-track to death. These girls are sold into marriage or raped when they are children. There's no contraception. Forty-one per cent of women in Sierra Leone have their first child between the ages of twelve and fourteen. And of course it's childbirth complications that lead to fistulas. Almost inevitable in underdeveloped bodies that have been subjected to female genital mutilation.*

It was a jaw-dropping tirade.

And that's why they call you Cunty? Logan was struggling with the comedy of his own misapprehension. *I assumed you were a gynaecologist. Or a bit of a ladies' man.*

Good God, no. Cunty tugged a pair of white briefs into position. *Happily committed, thank God. My interest in vaginas is purely sociological.*

Purely sociological? Logan couldn't imagine any man meaning such a thing. It was surely a line concocted for women, which Merriweather had adopted and practised so rigorously that he spewed it out even in all-male environments.

Yes. It's interesting, don't you think? How women in that culture are valued entirely through the commodity of a working vagina. *That there are still countries where half the population are utterly disempowered through the accident of their gender.*

Women must find this stuff incredibly attractive, thought Logan. As if Merriweather's impressively toned body weren't enough.

But… purely sociological?

Cunty laughed. *Oh, I see! No, of course, I appreciate a vagina on a personal level. But it's not about body parts, is it? It's about the person. You should meet Jules. You'd like her.*

And Logan did. He liked the way she leant over her fiancé's shoulder to put his dinner in front of him, kissing him on the neck as she did so. He liked the tenderness between them, the girlish laugh she exchanged for Merriweather's frequent compliments. And he liked the way she piled her long, cream-coloured hair up on her head with a barrette, as if one pull of its pin would undo her, set her off like a grenade.

Father.

The formality is mocking.

To Logan, Tom looks disarmingly like a younger version of himself recently emerged from a tumble dryer: dishevelled, disoriented, carrying a higher-than-average charge of static. There is something odd about his glasses.

You're rather late, Logan says mildly.

Tom shrugs. *Bus. Traffic.*

Lack of planning, thinks Logan. Reluctance to come in the first place. *If we'd met on campus, you wouldn't have needed to get the bus*, he says. Nearly two decades of barely parenting the boy, and still he can't escape the urge to tell him off.

I was across town. Seeing someone.

A woman? A psychiatrist? Logan decides it is better not to ask.

I hope he or she was worth it, he says.

Worth what?

Being late for your own father. He hopes to sound funny, but his anxiety turns it into a scold.

Tom hovers there. He stares at beer stains on the carpet as though they are Rorschach blots.

Are you going to buy me a drink? he mumbles. His hands jiggle in the pockets of his oversized parka. *I'm a bit short.*

It's the beginning of term, says Logan. He notes again the urge to criticize.

The boy's face says, *And?*

Logan digs out his wallet and peels off a tenner. *Get yourself something*, he says. Even as he hands it over, he understands that his failure to go to the bar himself will be read as unfatherly.

The pub has returned to normal. Fred and the squawker have gone. The horse brasses are tacky, the beer mats decipherable, and his dead daughter has returned to ash on the carpet. He's not sure why there's ash on the carpet. No one has smoked there for years. Tom returns with a house double that looks like vodka. So he'll be able to knock it back and get away quickly if necessary, Logan supposes. There is really something not right about those spectacles.

What's with the glasses? Been studying too hard?

They're not for sight correction, says Tom. *Did you want to see me for a reason?*

Only the usual.

What's the usual?

His son seems to be spoiling for a fight. Logan takes another tack.

Well, I was meeting someone about four hundred yards from your front door. In the circumstances it would be rude not to see your own son, wouldn't it?

Wouldn't bother me, Tom says. His eyes say otherwise. No eye contact, but they have the air of dark, roiling water, broken by the fins of sharks feeding just beneath the surface.

But it would be crazy not to say hi.

Hi, Tom says, washing down the greeting with a swig of vodka.

What do you mean, they're not for sight correction? Logan is just catching on.

They're NetSpex. So what was your meeting about, work?

Work, yes. NetSpex? So you're sitting here with me, what, reading e-mail or something? Tweeting?

Jesus, Finlay, tweeting? Twitter's so old.

His forename in his son's mouth is a slap. The rebuke even more pointed now that Tom's the only person on earth who might call him Dad. Such a finickety name, the way he says it. A name ruined years ago by his mother's telling-off. Made stupid by the kids at school: *Fin, Fin, swims like a fish.* Only Jules could make it tender. He stares into his son's unfocused eyes.

Take them off, for God's sake. It's hard enough…

Tom knocks back the vodka.

And how the hell do you afford those, anyway? Jesus, no wonder you're broke. Jesus… It's there, the terrible momentum of a lecture beginning to build, and it takes every ounce of strength he can muster not to be swept away by the surging current of it. Tom's leg starts vibrating. Through the ghost of a website, he's eyeing the empty shot glass. Logan knows he has only seconds to save himself from another toxic injection of regret.

Look, never mind. Can I get you another? They are nowhere, and his son looks like he is about to bolt. *Let me get you another. Same again?* Tom finds it hard to confront him, he knows that. Even to the simple extent of saying no to a drink.

Waiting at the bar to be served, Logan glances back. In his absence, his son has finally removed the glasses. He is shredding the beer mat, peeling it layer by layer with bitten nails. Shrunken inside the coat he still hasn't shed. What is it about being with his son, Logan wonders, that turns him into an arsehole? He knows that's how Tom sees him. He intends to be otherwise. But whenever he's in Tom's company, that's all he can be. As though, for all Tom's apparent vulnerability, his reality strong-arms his father's into a half Nelson, and Arsehole (the role Tom decrees) is the only option available. Fronting the drink won't help, but it could buy Logan a little more time. The opportunity, maybe, to say something right. Or kind. Or useful.

You're looking better, he says, rejoining his son.

Better than what?

Than a horse that's condemned to the knacker's yard.

Than you were. Last time we saw each other.

Probably the Anesthine, Tom says flatly. *Started a couple of days ago.*

Your doctor's put you on Anesthine?

I put me on Anesthine.

How does that work?

Tom focuses his eyes directly on his father's. A familiar contempt is burning there.

You go to the doc, you say I'd like to go on Anesthine, and they say Okay.

Logan is depressed by the psychological skills of his son's primary health carers.

That's it? They just say Okay?

They say Read this leaflet, you say I have, and they say Okay. Repeat prescription. Problem solved.

You don't seem that *much better.*

Thank you.

I mean… what about other routes? Have you considered EFT?

That 'tapping' bollocks?

Yes, 'that tapping bollocks'.

Two-year wait.

What about the student counselling service?

Logan is aware his concern has morphed into veiled criticism and unwanted-advice-dispensing.

You really are an arse. Tom's nascent anger is mostly contained, magma-like, under a crust, but Logan has managed once more to break through it by stepping where he shouldn't with his big volcano-scientist's boot. The magma, now spilling and spitting fire into the oxygen-rich air, is in danger of eating through the asbestos welly and taking his metaphorical leg off. *The student counselling service is all trainees. Doing degrees in it. You think I want to be someone's dissertation? Never mind being meddled with by a beginner.*

Logan considers whether he would want that himself. He doesn't even want to be meddled with by a professional.

Has it ever occurred to you, Tom says, *that I'm only like this with you?*

You're on Anesthine.

Yes, and it's stabilizing. Except under extreme conditions.

His facial expression lets Logan know exactly which extreme conditions he means.

Maybe, Logan tries to say cheerily, *this challenging time in your life is going to lead to some real revelations for you. An understanding you might apply to other people. I mean, who knows, you could even specialize at the end of your degree, change tack a little, and become a psychologist, like me.*

Tom's contempt crests its peak.

You can be absolutely sure, he says, *that I will never do, or be,* anything *that makes me like you.*

Surface

April is picking her fingernails apart with forensic precision. The cuticle of her ring finger is bleeding.

Logan searches for something in his briefcase. It is hiding. He has to shuffle through the same papers three times before it appears. As if it is trying to tell him, *This is a bad idea.* Ignoring the message, he roots it out.

I thought, if you liked poetry... I wondered what you'd think of these?

He pushes the volume towards her. She stops demolishing her fingernails, leans forward and scrutinizes the cover.

A smile crawls across her face, looking for a stone to hide beneath. Her eyes say, *Really? Sylvia Plath?*

I thought your poetry showed some similarities.

He waits for her comment. She has options.

- Smartarse: *Suicidal ones?*
- Sceptical: *Flatterer.*
- Academic: *Barring the father complex and violent line breaks.*

But April gives her standard response. None.

What he doesn't understand is that if April opens her mouth there is a danger her entire brain will empty itself like a suitcase whose catch has failed, snagged on some protrusion as it journeys through baggage handling, its contents spilt and strewn in a nonsensical confusion of objects and colours, the personal and the improbable, flotsam and wreckage. A black polo neck, twisted on the ground like the outline of a murdered corpse. A chlorine-eaten swimsuit, slung on a piece of machinery. Shower gel, the lid cracked, oozing jellified Ocean Breeze onto practical flooring. A broken-spined romance. It's the pool party.

He hasn't noticed it yet, the reference crouching among her other journal entries like a quiet tumour. Has read it as art, perhaps, rather than biography. He quotes lines from her poems, but never that one. Oblivious, he holds the key to her silence between his palms. Flicking past it, forwards and backwards, running the paper-cut edge of it under his thumbs as he lands on some abstract expression of pain, but not on the cause. How effectively she has disguised its ugliness as beauty, corseted her trauma in metre and rhyme.

Yet still she is afraid of it. Cannot open her mouth because any word might lead to it. Every word is a scent marker, pulling the brain down a darkened path, and the pool party is a terrifying animal that should never be hunted down, should never be cornered.

She watches him speaking to her now, as she practises the skill she is perfecting of concocting such a furious buzz in her head that his voice cannot penetrate. She thinks of bees, a whole colony, unhoused, tipped out of its chimney by some exterminator. Perhaps she is the exterminator. Perhaps she is the bees. It doesn't matter, so long as the buzzing continues. Not an angry buzz. There is no emotion in her now, the detonation exploded it out of her. She is a vast emptiness, filled with the buzzing of bees. Perhaps she is the chimney; the bees are just a memory. He thinks she is silent, but he is mistaken. She is nothing but noise.

Some of that noise is the pool party. For now, she is keeping it under the buzz. Like holding someone's head under water.

She wishes they had held her head under water.

There it is, breaking the surface for a gasp of life, its face blue and contorted. She pushes it down again: it must not breathe. She will not let it live. Soon, she hopes, soon, it will stop kicking entirely. Will sink in its heaviness to the very bottom of the deep end, and no one will even notice it's gone. Because only she ever knew it was there.

She watches Logan's mouth through the thick glass of a seaquarium. She will not lip-read. She likes the shapes of his words to remain as meaningless as the mouth shapes of suckerfish cleaning their tank.

¤　　¤　　¤

April, I have an idea, he says. *I have a friend* – is he already calling Dr Salmon a friend? Or is the word only to reassure April? *I have a friend, a scientist—* How does one broach this? Why didn't he find the form of words before their session? Because he didn't know he was ready to offer it. He has besieged her, he has failed to scale her mental ramparts, and now he is changing tack, setting up a stall of delicious-smelling fare and stepping away.

April, I want to offer you something. It's a way of connecting directly with God. I know (he is trying to read her inscrutable face) *you have your own way of connecting, the automatic writing, but I think this process might be even more powerful for you. I think it might help you in all sorts of ways.*

I'm going to leave you a letter from Dr Salmon, about the process.

I would like your permission.

I have already asked your mother and your legal team. Everyone else is willing to give it a try.

But you have to be willing as well.

April.

April.

Later, the forest paths unfold under his dog's muzzle. The dog travels forward, pulled by its nose on an invisible cord of scent: bunny and roe deer, brock and vixen, pony and vole. Were here, were here, a moment ago, some minutes ago, an hour ago. The spaniel stops briefly to sniff at a dropping. Logan has no idea what kind of animal dropped it, has no countryside expertise, but the dog knows. Innately, the dog unravels from a pile of shit the maker's species, gender, approximate age, health, fertility, recent meal.

How to unravel April, Logan wonders. How to close in upon her, fact by fact, as the ropey scent of a distant doe reels his dog along the darkening path. To win her confidence. To unleash her tongue.

It could hardly be more of a challenge, surely, than stealing his wife from the perfection of Simon Merriweather.

This was the story he could never share. The public version, the sanitized answer to *How did you two meet?* was laced with only the merest decorative trappings of the truth: *Through a mutual friend*, they would say, *I resisted his charms for a good long while*, she would say, *But I won her round*, he would say, *with a flower*. If he judged the company appreciative, he would show them the top of his buttock. A single tattooed rose.

A test, she'd confirm to the curious.

I passed, he'd say, buckling his belt.

A simplistic, fairy-tale retelling, their mutual shame erasing the only obstacle, Simon Merriweather. Or more explicitly, Jules's love for, her devotion to, Simon Merriweather. The story was repeated and polished until they had themselves almost forgotten the identity of the unnamed mutual friend who was the cause of Jules's long resistance and the unwitting source of the buttock flower. Logan marvelled at her collusion in their revisionist history, but she needed the rewrite more than he did. He could play the rutting stag, slave to his masculinity, provoking feigned disapproval tinged with admiration. But Jules wore the gown of a good and loyal woman with conviction because it was her essence. The chief person she had betrayed was herself, and betrayal didn't fit her comfortably enough to be worn out of the house. Only in private would she admit it. In good humour, provoked by his failure to wash up, it was her quiet needle; in high dudgeon it became her shitty goodnight, her stiletto-blade stab in any argument she was losing. *I should have stayed with Simon.*

But she hadn't stayed with Simon.

What had she let go? A man who could cook a Thai curry from scratch: not spooning the paste from a jar but blending it fresh from garlic, ginger root, galangal, lemon grass. A man unashamed to cry when big-eyed, fly-haunted children appeared on the news, whose phone calls moved trucks across Africa. A man who would drive anyone anywhere; foot rightly balancing accelerator and brake, ear patient, mouth incapable of platitudes; who would answer your call at four in the morning, and happily set off to Nottingham to pick up your freshly widowed aunt. A man who could listen to you unleashing your misery without making a joke of it, changing the subject, or offering a 'solution' beyond the tissue he pressed wordlessly into your hand. A man of boundless compassion. And as his reassuring presence returned your breathing to normal, you knew that simultaneously, thanks to this man's direct interventions, a surgeon in Sierra Leone was repairing the urinary tract of a girl raped by her uncle at twelve.

No wonder male friends had christened him Cunty. Because beyond the reference to his fistula repair charity there was the tacit acknowledgement among them that he demolished the masculine stereotypes upon which they relied to excuse their shortcomings. Any appeal to genetics or testosterone dropped like a shot pigeon in the wake of his existence. And it was worse than that. The least Cunty's friends might hope for was that all his feminine traits left him a eunuch in the bedroom. Yet by all accounts he was both well endowed and skilled with his endowment. On the nights when she lay beside Logan's unresponsive torso, Jules remembered her former lover's tenderness, his willingness to serve her desire, how the entire canvas of his skin was alert to the brush of her fingers, how full and complete she felt when their flesh was joined. No man could get closer to perfection than the man they called Cunty. On such nights, Jules could only mourn her incomprehensible surrendering of that perfection.

Perfection was where Logan began his campaign. For Logan understood that perfection is uncomfortable to live with. One assumes that proximity will reveal the seemingly godlike creature as a mess like the rest of us. But the closer to perfection one gets, while finding no visible flaws, the wider one's own cracks appear. The woman of such a man, he reasoned, must surely be harbouring a slow leak of inadequacy. Beneath their palatial love, their sound foundations, would be an increasingly damp cellar neither of them ever visited. Unlikely she would conduct her own structural survey in front of him and expose her deficiencies. No profit in frightening an enthusiastic buyer into pulling out. Thus, in the secret of her dishonesty, the seed of her future loneliness was sown. She was watering it herself. Logan had only to warm it, unfog the window to admit a little sunshine, encourage it into the light.

That

April is hyperventilating. He has taken her paper away. And her pen. The obligatory walk round the garden, and when she returned, they were gone. She mimed her distress to the bosomy guard, who sneered at her. *No pen, no paper, Dr Logan's orders.* Now the trouble starts. Now the trouble starts.

Dr Logan is a bastard, she wants to say, but cannot write it. *He is a bastard!* The words are rattling the bars of her head, huge strong hairy hands they have, and the bars are rustier than she realized, are winnowed thin where the rain pools at the edge of the imaginary, glassless window. There is a danger, a real danger the bars will snap and the words will free themselves, burst onto the world. And others will follow, bringing mayhem.

She prays, *Give me peace, give me peace.* In her head *Shhhh shhhh*, a mother to herself, *peace, peace.* She can still talk to God. She can still talk to God. But if God is talking back, she cannot hear him. He is never in her ears. He was only in her hands. And her hands need paper, a pen.

She tries not to think of Dr Logan, of tensioning her words into a cord of obscenities wrapped round his throat just above the Adam's apple she watches bobbing on the sea of his silent words.

Peace, peace. Shhhh.

Perhaps this is the moment she will make the transition. She knows, through history, there have been those who hear God directly. She envies them, those possessors of a whispering intimacy with the Almighty. But maybe this is how she will join them, necessity stinging the cells of her brain into change: the malleus, incus and stapes of her inner ear at last sensitized and vibrating to His higher, heavenly, frequency. Ask, says the Bible, and it shall be given you. She is asking. Her asking is fuelled by a powerful need and surely, surely He will answer. *Speak to me*, she whispers, flicking her eyes to the door's observation slot. Turning her face to the wall, screwing it up to intensify the transmission: *Speak to me.* But there is nothing. A terrifying silence devoid of anything holy, of any sound at all but the guards' passing footfalls, an inmate's cackle.

The line has been cut. Or God has put down the receiver.

A day, a night, a day, and now she is hearing one word.

Forsaken.

Forsaken.

It is her voice. It isn't God. It is the absence of God, and what she has made of it.

A night, a day, a night, and now she is frightened. Truly frightened. Because something unwanted is surfacing in the silence, something only the words of an omnipotent being could soothe.

It is the pool party.

First the music begins. Madonna's 'Like a Virgin'. She wants to vomit. Her head seems detached above a stomach tricked and triggered into a violent and involuntary series of spasms, the contractions of birth. Something terrible, something toxic and jagged, is about to be born. The birth canal is her throat. Her mouth is the vagina. The whole night of it, every bilious chunk of undigested experience, is about to empty itself into her sight.

She falls to her knees, *God, no*. But God cannot speak. No pen. No paper.

She crashes her head against the metal bedstead, once, twice, hard enough to smash stars onto her eyelids and spatter blood over the sheet, but her brain remains stubbornly conscious. It is too late. In her head, the bars are broken, bent back, the cell is empty.

And here it comes.

She throws up. Fragments of ridge-cut crisps, the stench of vodka. The nicotined hand of a stranger on her forehead, the other muscled palm at the back of her neck, keeping her hair from the puke. Dismembered hands at first, but they grow wrists, arms, a torso, then the rest of the man, the toilet cubicle she is kneeling in, and just beyond the walls, an amplified thudding, hysterical laughter. She is back there. *God*.

God, he says, *you're properly ill. How much have you drunk? I haven't – I don't—*

She can't say *drink*. Speaking makes her nauseous.

The man laughs and his voice cracks into a higher octave. He is hardly a man really. Two years older than her, but like everyone else there, barely legal. It is Joey's eighteenth.

You've had the bloody punch, he says.

She didn't know. Too inexperienced to detect the alcohol under the fruit.

He laughs. *Fancy not knowing. I thought all the Shipley girls were boozers.* She wants to address him, but is too sick to speak. Worse, can't remember his name. Jack? Jake? She transferred into the sixth form only a month ago. A lost sheep, hiding under her fringe, making friends, but slowly. Didn't belong to the confident, hair-flicking crew. Didn't presume. Didn't know why she was invited to this party of people she can barely identify, but was stupidly grateful. Now she knows. Because the hand that was keeping her hair from the puke has slipped to her breast.

You're not even with us, are you?

She wishes she wasn't.

Come on, there's a lounger in the pool house, you look like you need to lie down.

Joey's parents are away. Joey's parents are idiots. Joey's parents said, *Look after the place.* Joey's parents left wine in the cellar, beer in the fridge, and the pool house key on the hook.

Jack, Jake, manoeuvres her onto the lounger in the pool house. Strewn clothes on the floor: the sloughed-off skins of drunken girls who are now on their way out of bikinis. She nearly slips, he steadies her.

Gently now, he says. *That's it. Lie down.*

Again, his hand brushes her breast, and the worst of it is – this, she didn't want to remember – her nipple tingles in response. Tightens. She hopes he hasn't noticed but he says, *Mmm, not completely out of it then.*

Horizontal feels good, she is grateful. The room is spinning, and she closes her eyes. She knows if she were sober, she would let him kiss her. As it is, she just wants to sleep.

The light, she says.

Hurting your head? He turns it off and sits there. She focuses on his breathing, counting his breaths, to anchor the sickening lurch in her brain.

Let me get you some water, he says, and vanishes. She doesn't open her eyes. She wants everything to go away. She just wants to sleep, she just wants to sleep.

Water. He sits her up, tips it into her mouth, but he pours too fast, her lips don't catch it all, and she feels it splash onto her top; a hand-sized patch that clings to her. *Sorry*, he says. A pause. *Better take this off.*

Why does objecting feel babyish? Because he is looking after her? She just wants to lie down, very still. The insides of her head heave about like unlashed cargo in a storm. The top is peeled off like a child's vest, over her head, and next, next—

No, no, no – briefly back in her cell, gripping the bedstead before the gravity of *next* sucks her into its dense misery – next, his mouth over her mouth, her nose stuffed up with the pillow of his cheek, she is struggling to breathe, she breaks free, she gasps—

And the gasp is a trigger for *God, you want it as much as I do* and the whole force of him unleashed on her, his whole heavy body suddenly pinning her down, his mouth again clasped on her mouth, his tongue muscular and persistent, miming a penetration she can already feel building in his groin, accurately positioned.

She twists her head away, says, *Stop, please*, but so quiet, so muted by terror, she cannot make it louder. Can he even hear her? She begins to cry. *Please, please stop, please stop*, and he hears the *please*, and he doesn't hear *stop*. He is unbuckling himself. She tries to push him off, the motion so ineffectual it makes him laugh. *God, you're wild*, he says, one hand gripping her wrists, the other pulling up her skirt and pushing the gusset of her knickers aside. Fighting him, she feels like a child fighting a giant, a wasp in a jar, a cat being stuffed by its neck into a sack. Every struggle proves her powerlessness.

His pushes his fingers roughly inside her. The sobs arrive even though it's hard to breathe with his weight on her chest: huge, involuntary sobs, loud with impotence. *Shhh*, he says, *you don't want the others to hear*, and grabs a damp towel from the floor, stuffing into her mouth the taste of laundered cotton, the anaesthetic odour of chlorine. The towel covers her face. She is not even there to him now, she is just a body, decapitated. Still she fights. But she is losing count of his hands. Though one is hurting her with its insistent fucking motion, when she breaks her wrists free they are recaptured by two more. There is whispering. There are others. Every kick, every twist of her body lurches her stomach. She's afraid of being sick again, of suffocating on her vomit under the towel. And the more she fights, the more she fuels him. In place of his fingers, now, a more potent weapon. Her struggle doubles his desire.

So she stops fighting. *I am not here*, she whispers to herself. She draws a mental line across her neck: *Everything above it is mine. I feel nothing below. I feel nothing below.* He penetrates her; she is dry, unyielding, yet he makes her yield. *I feel nothing. I feel nothing.*

But she does feel. She feels the crashing weight of him, the friction of his violation rasping and burning her, the whole foul flesh of him inside her, and all ten of his fingers and thumbs viciously clamped into the muscles of her buttocks, thrusting her against him as though she is his puppet. Another hand furiously twists and pinches her nipple. And still she cannot free her wrists.

Oh God, oh God, oh God marks the end of him. The beginning of another. This one bites her. Lubricated by the first's manifest desire, he fucks her with the fury of the scorned. Mistaking another man's semen for her consent, he tells himself *you love it, you love it, you love it*, until the self-deceit reverses evolution and he is beyond language, fully animal.

Her arms are released. The one who held her wrists rolls her over onto her face, determined to break a new virginity. He pulls the towel out of her mouth so he can hear what his size sounds like. He makes her cry until she is sick.

They take her arms and legs and carry her, like a murdered deer, to the edge of the pool. She is swung and let go. Falls through the air. Falls through the water like a stone. Falls to the bottom of the pool. The water is cold and compassionate. It muffles their laughs, holds the dumb thump of music at bay. She must never surface. Breath leaves her body in a musical stream of bubbles. She squeezes her lungs until they are tight and needy. All she has to do is breathe water. The water will fill every emptiness inside her. It will turn her a beautiful chlorine blue.

She knows she must inhale. But she swallows.
She knows she must sink. But she floats.
She knows she must die. But she lives.

Contract

I want to talk to God, she says.

Logan is congratulating himself so loudly in his own head that he doesn't immediately respond.

I want to talk to God, she repeats.

You need to sign a consent form.

She thrusts out her hand. It is shaking. *Still largely non-verbal*, he notes. *Still avoidant.*

He extracts the consent form from his briefcase and slides it solemnly across to her.

Her fingers mime a writing motion.

Pen, she says, irritated.

I think you should read it first, he says. *It's an experimental procedure. There may be risks. None of us will be held legally accountable should there be – should the results be – unwanted.*

She flicks her eye over the first page of clauses. Glances at the second and third.

My lawyers have read it?

Yes.

Pen, she says.

Lost

Cunty was a good man. Cunty deserved better friends than the one who sidled up to his fiancée at their Christmas party and whispered, *He's utterly flawless. How do you stand it?* Cunty deserved a less gullible mate than the woman who answered, *To be honest, it's not easy.*

As always, Logan moved slowly. This early in the evening, he would not so much as lift the corners of the gift she had given him. Cunty himself was deep in a vaginal conversation: the complexities of surgery, the costs of obtaining appropriate expertise. Now they were observing him together, side by side, as though studying a rare zoo exhibit.

Have you ever considered you might be dating a saint? And I don't mean that as a figure of speech, I mean an actual saint, someone who might one day be canonized.

Jules laughed nervously. *He's not Mother Teresa.*

Of all the women under the infinite sky, Jules was the sea: contained, patient, pulled into or out of shape by the gravity of her most powerful satellite. The man orbited her and she watched him. And like the sea, Logan noted, her eyes changed their hue with the prevailing mood. Sometimes grey, or seeming blue, today they were an algae green. Logan caught their gaze as it flicked in his direction.

Faith is at the heart of his work, is it not?

He's a Catholic, yes. But he doesn't evangelize. Jules corrected herself. *About the spiritual side of it, anyway.* She popped a Hula Hoop into her mouth.

Doesn't have to, said Logan. *Deeds not words.*

Was she really more beautiful then? Had he dulled and blunted her through use? Perhaps it was something to do with the throwing of parties; something she loved and his weary misanthropy had put a stop to. Remembering a loop of hair balanced on her shoulder, he supposed she spent hours making herself beautiful that night.

Twirling another Hoop on her finger, *They'd never make him a saint,* she said, *the Church. He's a big fan of contraception.* She glanced up at Logan from under her eyebrows and frowned. *The girls, I mean. None of them would be having babies at twelve if they had contraception.*

Logan conjured in his mind a windowless slum with a dirt floor, a large African with broken teeth forcing his bulk on the girl he has bought from her aunt.

How does he square that stuff with a benevolent God?

¤   ¤   ¤

The dog pads ahead through the forest, muzzle a bare sliver from the earth, like the gap in a spark plug. The dog knows where they are going; Logan is lost. He calls the spaniel back to his heels, pulls out his phone and summons the map. He finds himself, a pulsing blue dot. Some distance away to the north, what looks like a road makes a crooked line on the screen. *Come on*, he says, and the dog slips ahead of him, connected to the circuit of the earth, the leaf mould sparking smells and stories into its nostrils.

Logan found relief in the nose-down challenge of April; tugged forward on her trail, barely glancing ahead. But her consent was the quarry, the full stop of opened-up pelt. Once it was given, he disconnected from the track and raised his head. He left their last session with a suppressed smile which he contained through twenty minutes of screenforms at her solicitor's, but allowed to leak from the corners of his mouth as he crossed St James's Park in the late afternoon. Then he noticed a little girl with her father, feeding the ducks.

Flora's death fell upon him like an unbuttressed wall. He was buried in the rubble of her loss. Unable to breathe, doubled over. A stranger he couldn't even bear to acknowledge helped him to a bench. The shame of it, the ludicrous dissolution of a suited man in a public place.

There is no fucking God, he said. Flailing his arms, scaring the geese. *There is no fucking God*.

For if there was a God, an omnipotent being, omnipresent, all-seeing, surely any deity worthy of worship would not stand by and let fifteen teenagers – atheists or no – board a bus that a lunatic planned to explode. If God was all He was said to be, He would jiggle the wires loose, pinch the fuse, break down the bus by the side of the motorway, kicking the occupants out into safety. A loving God, infinite options at His disposal, would surely inspire the students to seek a service station's vending machines, where they'd glug canned drinks behind cold glass, choking astonishment at the sudden fireball in the car park.

But God had done nothing. God had whistled with His hands in His pockets, and watched the carnage. Across the conflicted world, again and again, God had scuffed His shoes in the dirt, averting His eyes, neglecting to intervene as His children slaughtered each other. Or the simplest explanation of all. *There is no fucking God.* Because it simply wasn't possible that God the Father would smear your twenty-one-year-old daughter across a field in the Surrey Hills.

Logan was back in the empty cargo hold of the plane, watching the space where his daughter had been. Staring into the buffeted blue hole of sky she had passed through, strapped to her instructor, unaware of the random statistic they were shortly to become. Not that Logan had been at her point of departure, this imagined place he visited when he thought of Flora's last moments. Where he had been was heartbreakingly prosaic. Working back from information the police imparted to him when they knocked on the door, Logan had calculated that when his daughter hit the ground at over a hundred miles an hour, he had been at the kitchen table, eating a late bowl of cereal.

It is no wonder he has had little appetite since her death. That he has developed an aversion to cereal, and that milk, no matter how fresh Jules claims it to be, seems sour, and curdles in his mouth. The dog trots onwards through dead leaves and feather-coated twigs – former nests, from which branches, deranged by storms, have shaken themselves free. Rain begins to fall: large, solitary drops that make an audible splatter in the leaf mould, and on the shoulders of his coat.

It was hard to shake the strangers off, in the park. They wanted to fetch help, professionals adept at handling the mentally unstable. Had no inkling he *was* one. *Who can we call?*

No one, he said, *no one, I'll be okay.*

And when they persisted, suggested ambulances, *I'm fine. It was a thing, a moment. I'm fine.* Shook them off, walked away.

He could imagine their relief as they turned him into an anec-
dote, one to be recounted for a couple of days, then forgotten,
the man in the park who lost it. And then was fine.

Always pretence. The essential burden of maintaining the
pretence of normality for other people. Because the moment you
can't keep up the pretence, Logan knows, they lock you away.
Professionally, he knows what that entails. That if he allows that
to happen he will lose his career – his only protection from the
howling despair of his grief.

Dusk is gathering itself from the shadow of the forest, spilling beyond the edges. He reaches the road, clips the dog onto its
lead, and assesses his position. He turns east, responsibly walking along the right-hand verge. He passes a couple in walking
gear, earnestly orienteering towards the local pub, and nods at
them, *Good evening.*

He is clothed entirely in pretence. Pretence is holding him
together. A chaos of thought and feeling is only barely contained
in the fragile shell of *I'm fine.* He has shouted out loud, in a
public park, that *There is no fucking God* in the very same hour
that he promised a lunatic she could talk to Him.

What is he doing, deepening April's psychosis? The rope he
has thrown to this silent murderous girl, drowning in her own
delusions, is a massive, knotted, vanishing lie.

Dr Salmon?
   Speaking.
   He is alone in his study. The light has faded so quickly
that he cannot read the spines of the books on the closest
shelf, but he is happier not illuminated. His phone is the old
phone whose cord Flora used to twiddle in the hallway of
the London house. He twines the cream-coloured umbilicus
around his fingers.
   It's. He has to remember. *It's Dr Logan here. Finlay.*
   Did her voice warm noticeably?

Dr Logan! Good to hear from you. I got your message. Great news about the consent.

He pictures her working late in a well-lit lab, spinning a quarter-turn on a high stool, unsuitable shoes, legs crossed at the thigh.

I was very pleased about the consent, he says. *The thing is, I'm having second thoughts.*

The line muffles, as though she's put her hand over the receiver. Then she's back. *About what exactly?*

About the process. About putting April Smith through the process.

A pause. *What about it?*

Logan does his best to tread carefully. *I'm wondering if it's really helpful to deepen her delusion.*

Again, the line fills with silence. Then she says softly, *Finlay. What's happened?*

Logan is taken aback by the change in register. *What do you mean?*

Something's happened. To you. Wait.

Her voice is replaced by a Bach fugue. It takes him a few bars to realize, with incredulity and a rising fury, that he has been put on hold. He cannot fight the urge to hang up and replaces the receiver on its cradle with a venomous click. He stares at it until it rings.

Sorry, she says. *I was transferring you to my mobile, I think I messed it up.* She is slightly out of breath; from the movement of air on the mouthpiece, the crunch of gravel a few feet away, she is walking across a car park. *I want to come down and see you.* In her voice: something as hard to resist as the warmth of whisky in the belly.

When?

Now. Tonight.

Logan knows this isn't right or normal. But he isn't right or normal. And she can tell. Jules will be at her book group; he has no plans himself, other than work. He can tell himself this is work.

I can be there in about two hours, she says.
It's two and a half by car.
She huffs out a laugh.
Not the way I drive.

Found

Two hours twelve minutes later, he takes her coat and shows her into his sitting room.

You want a drink of something?

Water, she says. He brings water for her; a clean glass and the bottle of Laphroaig for himself.

You want something in your water? he asks.

Only if you want me sleeping on your sofa, she says.

Suit yourself. He settles himself into his customary armchair. Puts the bottle down beside him, close as a guilty man will keep his lawyer. She leans towards him from the sofa that threatened briefly to become a bed, elbows on her knees.

Tell me, she says, and lets the silence pool between them.

Tell you what?

What happened. To give you second thoughts.

He is careful. He picks a path towards her. Emotion swirls close to him, licks at his tentative footing.

I no longer—

Another step.

I don't know that—

In place of the right word, he substitutes the familiar burn of whisky.

It feels like deceit, he says, when he has swallowed. He is relieved to make land. *It feels like deceit.*

You think we'd be deceiving April? She clearly knows his answer.

Yes.

Because?

A swell of anger so powerful that his eyes water with the pressure of containing it.

Because God doesn't exist, Dr Salmon.

I think, she says, getting to her feet, *that after I have driven two hours to see you*, she picks up a footstool, *and come to your house*, she deposits it in front of his chair, *you might call me Gabrielle*, she sits down, *or Gabby. Or just Salmon.* She takes his hand in hers, as though that is a normal thing to do, and weighs its warmth in her palm like a Cornish pasty. He is too embarrassed to withdraw it.

I'm guessing, she says softly, *you were brought up in one of those Calvinistic communities in the Scottish Islands where emotions are buried under stones.*

He remembers a sandpaper wind ripping the skin off the beach at North Uist, a hand-knitted pullover itching him through his shirt, shoes half a size too tight, his mother an outline on the headland. Disconcerted, he says, *What are you doing now, reading my aura?*

She shakes off his sarcasm as a Labrador shakes off a dip in a river. *Your name*, she says. *I have an interest in names. Having a bit of an odd one myself.* His hand still in hers like a dead animal. *Plus I had a boyfriend at university, originated in the Western Isles, had something of your reticence. Listen*, she says, *I know you are a good man.*

He withdraws from her touch.

How can you possibly know that? It is a cue to refill his glass. He thinks, Even I don't know that.

Inside information, she says, keeping her gaze on his face as though to hold him in place and prevent him doing something rash. *Somebody loves you.*

He stares back at this smoky-voiced woman with her maroon-tinted hair and her chipped-varnish fingernails. And though part of him has already imagined their sliding into an anonymous, silk-sheeted bed, he is sure she cannot mean herself. Nor can she mean Jules, a woman she doesn't know, who loves only what she thought he was.

I'm sorry? he says. Understanding is so much his business that he has to apologize when he fails to do it.

Dr Salmon remains calm, steady.

Finlay, tell me about your daughter.

What do you— He is on his feet. *How did—* Words fly through his head. Unbelievable. Prying. *How could you— Who?— Where did you?—* Nothing completes. He is too frightened to think clearly. In his six-foot frame, now making random forays towards the door, the window, things he might throw, fright feels like anger.

It's okay, she says. *It's not what you think.*

Don't presume to know what I think. What do you know about my daughter?

He paces to the bookcase and, confronted with the spines of his wife's novels, stalks back to stare at the dark mirror of uncurtained window. Dr Salmon addresses her fingernails.

I know she's dead.

Who told you?

No one told me, she answers. *That is—* He can see her reflection speaking to his back. *Your daughter told me.*

Ha! His scorn is voluble. He wheels to face her. *My daughter? My daughter told you?* Incandescent. *My daughter?*

Now the good Dr Fish is posing as a medium. An idea strikes him as swiftly as the back of Reverend Holinshead's hand once stung his ear when Mrs Holinshead folded in half to pick up a Bible he'd dropped.

What's her name, then? What's my daughter's name?

I don't know her name, Dr Salmon says calmly, *but I know she died by falling.*

He is ransacking his brain for how she knows this.

This is some kind of trick.

Actually it's some kind of side-effect, she says. *Happens more or less automatically once the amygdala response is mitigated.*

The medical language is a tranquillizer dart. It punctures his protective rage, and the fury that propelled him to move, urged him to throw, drains away through the hole.

Side-effect?

Of the process, she says.

He examines her face for dishonesty but she wears an untroubled expression. If she is lying, it is a lie she believes. And she is examining him back.

You did read my paper, didn't you? Fully? You understand what it entails, this process? You understood it before gaining April Smith's consent, did you not?

Yes, yes, he says, although now he is confused, not so sure. *But what are you saying, exactly? This information about my daughter came to you – how?*

Dr Logan, this is important, she says. *If you're not clear about what the process entails, we need to—*

I need to know about my daughter!

The room rings as though slapped. Calmly, she asks, *Are you going to sit?*

They stare at each other. He remains on his feet. She relents and begins.

The last time I saw you, after you left, there was something left behind. A kind of— She casts her eyes around the room for help with the word, but it's nothing she can see. *Finlay, I realize this is hard for you to take, and it's not easy to say, either, which is really why I wanted to talk to you in person. All of this is pretty new to me, too. I used to be—*

It's okay, he interrupts. *Just explain what happened. There was something left behind, you say.*

He can feel his professional self resurfacing at last, the reassuring rhythms of his familiar tropes, the repetition intended to focus her on the essentials, waste less of his time.

It was – a voice. Since the process there seems to be more activity in my left posterior superior temporal gyrus, and to put it in plain language, I hear things.

Logan ticks the first item on a mental checklist. She laughs.

You're putting me down as a nutter.

He side-steps the disconcerting feeling that his mind is being read.

What did the voice say?

It said— She said— She hesitates. *She said 'I fell through the air.' I asked who she was.*

And she answered?

She said she was your daughter. I knew she was dead. When I asked her name I got a picture of flowers, not a wreath or anything, more like a posy.

Something cold runs through him.

Her name was Flora, he says quietly.

Oh. Okay. That's interesting. She is, he can tell, adding to the experiment write-up in her head.

Dr Salmon, how can you imagine that Flora is communicating with you when the thing that would generate that communication, her brain, is—

He sees her coffin slide again through the black curtains of the crematorium's chapel, imagines the gas jets of the furnace turned suddenly up to full. *The brain* generates *consciousness*, he says. *So Flora cannot have brainwaves, cannot think, cannot be, beyond the death of her physical brain.*

What you are citing as fact, Dr Salmon says softly, *is only theory. A popular theory, I grant, a mainstream theory that its proponents present as the only rational choice. But is it rational to cling to a theory when the empirical evidence soundly refutes it?*

What empirical evidence?

The evidence from NDE studies alone is sufficient to refute the idea of the brain as a consciousness generator. Patients accurately report operation-room procedures and conversations that occurred when there was no electrical activity registering in their brain whatsoever. They could apparently see and hear without the neural networks of eyes and ears. The brain was

*dead; the mind was not. There is no viable physiological expla-
nation for the data.*

The scientific aspects of Logan's psychological training
resist, kick back.

*I'm sure I read somewhere that oxygen deprivation, or carbon
dioxide levels—*

*Long ago disproved. Those conditions are neither necessary
nor sufficient for a Near Death Experience. These phenomena
are real, and they require explanation. Believe me, Dr Logan,
I could take you through the literature, but generator theory,
dominant as it is, is not supported by the evidence. The research
groups at the Alterman Centre believe filter theory has far more
validity. The idea that the brain is a transmitter-receiver unit
that filters out the vast majority of consciousness, leaving us
ourselves.*

He feels ill-equipped to argue with her. Her ideas are too
large, and the heaviness of grief has descended upon him.
Crossing the room, he dumps his body into the chair. Pours
himself a Laphroaig, aware of a tremor in his hand, an early
warning of pressure on the fault line. The bottle trembles on the
rim, and a thread of whisky pours itself down the wrong side of
the glass, pooling on the coaster, dribbling onto the side table in
a way that Jules will find upsetting if he can't remember to mop
it up before she comes back. But this, this is more important
than getting a cloth.

You feel sure you were communicating with Flora?

Yes.

What else did she say?

I wrote it down, Dr Salmon says, *so I would remember.*

She fumbles in her bag, brings out a small notebook, unleashes
the pages from the elastic that keeps them together. Logan is
afraid she will release him in the same manner. The way she
reads from her notes reminds him of a 1950s TV policeman:

*She said, 'He blames himself.' I said, 'For what?' She said,
'Not seeing more of me.' It's funny,* Dr Salmon says, breaking

off to look him in the eye, *but I can't tell sometimes, when it starts, whether it's my voice or someone else's. I know that sounds weird. But it's not – it's not a real voice, you know, it's not sound waves in the air, it's the re-creation of sound waves in my head so it sounds rather like me.*

Logan is thinking, *Paranoid delusions.* He is quietly working out whether she is dangerous. Whether he might slip away to the toilet and dial for backup – for Jules, sensible Jules – from the mobile in his pocket.

So what makes you think it isn't you? he says with calm professionalism.

Oh, I realized it wasn't me from the next bit, she says.

Which is?

I asked her why you didn't see more of her and she said, 'Because I was an accident.' The phrase hooks into Logan, but Dr Salmon rattles on, *And* I'm *not an accident, God knows my mother bent my ear enough times about how she shagged for England trying to conceive me, had all those investigations they do, even tried the test tube route, ran out of money, gave up... and bang.*

The bang, illustrated with a fist against a palm, is Dr Salmon being conceived. It seems an appropriately dramatic conception for someone who has car-crashed into his pain. Logan is almost distracted from the main point, and then it comes back to him.

You're sure the voice said she was *an accident. Not that she died in one.*

Dr Salmon pushes a strand of hair out of her eye, the same rebellious strand that had bothered him when they first met.

No, she said she was *an accident.*

His throat dries.

Flora's face in the car. Their last conversation.

Accident

Biblical rain.

Biblical rain blasts berries from the rowan that leans like a curious neighbour over Rachel's gatepost. Vanishes birds, cowers cats under upturned wheelbarrows. Drums worms from their suburban burrows to swim in an ecstasy of water. Hammers flat the drilled and refilled tarmac of Burnthope Road. Astonishes storm-drains into spewing fountains of its own excess. Dissolves the smug bay-windowed smile of Rachel's house. Paints the settled compass of her life after Logan as veiled, indistinct; the window at his leathered elbow now an ancient TV with poor reception. The car roof thunders with applause.

Flora appears as a brushstroke of colour, an impressionist smear. She runs towards him through the deluge, raincoat cantilevered over her head. Scoots round the bonnet, a smudged embodiment of love through the weirs and waterfalls of the windscreen, to the passenger door, which she pops open like a briefcase even as he leans for the handle. She slides into her seat, damp and panting, all in one movement: a try or a touchdown.

Dad, you idiot! Did you not see the rocks?

He growls at her, *Or alternatively, Hello Dad, how are you?*

She leans over to kiss him: a waft of the scent she habitually wears, something he himself bought for her at her insistence when she turned sixteen *because I'm going to be a woman.* Called some ridiculous name, *Devotion* or something. She settles a hessian shoulder bag into the footwell, snaps her seat belt together.

Dad, really, I'm serious. Twenty years of this, and you're still driving Mum crazy.

How so?

Parking on the verge. It wrecks the grass. Did you really not see? She put rocks there to stop you.

I thought the grass was a bit bumpier than usual. To stop me in particular?

You're pretty much the only person who does it.

He puts the car into gear, releases the handbrake and moves off, focused on the quarter-arc of view which windscreen wipers are valiantly labouring to clear.

Pretty much?

Apart from delivery men. And they're trying not to block the road with their vans. What's your excuse?

He glances at her questioning eyebrows.

It pisses your mum off. A pause to test her reaction. *I'm kidding. I don't think about it.*

Well, maybe you should, Flora says. *For the sake of peace. Mine, not yours. I'm the one that gets the flak, you know. I think you like being stuck in her craw.*

Sorry, he says. And he is.

You should be. You're lucky the ground's so wet, it's swallowed them up. A drier day, and you'd have dented your sill.

What do you know about sills?

John, she says.

The hairy one?

Yes, she sighs, *the hairy one.*

That's right. Into cars.

Obsessive, she says. *Was restoring an old Jag. Spent half the time he might have been with me prostrate in his garage, wrestling with six kinds of rust. That car was in more pieces at the end of our relationship than it was at the beginning. I'm sure I moaned to you about it at the time. Do you not remember?*

Vaguely, Logan says. When she talks about boyfriends, he tries not to listen. He doesn't want to think of them touching her.

She pulls down the sun visor, peering into the mirror to rearrange the damp curls on her forehead.

Where are we going, then?

The usual.

That would be a good name for it, she says. *The Usual. The Usual and Commonplace. That's what they can call the Rose and Crown, come the revolution.*

Lunch at the Rose and Crown arrives in unsatisfactory pieces. His starter is garnished with pistachios, though he specified his allergy. The atoms that make up his steak and ale pie are overagitated by the microwave and furious enough to strip two layers of cells from the roof of his mouth. The spinach, boiled beyond any hope of texture, lies dispirited at the side of his plate like a pile of discarded school jumpers.

The wine, however, is surprisingly good. He can forgive the food in the clean wash of a good Pinot.

Dad, seriously? she says, as he pours himself a second glass.

Thin people have a fast metabolism, he answers, *the first glass will be thoroughly processed by the time we've had pudding.* He is thinking only of driving the car, a function he trusts to his subconscious. He is not imagining the perils of losing control of his tongue, of crashing the conversation centres of his brain into the tree trunk of a hidden memory. Her face is animated with the details of her three-month sojourn in Thailand, framed by earrings that successfully draw his eyes from the plaintive flashing of a playerless fruit machine. A staff member polishes the bar a few years away. Years, yes, it is almost years since he sat opposite his daughter in the Hope and Disaster, the Johnny Come Lately, or whatever republican name she was giving it that time around. And he is still savouring the Pinot as it unlocks a train of thought that will lead him to a disastrous noun.

... so I left him in Koh Samui.

Who?

Adam. Dad, aren't you listening?

Of course I am. I lose track of all your boyfriends. Why did you leave – Adam – in Koh Samui?

She screws him a look, but continues.

He kept fondling ladyboys when he was drunk. Thought it was funny. He was a total child.

She has stripped her plate clean somehow, though he swears she didn't once stop talking. She signals to the barman to throw her a bag of crisps. Logan wonders if one of her Thai souvenirs is a tapeworm. No one her age goes travelling now. They stay in, do everything virtually. Though he will lecture the children of friends on the benefits of Real Life, he wishes his own daughter were less adventuresome.

Men your age, he says, *men in their twenties, they're boys, really. Women grow up fast, but men stay children for a long time.*

She squeezes the bag until it pops.

That's exactly how Mum explains your behaviour.

He is rankled.

My behaviour?

Flora's eyes, vivid green in the light of a rain-curtained window, are soothingly matter-of-fact.

You know. Leaving women the minute they have your babies.

Hardly 'the minute', Flo. You were – Tom was – Furious calculations thwarted by a memory of Rachel in tears, empty-ing a nappy bucket.

I was three.

Three years with Rachel had felt like a decade. Considering their relationship was over the night Flora was conceived, Logan thought he had done an extraordinary job of sticking with it. At least he saw her through the gruelling bit: did his fair share of jiggling and soothing and four a.m. pacing with a colicky bundle hiccuping on his shoulder. But what had gone wrong with Johanna? Guilt bubbles up, and he severs the thought with a platitude.

Something happens to women when they have children.

Yes, they stop mummying you, Flora says, and looks at him mischievously.

He splutters to defend himself, and a laugh explodes out of the side of her mouth, carrying with it a tiny shower of lobster and pesto crisp.

It's hardly funny, he says.

Oh, Dad, you're very funny, she says, *you just don't know it.*

The trouble begins back in the car. Logan is a little drunker than he intended. Probably over the legal limit, but he feels only gently softened at the edges. He is sure his instincts are sharp enough. He will reach the end of this journey physically safe, the car intact. But he fails to register the humming presence of a far greater danger: that half a bottle of wine has chemically reacted with their earlier conversation and will soon catalyse his speaking to her with an honesty reserved for friends. No, not even friends. Reserved for himself.

There is another factor churning in his stomach. He has finally noticed that his daughter is a woman. A woman so beautiful, both inwardly and outwardly, that any man who meets her and fails to fall in love with her must surely be a fool. Logan can hardly believe she is his flesh and blood, let alone that he created her. How could half of him plus half of Rachel possibly equal this infinitely glorious being? Her very goodness means that *he* must be good. In her presence his sins are understood and forgiven. She is the only woman he can trust himself not to hurt.

He tells her to wait under the porch, and drives round in the still-pouring rain to save her getting wet. But she has abandoned cover to help someone in the car park manoeuvre his elderly mother out of her wheelchair. Flora lands on her seat and slams the door, shaking herself. Rain has separated her loose curls into ringlets again and just for a moment her six-year-old self is equally present. He is protective still, wants her smaller than she is, so he can tease and chide her rather than the other way around.

Oh, I nearly forgot, she says, as she's about to strap in, *I'm doing a thing.*

A thing?

She lets go of the seat belt so she can lean forward.

A drop.

A drop?

She fumbles in the shoulder bag between her feet.

From an aeroplane. *For charity. You know.*

What charity?

She surfaces from her search waving a piece of paper.

Does it matter? I'm jumping out of an aeroplane, *Dad!*

Big grin, nine-year-old grin. She hands over the sponsorship form, follows it with a chewed biro.

He cannot miss the name of the charity, printed beside its safely neutral logo. Freedom from Fistula. Simon Merriweather's charity. He scans her face for a hint that the joke is about to unravel, but she's clueless.

I know the man who set up this charity.

Really? she says, uninterested. *A friend from uni has gone to work for them. She's organizing the drop.*

Coincidence, then. Just a weird coincidence. He duly fills in the details of his donation, ensuring it's double Rachel's.

Rather you than me, he says, handing the form back to her damp, ink-smudging hands. *What were you doing to get so wet?* he asks.

The man was having trouble, she says. *With his mum's wheelchair. First time he'd taken her out in it.*

Logan eyes the box-ugly car hesitantly nosing out of the car park. He knows that shape of car is favoured by those who barely have the confidence to drive, let alone abduct young women. Nevertheless, as he follows its tail lights out onto the main road he can't help saying, *You should be more careful. It could have been a trick. He could have bundled you into the back and driven off.*

Flora guffaws. *With his eighty-year-old mother in the car? Come on, Dad. I think I can tell the weirdos from the psychos. Anyway, you're forgetting my chip. They can track me from space, if needs be.*

Chip or no chip, you shouldn't put yourself in the way of danger. Sure, they can track your body, but it only takes seconds to kill someone.

My, we are jolly today! I helped a guy with his disabled mum. Where's your trust? I've been halfway round the world on my own.

He considers this reality and shivers.

You shouldn't have left whatshisname while you were still out there. In Thailand. It isn't safe for a woman to travel alone.

His daughter demonstrates with both hands the evidence of her safety: the wholeness of her body, the absence of stab wounds.

Yes, okay, you didn't die, he acknowledges. He skirts a mini-roundabout carefully, feeding the wheel correctly through his ten-to-two hands as though he is being examined.

Most people are friendly, she says. He lets his disapproval leak into their small box of air. Words are hardly necessary.

You can't Daddy me now, she says in response. *You can father me, certainly, but Daddy went the way of Pippi Longstocking braids, gappy teeth, and chewing gum under the dinner table.*

It takes him a moment to realize what she's said.

That was never you.

Who else did you think it was?

He says nothing.

Tom! she says. *Jesus, you thought it was Tom. You didn't punish him for it, did you?*

Tom's howls of indignation at his pocket money being stopped every time a new piece of gum was discovered. How he never completed his collection of *Lord of the Rings* die-cast figures as a result. The furious denials. The tears. There had been another layer of punishment *just for lying*.

Sorry, Dad. Christ, I'll have to say sorry to Tom too. Why didn't you challenge me about it?

I had no idea it was you. You were too angelic.

She snorts.

I would have confessed. I wanted you to notice. To say something.

You wanted me to say something?

Flora slaps herself on the thigh.

Of course!

Like what?

*Like 'Flora, why do you keep sticking chewing gum under
the table when you know it upsets me?'*

And what would you have answered?

She looks at him sideways. Then turns her face to the sliding
past of suburbia.

*Oh, Dad, you have no idea. Jesus. I was cross with you.
You had this perfect home with Jules and Tom and I wanted
to mess it up.*

I had this perfect home?

It looked that way to me.

They are only two turns away from Rachel's road and he is
not done with her. He is only just learning disquieting things
and needs time to re-map himself onto her childhood. Indicating
left, he pulls over to the side of the road and switches off the
ignition. The wipers halt halfway up their arc and rain fills in the
view as rapidly as ticket-holders taking their seats for a cup final.

Flora, he says, *I'm sorry. I didn't realize you were unhappy.*

That was because you told me not to be.

I told you not to be?

Flora presses the button next to her: her window slides down.
She presses it a second time: it slides up again, miraculously
clear. She won't look at him.

This is what you get paid for, isn't it? Playing the echo.

He feels the temperature of her disdain. Almost her mother's.

Yes, she continues, *you told me not to cry. Because it upset
you. Don't you remember?*

Logan rifles through the mental kitchen drawer of his mind
from just after leaving – broken promises, doorstep rows, torn-
up letters, keys removed from their key rings. No instructions
to a daughter.

No, I don't remember saying that.

She lets out a sound like a small rodent expiring. *I guess it
didn't mean anything much to you. It meant a lot to me. It really
stuck. You didn't want to know how I felt so I kept it to myself.
But I let it out in other ways. And yes, after you and Jules bought*

*the house in Streatham, I stuck chewing gum on the underside
of your dining-room table.*

Why?

Revenge.

Revenge?

She turns to him.

*Do you know what, Dad, if you're just going to play Dr
Psychoparrot I'm getting out and walking.*

No, he says, *no. Don't do that.*

He restarts the car.

I'm just surprised. Revenge seems a little strong.

Flora says nothing. In his peripheral vision, he can see her
jaw jutting out, her lips tight with the pressure of the unsaid.

Not Flora, he thinks, not Flora too. It's bad enough with Tom.

Flora, where has this come from?

For a while she lets the windscreen wipers answer him. Finally
she says, *It was always there. The gum should tell you that.*

They are turning into her mother's road.

But you *didn't tell me. So why now?*

There is a small fist of fear in his stomach, tight and cold.
It is connected to a memory. He remembers the mouse in his
father's bedsit: a trap-savvy bin-raider known only by his nib-
blings. They never caught a glimpse of him. Then his father went
away for work and Logan stayed with Aunt Pam for a couple
of weeks. When they returned, the mouse was curled up in the
fluffy hearth rug, stone dead.

It doesn't matter, she says.

Of course it matters.

In less than a month he will understand, thanks to the post-
mortem's revelation of a small clump of cells that changed his
daughter's perspective.

Will understand, but will have no way of making amends. For
now, he can only drive more thoughtfully, pulling up alongside
the kerb with all four wheels on the road. He sees the rocks
now, compacted into the mud by his tyres. Though still falling,

the rain has lessened enough that Rachel's house is no longer a fuzzy unreality.

Flora says, *I never used to see Mum's point of view. I was a real Daddy's girl. I thought she'd driven you away with her craziness. But now I think you were the source of it.*

He silences the engine's grumbling.

She wasn't very stable when I met her, Flora.

Well, I think you destabilized her more.

He is about to defend himself when she continues, *We talk now, you know. She said you never meant to stay with her.*

That's true, but—

So why did you get her pregnant?

The Pinot greases his defence: the long-gestated fact slides out all at once.

I didn't get her pregnant on purpose.

No?

No! Jesus, Flora, you think we were a storybook couple? You think we were a perfect match, and everything went wrong after you were born? What kind of nonsense has your mother been spinning you? You were an accident!

As a child watches a kicked ball sail towards a window and punch a hole in it, he watches the understanding land on her face. Her eyes open painfully wide, and in a blink, two teary blinks, are emptied of love and stuffed to their lids with shock. The bag in the footwell is pulled into her lap as though it is a helpless mammal he has injured. For a moment, she is completely still. He watches her as one might watch a small plane, thousands of feet above the earth, whose engine has stuttered into silence. Then she's gone, the door slammed, her boots stomping up the wet path, and he is out almost as quickly, running after her, calling *Flora!* but she has reached the door.

Flora! he says again. *At least let me explain!*

She inserts her key in the door, steps inside and swivels on a heel.

Let me explain for you, Dad. You're a real arsehole.

He stares at the closed door.

Arsehole. The last word she ever spoke to him.

Finlay?

A soft voice through a long tunnel.

Finlay?

He can't remember the last time anyone said his name so tenderly. The tenderness alone is enough to spike tears, and lifts him like a helpless infant from the dread inevitability of memorial replay into Dr Salmon's compassionate gaze. Though he has been far away, only seconds have passed. His hand is gripped so tightly on the whisky tumbler that it is almost slipping away from him and he replaces it, shakily, on the sticky coaster.

Dr Salmon—

He cannot find any words.

Yes.

Her eyes are too intense, so he looks at her shoes, as unscientific as her nails: pointy and scuffed.

It does seem… It would seem… He tries again. *The last thing I said to my daughter. The last thing I told her—*

He can't say the terrible words. Has tried for eighteen months not to remember them.

But I don't understand how…

No, says Dr Salmon, *we're a long way from how. I don't have a how for you, I'm afraid. Only observations and theory. No mechanism.*

There are questions, but grief disturbs them, shakes them up into a bag of crumbs he cannot wrangle into sense. Somewhere in the bag of crumbs he locates a reasonable objection.

You say mind and brain are not the same thing. But how can Flora's mind exist independently from her brain?

As I said, we're years from the how. Steingarten and Rodgers postulate—

He holds up a hand to halt her.

Give me something I can understand. An analogy, not citations.

She gazes at him as though she is drawing the analogy out of his head, rather than hers. Takes a breath, then releases the words.

Say you were listening to someone talking on the radio. Then your dad comes in and smashes it up with a hammer.

Nice.

So it stops working. Does that mean it was generating the voice? Was the person you were listening to in the radio?

Of course not.

So when a radio breaks, is the broadcast still there?

He nods slowly. Each nod is the idea bouncing on the surface of his thinking. When it settles, she continues, *And to hear that voice again, one would only have to get another radio and tune it in to that frequency.*

Logan considers her meaning.

You're tuning your brain to Flora's frequency?

She smiles.

If the brain is a filter, let's just say that since the process my filter is a little wider than it was. Increased bandwidth, if you want to think of it that way. When I'm tuned in to you, and clear of static, I can pick up on Flora. As though— She reads his face, choosing her expression carefully. *Well, let's say the broadcast is being beamed towards you, but it's bouncing off.*

Bouncing off what?

At a guess? Your grief. Your belief in loss and separation.

Logan picks up the whisky glass and turns it slowly in his hand.

My atheism?

The centre of caramel liquid revolves; the edges cling to the side.

Yes.

Lodger

Sometimes her husband murmurs her name in his sleep.

Jules?

A soft question thrown against the long darkness. She is glad it's not some other woman's name.

Yet it might as well be. For if she wakes him, thinking she's needed, that he's drowning, that her love is the rope he wants her to throw, he greets her with confusion. She has invaded his grief, yet again, unwanted. Yet some part of him, a part that wakes up alone in the dark, is asking for her. For that part of him, she stays. Opens the curtains, dusts the hall table, makes tea.

Months ago she dreamed they had welcomed a homeless street-drinker into their house. Out of pity, and just for the night. His name was Brian. But Brian wouldn't leave, and she was too scared to ask him. Her husband was nowhere to be found, and the unwanted lodger festered in his room, drunk on the contents of their spirits cupboard. Raging and bearded, leaking anger, shouting at no one. Or maybe, at her. She tiptoed past Brian's closed door, flinching at the smatterings of violent self-talk that might explode any moment into murder. She woke in tears, reviewed the dream, and knew: *Finlay is Brian. I am married to Brian.*

She began an anonymous blog, *Wife of Brian*. Her username is brianswife. It is a place to log her loneliness. Ask advice. Crack bleakly funny jokes. What she used to share with Finlay, she shares with the internet. A growing band of commiserators follow her posts and leave their comments. They cheer her on, commend her strength. Sometimes they urge her to leave him.

Yet when she drills down, under the hurt and tears, she finds love for her husband. She is married to Brian, but somewhere inside him is Finlay. Though her husband feels utterly gone, dead as his daughter, that is the trick of grief. Finlay is buried alive, and his coffin is Brian. He is rattling around in his own monstrous craw like a pea. She glimpses him from the corner of her eye. He flicks out of existence under her focus, but faith is restored: *her husband exists!* But is trapped inside Brian. She forces herself to remember the difference: there's Brian and there's Finlay; one is not the other, the monster is not the husband, even when the monster has swallowed the husband whole. Even when, eyes aside, they look almost identical.

When her husband is swallowed by a monster, the good wife waits. There is an old folk tale, Tam Lin. A beloved husband is cursed by a witch. The curse can be broken only by love. The husband's first disguise is a tree. So the wife hugs her wooden, unyielding husband, declaring her love. But it is easy to love a tree, and no test of your trueness. The tree will not love you back, but it's harmless. The witch's curse tests love more completely. The husband will keep changing form, and the wife must hold on no matter what form he takes. If she drops him, he's lost, stuck forever in the shape that his wife couldn't tolerate. Whether she finds in her hands a poisonous snake or a razor-sharp blade, a slippery eel or a white-hot poker, and though she cannot know what terrifying transformation will follow, the wife must grip fast, keep faith that *this* is her husband. Only when her love has been tested to its end will her husband be restored.

It has been eighteen months since her stepdaughter fell from the sky and demolished their marriage. She strengthens her resolve by remembering the man she fell in love with. Before Fin, every love was a sham. Before Fin, she was all front and hiding. All lipstick and capability to her man, but privately punctured, spilling secretly in the darkness like a packet of rice at the back of a cupboard. Somewhere in her adolescence she had swallowed the cultural pill that led girls to mould themselves into what men desired. Whereas every cell of Fin whispered,

I want YOU.
Who are YOU?
Give me YOU.

Clandestine coffees, museum picnics: she was hungry for his questions, the answers to which she could only discover as she reached them. Conversational spaces, which other men filled with themselves, he left open for her. Never trespassed, but waited until, at last, she stepped forward. Six months she called him from car parks and playgrounds: colouring herself in. Discerning at last who she was. Not daughter, girlfriend, partner, fiancée, but Jules.

The freedom she found in his love was intoxicating. But it dragged fear in its wake as a luxury yacht tows a dinghy. For how could he need her at all, this man who demanded so little? If she wasn't required to complete him, would he not simply moor her to some shoreline post and vanish to a new adventure? She had challenged him to offer something permanent. He had given her the buttock rose. Which seemed generic, something he could offer any woman, until she noticed its petals spelt out her name.

Such a love cannot have evaporated into nothing. It is no more possible than that the Great Wall of China could prove itself a thousand-year-old illusion and vanish in a whiff of cordite.

But now he walls her off. She cannot access those spaces where she found herself. She plays conversational tennis against his surface, but the words bounce back. There is no opponent. No one to equal and call, *All*. No one to beat and call, *Love*. She is furious with Flora for dying.

We shared him, she tells the mirror, strangling the toothpaste tube into relinquishing yet another squeeze of itself. *I was happy with that*. Snatching the relegated kitchen sponge from its hiding place to polish to oblivion the fingerprint smear on her reflected face. *But you had to go and die*. Buffing the taps under their four brass chins like a furious barber. *And now he's bloody gone*. Filling the sink with hatred and steam, drowning the flannel. *Bloody gone*. Wringing it out, burying her face in the heat of the cloth until the lump of uncried tears in her throat begins to ease.

And it's bad enough she has to watch him pretending to eat breakfast in the kitchen, pretending to read in the study, pretending to lie by her side. But tonight she returns from cava-fuelled discussions of a novel about a serial adulterer to find her husband talking volubly to a red-haired, red-nailed woman at least a decade his junior and asking her, his wife, to make up the guest bed.

Could be worse, she says, nodding to reassure her reflection, running the movie where she finds them in the marital one. But her heart sags and splits. She has loaded herself up with too many sharp-cornered containers, carried herself too far, waited too long.

Nevertheless, she makes up the bed. All the love she feels for her husband, that cannot go anywhere, she channels into selecting the guest towels. Her dismay, she folds and piles neatly on top of the blanket box. Overwhelming fear, where can that go but into the careful positioning of a fish-shaped guest soap on the unused sink in the en suite bathroom. She dusts the ceramic with a folded square of toilet paper. And in the guest bedroom, a single tear spots the bedspread before being folded back on itself, the ocean it escaped dammed up by the small acts of decency she would gladly give anyone but her husband's future lover.

Trees

Now Logan has company in the forest. Gabrielle, hair still wet from his shower, in a grape-coloured Afghan coat. The dog pads ahead of them, dragging its ears over mud.

Your dog is okay by the road? she asks.

Achilles! he calls.

She laughs.

What?

I like the name. Your joke?

Yes. My wife's dog. My joke.

Go on, says Gabrielle, *give the command.*

He glances at her.

I can't, he says. *My wife did the training. She won't listen to me.*

Your wife?

The dog.

Achilles is a she?

I thought we were getting a boy dog, he says. *And I liked the name.*

Achilles detects their usual path and switches onto it, pulled by the electricity in her nose. October has stripped the canopy above them, exposing them to a shocking blue sky. Only nine on a Saturday morning, and already the smell of bonfires. Gabrielle, in Jules's borrowed wellies, kicks at the leaves.

She seems very nice. Jules.

Nice. A word his English teacher, Miss McAlpine, banned.

She is very nice.

The cloud of his words condenses, evaporates.

How long have you been married?

A while. He reads a flicker of emotion in her face, and softens his voice a notch. *I'd rather talk about you. How did you get into this? Consciousness studies.*

Ah. She laughs. *The sense of being stared at.*

He instinctively glances about them. They are alone.

Explain?

Gabrielle lunges for a stick that is resting against a tree trunk, as if she were afraid he might snatch it first. She was not an only child, he concludes, had at least one brother. Rather than use the stick staff-wise, she drags it behind her like a stiff tail.

When I was a child, I thought science would explain everything. That's why I loved science. I wanted to know – everything. But when I was an undergrad, the lecturers poured everything science knew into my head and I realized there were things it couldn't explain. Like, how do you know when someone's staring at you? Because you do, don't you? You can feel when someone's staring at the back of your head, and you can turn and pinpoint them exactly. Exactly! Lock eyes with them. And science can't explain it. Elizabethans thought the eyes emitted beams. But modern science has no truck with eye beams. Eyes are passive receivers of light waves. So how can you explain our sense of being stared at?

I don't know, he says. *How can you explain it?*

Is she demonstrating eye beams? It's a strong look.

It's early days, Logan. So no hows. Only hypotheses. Swishing her stick-tail, side to side.

Throw me a bone, he says.

She plods ahead, dropping questions behind her. He's familiar with the measurement of brainwaves? Does he imagine brainwaves stop at the skull? Does he know there are more than five senses? At least seven more? And that there may be others? Has he considered the evolutionary advantage inherent in a social primate sensing when he or she is the focus of another's gaze? They have reached a small stream and she stabs her stick into the ground, a pennant.

You are saying there is a sense of – Logan hesitates – *what would you call it?*

Skoporeception. Beaming from his wife's wellies to her unbrushed teeth. *From skopos, attention. It has been suggested.*

But there's no proof we have such a sense, Logan says.

Only in the experience, she answers. *I experience it rather frequently. Don't you?*

No, says Logan. Though it makes perfect sense, looking at her, that she's the focus of a stranger's gaze more often than he is.

She giant-steps over the stream, the stick now a lever propelling her forward.

Proof in terms of mechanism – if that's even achievable – is years away. This is hypothesis. But that's what you need before you start looking for proof. Goodness knows, we need more sensitive measuring equipment. Assuming we're even measuring the right thing. And there's something else.

What?

He follows her, but catches a foot on the far bank, dousing his walking boot. Unbalanced, he stumbles forward, and when she turns to answer him, she has to put a hand on his chest to stop them colliding.

I'm not even sure about the concept of proof in a quantum universe, she says, stepping away and moving on.

He is conscious of the coffee on his breath.

Why?

She sets off again.

The Observer Effect, she says over her shoulder. *Heard of the double-slit experiment?*

He has, but he doesn't really get it.

Subatomic entities behave like waves until they're measured, she tells the trees. *They then behave like particles. They don't exist in any particular state until they're observed. Until then, they're just probabilities.*

He is beginning to feel distinctly unfit. His breath is ragging, strips of it left hanging in the undergrowth.

And this affects us how exactly?

Logan! she says, wheeling to face him. *We're talking about the building blocks of everything we call reality. The entire physical world is quantum mechanical. This stick. That dog. Your face.*

Okay, he says, not getting it. Because whatever she is trying to tell him, and no matter how important it was, he can no more fit it into his brain than he could squeeze an elephant into a matchbox.

But surely proof is still possible?

If we influence what we observe, what are we proving? In her eyes, the sharp hook of the question mark. *You see it all the time – one study 'proves' salt is bad for you, another 'proves' it's good for you. Bisexuality doesn't exist, bisexuality does exist.*

Sorry? Logan is confused to hear the syllable sex. Why would she—

It's a bugbear of mine, she says. The stick is finally a staff. *An old boyfriend—Never mind. Let's go back for that breakfast you promised.*

She is always in the lead, it seems. He's not even sure they are going in the right direction. She is striding ahead with the spaniel invisibly tethered to her ankles, almost sheltering under the grape-coloured faux fur of her coat as it swings open in time with her gait. There is something Flora-ish about her. Was there always? He rolls his mind back to their first meeting and he can't detect it. Perhaps he simply couldn't see it, through the initial fizz of sexual attraction; a man never wants to see echoes of his daughter in a woman to whom his groin is responding. Or maybe—

Could it be that in receiving Flora, she is now partly Flora? Is she channelling his daughter's physical confidence, her manner, her way with him, even her stride?

Salmon! he says, jogging a few steps to catch up.

Logan, she answers, smiling at him sideways.

Stop a moment, he says, pulling his phone out of his pocket. *Explain where consciousness comes from, if it's not generated by our brains.*

Big question, Logan. You want all the answers now?

Kind of, he admits.

You're not going to give science a hundred years or so to work it out?

I'll be dead by then. Best guess?

How many dimensions are you aware of, Logan?

Three. No, four, if you include time.

Very good. You know how many dimensions string theorists suggest? Eleven.

So?

Perhaps one of those dimensions is consciousness itself.

Which comes from where?

He is looking at his phone, and she laughs.

You want GPS co-ordinates?

I'm just working out where we are so we can find our way back, he explains. *GPS co-ordinates for what?*

For God.

That's your explanation?

It's just a label for everything we don't understand. Traditionally God is omnipresent. Is everywhere. I say God is consciousness. And Logan? She fixes her eyes on him until he looks up. *I know where we are.*

Gone

Jules has laid the table for breakfast and vanished. There is a fresh granary loaf on the bread board, and a bag of croissants from the village bakery. Beside the kettle the spherical chrome teapot, whose insides are heaped with the correct quantity of loose leaf Twinings Assam, gapes like a patient at the dentist's. Gathered in the centre of the kitchen's reclaimed oak table, a cluster of home-made jams bought at the Women's Institute Fayre, complete with their rubber-banded paper mob caps. Flanking the jams at perfect ninety-degree angles: two black slate place mats, which slide-rule precision has arranged with two square white side plates, two best-set knives, and the cup and saucer pair he brought home from Paris one long-ago Valentine's. His wife's more prosaic breakfast crockery is dripping itself dry on the draining board, and the car is missing.

Logan feels a pang at the orderliness of it all. *Will you make up the guest bed?* was all he said. And *Of course* was all she replied; no emotion in her face, no drama. It was he who was afraid.

Gabrielle had been tired and ready to leave. The crunch of tyres in the drive provoked his guest to notice the time; the first words of excusal from her lips and his stomach began worming: *What if? What if?* No other words, and he buried the worm under good manners, but as she reached for her coat from the hall banister and yawned, the sentence completed. What if she fell asleep at the wheel? What if she – this person who could speak to his daughter – wrapped her car round a tree? She'd be lost to him. It happens. These things happen. He had taken the grape Afghan from her, as if he was about to help her into it, but saw a rash of blue lights, pneumatic cutting equipment, Gabrielle's white, uninhabited face. He folded the coat over his arm.

Please stay, he said. *It's too late for driving. Tomorrow is Saturday. You can stay in the guest room.*

At which point, a key turned in a lock and Jules walked in, a book under her arm, wine on her breath. Saw him, saw Gabrielle.

This is Dr Salmon, he said.

Just arrived?

Just leaving, said Gabrielle.

And words fell from his mouth: *No, please*— too quick. Too desperate. A veil fell over his wife's gaze, as though she had kicked herself into neutral. In response, Logan found a more rational gear.

I'd rather you stay, Dr Salmon. I'd worry about you driving back so late.

Jules cut a wake between them, making for the hall closet. Her back to them, she began to hang up her outdoor trappings.

Where has she got to go? she asked, erasing Gabrielle from the hallway.

Brighton, said Gabrielle. *It's okay*—

Logan reached for her arm. *No, no, you'll stay. Jules, will you make up the guest bed?*

Of course.

And his wife had passed back between them and ascended the stairs, and he had hooked his guest's coat safely into the closet on top of his own. And later, had lain like a rotting log beside his wife's awake but unmoving body, not knowing what to say. Because how do you explain the sudden appearance of a young woman with red hair, red fingernails and impractical shoes to a wife with whom you can barely discuss curtains?

How can you communicate, without appearing insane, that you believe this archetypal Other Woman has been conversing with your dead daughter? And if this suspect guest offers even the smallest possibility you could talk to your dead daughter too, how can you serve up the fragile dish of your hope to someone so likely to dash it?

Jules not here? asks Gabrielle, flamingo-legged on the threshold of the back door, levering off the borrowed wellies with difficulty.

No, he says, watching her Flora-ness with unease.

Before long, she is back to being Dr Salmon, buttering her toast with an unforgiving enthusiasm that tears it up like galloped turf. She lines up the jams, twists their labels before her, then singles out the blackcurrant, undressing it from its Victorian servant headwear and popping the underlying clingfilm with glee.

This is nice, she says.

That banned word again.

You haven't tried it yet.

No, but they're all nice. Look at them. Handwritten labels. Countrified. Made with love. Old school. My mum used to do this kind of thing for a bit.

For a bit?

Until she got tired and buggered off.

You went with her?

No. Well, only after Dad hanged himself.

She is knifing a generous dollop of blackcurrant jam onto her plate.

Oh my God, says Logan. *I'm so sorry.* The professional response would have been, *Your dad hanged himself?* But instead he is fighting a prickle of tears.

Why are you sorry? she asks, looking up. Then understands. *Ah, right. No. It's me who should be sorry. I forget, this upsets people.*

Doesn't it upset you?

Not any more. A bite of toast. Two dark purple globes kamikaze to the plate. She chews, swallows. *I know, it must seem strange. Six months ago I wouldn't have believed it myself. I mean, I can still see him swinging there. It just doesn't have any feelings attached to it any more. The memory is further away, fuzzy, black and white, like an old film of something that was never anything to do with me.* She scoops the two escaped blackcurrants back onto the toast and chomps off another corner.

You were the one who found him?

Chew, swallow, slurp of tea.

Yup. Bad planning, eh? I guess he didn't think through to the discovery, and who would be traumatized. I suppose if you're about to do yourself in, you're not rational.

Logan butters his own toast with the care and precision of a carpet layer. Each thin curl of butter unrolled into its place and pressed down.

So what happened? he asks. *What did you do?*

Went into shock, she says. *Closed down. For about twenty years, if I'm honest.*

It seems to Logan she is always honest.

And it affected you how?

Nightmares. Flashbacks. An intense interest in neurology and the afterlife. She pops a final piece of toast into her mouth like a full stop. Then remembers something else, and says, toastily, *Oh, and a massive, massive fear of abandonment. Which made me rubbish in relationships.* She swallows, licks her fingers and grins.

And now?

All gone! she says cheerily, mimicking the tone of a mother to her toddler after the last spoonful of puréed fruit. Logan isn't sure if she means the toast, the fear, or the relationships.

All gone because of…

She fills the gap left for her answer with a dipped head, raised eyebrows, widened 'you know' eyes.

The process? he ventures.

Dr Salmon leaps up. *Shall I make more tea?*

Logan nods and reaches for the Duerr's thin-sliced marmalade he had to fetch, separately, from the cupboard. He has been eating the same marmalade for twenty-three years. Astonishing how his wife failed to put out the marmalade, but furnished the table with a bowl of sugar lumps, which he bought by mistake six months ago from the village shop.

So how is that possible? he asks.

Distracted by tea-making, *What?*

That this process of yours could just— Not understanding what it's done, he isn't sure how to finish.

I don't know, she says. *But I intend to spend the next few years finding out.*

Logan spreads the marmalade squarely, to the border of the crusts, no further.

Did you try talk therapy of any kind?

She laughs. *Oh yes, I've had plenty of abominably expensive chats. Sorry, it's your business, isn't it?* She returns to the table with the chrome globe, full and hot, pours both of them a fresh cup.

So do you think the process somehow synthesized all the work done in those sessions?

Sure, that's right, nothing works for twenty years. Then I undergo this new process, am immediately released from pain, and I should credit the things that didn't work? Come on, Logan, you're not serious?

He is staring at the toast, but has lost his hunger. His stomach is tight as a child cringing from a blow.

But how could anything work so fast?

Gabrielle has balanced two sugar lumps on the side of her cup, like swimmers on the side of a pool. She pokes each one in with a small brown splash.

Perhaps it didn't know it was supposed to work slowly, she says.

Logan wants to get a cloth. Desperately wants to get a cloth. Controls himself.

But people spend years in therapy overcoming that sort of thing.

And not overcoming it, either, she says. *You assume psychological change can only be achieved slowly, because that's your experience. But perhaps it's only slow when the methodology is wrong.*

He can feel himself bristling. *In what way, wrong?*

Say you want to move a mountain of salt. Takes years with a teaspoon. Takes minutes with hot water.

Now she is on to the croissants, tearing one apart in its sections like a pastry crustacean.

We use electrical stimulation, Logan. And electricity isn't slow. It's instantaneous. Switch on a light – pow. Same in the brain. You know how I see it?

Logan knows he is about to find out.

In the nineteenth century, she says, *medicine was biology. We're at the organism level. Leeches and bleeding. Something wrong? Cut it off with a saw. Then comes twentieth-century medicine, and it's chemistry. We've gone down a layer to the molecular level. Something wrong? Take a pill. And another pill for the side-effects. Twenty-first-century medicine will be physics. Dealing with matter in its fundamental form: energy. Brain stimulation. And goodness knows what else.*

The tail of the crustacean: scooped through jam and popped in her mouth. Logan feels queasy, disoriented. The delayed effect, perhaps, of last night's whisky, reactivated by tea and without the salvation of solids.

For mental health issues, he says, staring at the toast.

For physical ones too. Because what is the biggest underlying factor in all health conditions? Stress. And what is stress but emotional overload? Thoughts and feelings, Logan. Electrical charge.

He cuts his toast into six small squares, in the hope miniaturization will make it more appetizing.

It sounds like you're intending – stretching for a lightness he fails to achieve – *to put me out of business.*

Oh Jesus, she says, *don't worry, it'll take years before any of this becomes mainstream. First hurdle is putting together large-scale double-blind peer-reviewed trials. Given that most of the funding is controlled by the pharmaceutical companies, and this kind of research gets automatically dismissed by orthodox journals, you'll die before it's widely accepted. In the meantime, plenty of unbalanced people will get to commit insane-looking crimes, and you'll get to assess them.*

Logan considers the unnecessary murders she is countenancing so cheerfully. *And this doesn't bother you?*

Another segment of crustacean, popped, swallowed.

Would there be a point in it bothering me? Would my being bothered make the world change any faster? Or just negatively impact on my well-being?

She has a point. Nevertheless Logan is feeling increasingly nauseous. He's beginning to realize the cause is not undigested whisky but Dr Salmon's relentless positivity.

Dr Salmon, I—

Sorry, I'm going too fast. Too much to take in. I appreciate that. But can you allow that we don't know very much? The tide of nausea is rising, but she continues. *As much as ninety-five per cent of the universe is dark energy and dark matter. Dark as in obscure, we have no idea what it is, cannot account for it. Ninety-five per cent!*

Water begins to pool in his mouth and he realizes he is only seconds from vomiting. He rises in a panic, knocking the chair onto its back. Runs from her astonished face for the downstairs toilet, kneeling at the bowl just in time for the retching to begin.

Beans

When he returns, he finds his guest on the sitting-room sofa, trying not to read the free paper Jules brought into the house yesterday. He can tell this because she has left it on the table, rather than pulling it onto her lap, but has nevertheless been hooked by one of the headlines and is leaning forward to take her dose of national misery. He has the same problem: a compulsion to ingest whatever text is available. Advertising flyers, food packaging. She bounces back upright, as if his entrance severed a cord.

Are you okay? she asks. *Can I help?*

Yes. No. Yes, I'm okay, and no, you can't help. He positions himself by the fireplace. *Though I appreciate the offer.*

She pulls her bag onto the sofa.

I was thinking it's about time I got going, she says.

And again, even though it is not late, or dark, or icy, he feels a tiny shudder of alarm. Ridiculous, he tells himself.

Before you do, he says, *there's something I must ask you.*

Go on.

Last night, he ventures, picking up a glass tortoise Flora bought Jules for a birthday, then becoming conscious of his action and replacing it, *last night you said you thought I was a good man.*

I know you are a good man.

How do you know? How can you know this about me, for certain?

He wants a nail to hang his self-esteem upon, some external proof that he is worth saving. But Dr Salmon disappoints.

Since the process, it feels like – I sense the good in pretty much everyone.

He points at the paper she was trying not to read: someone with narrow-set eyes recently elected to the European Parliament and promoting the violent removal of France's Roma population. *Him? You sense goodness in him?*

Not from the photograph. But I suppose if I was put in his company.

Logan thinks of some of the people he has been asked to assess. The bullies and domestic abusers. The premeditated murderers. And those rare but disturbing individuals who simply exude evil. To be in the same room with one of those people is to feel your blood cells rush faster through your veins, away, away, as though they drag their victims' ghosts around with them and those ghosts are screaming, unheard, in your ears. Just sharing the same air with one like that draws your thoughts into disused warehouses where meat hooks swing and terrible things are done, or moorland at night, the chuck of a spade, and you know you cannot be long with them, the air is visibly darkening, you are being sucked into whichever circle of Hell they inhabit, and your wife and children are already at risk.

I don't suppose, he says, *you have, since completing the process, met a psychopath.*

Not to my knowledge, she says.

Someone truly evil.

I don't know if I believe in evil, she says. *I believe more in – the absence of good.*

And he thinks again about the absence of good, so absent it is a vacuum, sucking you into its horror. He takes refuge in his armchair, the sturdy comfort of a Chesterfield.

So it's not that I'm an especially good man, he says, *but just that you now think everyone good.*

Don't take it as an insult, she laughs, digging into her bag for her car keys.

It has nothing to do with my daughter, anyway.

I don't know, she says, clasping the keys and placing the bag on the floor, *maybe it does. It was what I felt moved to say to you. I felt it strongly after she – can I call it a visit? – visited me.*

Strictly speaking, one would call it a visitation, surely.

Only if you wanted to call her a ghost. She rotates the key ring – a plump brass heart. *And I don't think— I mean, maybe that's what ghosts are, but I think the idea of a ghost is misunderstood.*

Ghosts are classically misunderstood, surely, that's why they come back, right?

Logan believes nothing of the kind, but hopes to lighten her seriousness.

But I don't think they're ever gone, she says. *We have this idea of separation. But it's wrong.*

How can you speak with such certainty?

Because I've experienced otherwise. As certainly as you experience that chair.

Others can experience this chair.

She stands.

I am not alone, Dr Logan. The non-physical world is perfectly real. Just because you don't have access to something, or equipment sensitive enough to measure it, doesn't mean it's non-existent. Someone who couldn't bend their legs or hips could never sit in that chair and experience it as you do. It wouldn't mean it wasn't real.

They could see it with their eyes.

Not if they were blind. In equivalent terms, Dr Logan, you are blind and cannot bend. You deny the existence of the subtler senses despite a plethora of phenomena that cannot be explained with the more obvious five. You think the rationalist/materialist viewpoint the only sane perspective and all other positions the domain of kooks—

Hold on, hold on! He is glad to have rattled her. It reassures him she is human. *I'm not saying you're a kook. I'm just trying to understand.*

This is not something you'll get your head around. You have to experience it to know it.

Do the process, you mean.

Do the process.

And if I did, you think I would be able to speak to Flora myself?

Maybe, she says. *No guarantees.*

He follows her to the hall closet.

No guarantees?

It's experimental. You know this.

He helps her thread her arms into the sleeves.

Of course, of course. In her strong advocacy, he had almost forgotten the nature of it. *But it might be possible. For me to communicate with Flora.*

She tugs his front door open.

Possible, yes.

When he has watched her pull out of his drive, he sends a text to Jules.

Okay?

Eventually she responds.

In Tescos. Want green beans?

Song

Since the pool party surfaced, April has been humming. All day, and all night for as long as she can stay awake, humming any tune that will give her refuge. She begins with hymns. 'Onward Christian Soldiers': strong, circular, and, for a few hours, a ring of courage no memory can cross. An image flashes into her head: she hums louder. The tune summons Archangel Michael and his sword. Snicker-snack, and another boy is decapitated. No words. The tune alone obliterates. When it wears off, she falls upon 'Lord of the Dance'. And when that tires, 'Dear Lord and Father of Mankind'.

Hymns are the world safe and simple. Primary school assembly, a whole school in grey pleated skirts and shorts, cross-legged, naked knee to knee, the smell of waxed wooden floors, the sinewy hands of Mrs Grover plonking the piano.

But the hymns wear out. After three days she is running through one after another, abandoning this one mid-chorus, that one mid-verse, a dozen after only a lungful of bars: a desperate chorister flicking through her mental hymnbook to land on something, something… but the faces are breaking through, and the smell of chlorine, and a tightness around her wrists, and something jagged as broken glass stuck in her throat. And she is lost, drowning, until she finds, at last, a tune that quells the panic. At first she can't identify it, but as the fear subsides she can think again. It's a nursery rhyme.

'Three Blind Mice' at a gallop lasts until she tips into sleep. In the morning, it's 'Oranges and Lemons' until the sunlight slopes off the end of her bed. And then one that sticks. One that counts, and needs its words.

One, two, three four five, once I caught a fish alive.

Any incursion of memory, she only has to sing a little louder and she's back into numbers.

Six, seven, eight nine ten, then I let it go again.

A flash, a breath.

Why did you let it go? Because it bit my finger so. Which finger did it bite? This little finger on the right. One, two, three four five…

And all day, and all night, and all week it contains her. As long as she sings, she is safe. She eats around it, humming only for as long as it takes to swallow. She stares into the eyes of the staff, singing, singing. She knows they will take it as madness, though it is the opposite. It is what keeps madness at bay.

One morning a woman comes. A woman with forms, a hot chocolate voice, elf-shoes, and a case like a drill might live in.

It's the friend of Dr Logan's. *One, two, three four five, once I caught…*

With two guards, they travel to a private clinic with an MRI machine. The MRI machine is *Just to check we're in the right area*, says the woman. Are they in the right area? It's very white, very clean, very hold-still-while-I-remove-this-vital-organ.

Then I let it go again.

The woman opens the case and brings out something that looks like a hairnet, trailing wires.

Which finger did it bite?

The woman's words slip through the gaps between lines.

Non-invasive, she says. *Like a hat.*

She positions the hairnet on April, plugs the trailing wires into something in her drill case, then repositions the hairnet, twice.

One, two, three four five...

The MRI machine looks like it could kill you. Cook you from the inside out, like a microwave. April doesn't mind. That'll be fine. That'll be perfect.

Six, seven, eight nine ten...

There's a cage for her head. That is good, her head needs a cage. She lies on the tray as she's told. They will slide her in and cook her, she will come out done, they will slide her into the cooling rack at the morgue.

Once I caught a fish alive.

The machine swallows her and the noise begins. So loud, so monstrously loud, that her throat is surprised into silence. It is so very sore. She doesn't have to sing any more. There is nothing, nothing outside the noise. She closes her eyes. It begins.

What? The unravelling. The tugging of threads. Memories like rolls of film pulled out of her head yard by yard, unspooled into the light and dissolved in its brightness. Jigging on Grandma's knee. Sundress with a daisy wish spot. Musical teddy, toddled into the sea and rusted silent. Green and white gingham. Pushed over by the boy. Handstands on the wall, six of them, giggles, show-your-knickers. A slap. Nothing forgotten. All remembered and retrieved... but neutralized.

A wall of sadness hovers, threatens to break over her head like a giant wave. But it breaks instead on a television in the dim back room of an unknown kid in a faraway country. Countless moments of squashed-down emotion, lumps in the throat, crumble to the clean white sand of a tropical beach and a long, cool drink. Humiliation in a music lesson: erased, sheet music wiped of its crotchety spikes, now filling only with the pleasure of Allegro in G. First week at secondary school, too scared to get past the *No* of the dinner lady, wetting herself in afternoon assembly: undone. The two boys behind who spotted the wet patch, smelt wee, and for five years called her... whatever it was, it's already gone.

Then the school she transferred to for sixth form: corridors thick with privilege. Impenetrable friendships: groups and gaggles. No lab partner. Swapped to the sticky locker. They are in gangs or pairs and she's alone, but under a hundred eyes. Even as they rise, the memories fall like a sift of flour, blow into clouds that evaporate into the perfect blue of an azure, time-lapsed sky.

A perfect blue that darkens, liquefies, lit from below. It's coming. The thump of Madonna. It's coming. Her heart snags and gallops, her breath catches on the jag in her throat, but the film is speeded up, zipped through: there are the boys, gathered round a doll, a thing, a collection of meaningless parts. Jerking like idiot extras, they expend their dark energy. She isn't there but above them, drinking their histories. Now she knows them: guiltless babies, marinated in manhood, confused by pornography, and in each of their cores, a fear of being shamed. And each of them now, by this unravelled act, imbibing an essence as toxic as taipan venom, a poison that shadows the daughters and wives of their futures. She slows time to watch them carry the poor, poor dear to the edge of the pool and swing her into the blue, as if they can wash away what they've done, and she's sorry for them, for the misery they will know, and forgiveness is easy as breathing. All emotion washed free, she sees only a story: a culmination, and a beginning. The water that was blue is clear, and the image drains away.

For a moment she's back in her body: the clinical light, the astonishing noise. No thought, no feeling: she is almost clean. But there is something else, and it pulls up in front of her mind's eye, opens its doors with a hiss. She steps again onto the bus.

The atheist charter. So easy to join them: just sign on the trip sheet, Humanities noticeboard. She gives them her tenner, her backpack heavy with The Project. Stowed in an overhead locker. No questions. They don't know her, bar Rick, the mocker, the fucker. The anger puffs into light like a photo flash. But she's going with them. They're going with her. To meet God. So they'll see He exists. *Because He's her only, her only...* Fear, rising like the head of a cobra, widening its threat, and the panic that had her running down the bus to the just-closing door, mumbling, *I forgot, I can't go* – this fear and this panic are suddenly, simply, turned off. A switch, and the current has vanished. She is calm. Calm and cool and deep as a lake in the quietest mountains. So calm that when she hears the explosion her only thought is *release*.

2.

PSYCHOLOGY

Alarm

Logan wakes with a start. Nothing but the tender tick of his wife's clock, her noiseless breathing, and the absolute darkness held at bay by the curtains.

Something is wrong. His breath is ragged. T-shirt soaked. As though his body squeezed out its own water to chill him awake. What does it know? The clock adds its evidence: 4.27. Is he due in court? Has he forgotten some vital piece of testimony? He allows the day of the week to surface. Sunday.

Something is definitely wrong. Sliding out from under the duvet, he pads to the bathroom, closes the door before turning on the light wired to a thrumming extractor. The unfriendly smell of the wrong kind of sweat. He peels off his T-shirt, slips it under the lid of the laundry bin. Running a sink full of water, he dabs a hot flannel under his arms. Some thought sharked into his sleep. What was it? He blinks to accommodate the brightness, peers into his own reluctantly awake eyes... and knows.

It was her. Gabrielle Salmon. Too... too everything. Too alluring. Too clever. Too odd. Too perfect.

And too convenient.

Say you wanted to ruin a man. Say you wanted to test his allegiance to rational principle. Say you knew that his weakness lay in the female sex, in the conquest of reasonable objection and C-cup breasts. You would send such a woman. A beautiful Salmon, slippery and scaled. A woman named after an angel, the angel, not coincidentally, of communication. Who purports to communicate – God! – with your smashed dead daughter.

He grips the edge of the sink as the tendons in his legs lose their tension, thigh muscles shake; he sits on the edge of the

bath and then, as that feels too precarious, lowers himself all
the way to the floor.

She's a trap.

Scrambled

His filing is not what it was. It takes nearly two hours to locate
the thing he is looking for – not in the pile on the desk, not in
the five piles on the floor by the bookcase, not in his briefcase,
and not, certainly not, in the filing cabinet under A for articles.
But he finds it eventually, bookmarking a novel he was half-
reading on the train three months ago. Jules knocks, tentatively
opens the door.

You all right, love? You're up early.

Couldn't sleep, he says, waving her away. He needs to read
it. He needs to do it now. He needs to do it without his wife's
gaze boring into his forehead. She hovers for five or six seconds,
then clicks the door into place.

The article that led him to Gabrielle Salmon unfolds in his
hands. And attached to it – now he remembers – the yellow
Post-it that shepherded it into his view. In personality-free
capitals:

INTERESTING, NO? – S

He makes a call.

Sean? Logan.

Sean laughs. *Why do you always say that? Your name comes
up when it rings, you know.*

*I know. Listen, do you remember a few months ago, you sent
me an article about human consciousness?*

I sent you a what?

A scientific paper. 'Creating God in the Human Brain'?

Creating GOD? Logan, are you okay? Jules said you've been—
I'm fine. Never mind. See you next week.

So it wasn't Sean. He'd just assumed. Although why he'd assumed that, why he'd assigned 'S' to Sean, he now couldn't remember. His brain hasn't been working well recently. He's had to shut down so much of it to stop himself thinking about Flora. Protecting himself from the truth was an indiscriminate process: it began with avoiding the word 'daughter' and ended in an aversion to the smell of freshly mown grass. Painful fragments could attach themselves to almost anything. He wondered if this was where Alzheimer's began: a yearning for a specific forgetfulness that arrived obediently, but spread, by the process of connection, from neurone to neurone until the mind was a blank.

And now he has to think. 'S' wasn't Sean. So who had sent him the article? Who does he know whose name begins with S, who might want to ruin him?

Another knock on the door. Jules again, this time with a cup of coffee in her hand. Clearly not hers, from the way she is holding it: a little away from herself, like an offering to an angry god.

I thought you could do with it.

She places it carefully on his circuit-board coaster (Flora's gift), turns the handle towards him. He looks at her unmade-up face, the face he stole from happiness.

I'm making scrambled eggs, she says. *Do you want some?*
I'll come down, he says. She leaves.

S.

Simon Merriweather? But it's been years, more than a decade, since Jules left her fiancé crying in a National Trust car park. And maybe three years since their last awkward meeting, in the pasta aisle of Waitrose. And after Flora's death, didn't he send that card with the letter inside expressing his sorrow and regret? Surely he would have moved on long ago, a good man like that, raised to forgive, not avenge, a busy man with fistulas to fix—

Simon, he says to his wife's egg-stirring back. *How's he doing these days? Do you know?*

You care why? asks Jules, turning round.

Do you know how he's doing? he asks again. *Has he been in contact at all?*

She blushes. There's something there. She turns back to the eggs.

Not exactly, she says.

Logan sits down at the table. He watches her back. More stirring.

What do you mean, not exactly?

Her left hand moves to her hip. An unconscious defensive gesture.

I follow his status updates.

TwitFacing. He doesn't like it. Doesn't like her doing it.

Since when?

She goes to the fridge. Retrieves the packet of smoked salmon, slides out the foiled inner card, laces two plates with thin, pink slices.

A few months ago.

No expression at all in her voice. He's betting it's in her face, if only he could see it.

Any particular reason?

She shepherds the scrambled eggs onto the plates in two unequal piles. More for him than her.

He sent me a friend request.

Logan is waiting. The breakfast plates are ready, and any moment she will have to turn round.

And you accepted it why?

It's her phrasing. They have lived long enough together to echo each other's verbal mannerisms. He can see her breathing through at least three answers, her shoulders rising and falling as she takes extra air into her chest to fish out the right words. Finally, with a plate in each hand, she turns. Her eyes lock into his: engaging in battle.

Because he's a good man. And he was a very good friend to me. If I wasn't a good friend to him, and if he's prepared to overlook that, then why shouldn't I accept his friend request? And what would refusing it mean? It wouldn't say anything nice, would it?

She puts his plate in front of him with inordinate care.

It would say your relationship is over, says Logan.

He knows that.

So why did he send you a friend request?

I don't know! Her face is exasperated. *Maybe because he wanted me to know that he's happy now. He's met someone. A pilot. She flies supplies around Africa for one of his partner charities. They're engaged.*

She pushes the salt and pepper pots towards him in a single movement, as though the table is a makeshift battle map and she is miming the advancement of artillery. Logan is surprised to see tears in her eyes.

What?

I can't believe you're jealous. I can't believe you actually care enough to be jealous.

The dog, who has been watching them both with concern, flicks her eyes to Logan. *Don't you start*, he thinks at the dog.

You do all the shit stuff to perfection, don't you, she says. *All the relationship shit. Why can't you do the good stuff, too? You're worried Simon might steal me back? Then why don't you treat me like you want to keep me? For God's—*

She stops. Pushes her plate away, and leaves the room.

He wants to go to her, but she's angry. And he can't in any case give her what she wants. Which is simply, he knows, himself: a version of himself he can't access, an older version written over by the new release, a version not hampered by guilt or skewed by self-loathing. And to go with her with his hands empty, with nothing to offer her, will only increase her despair.

Logan looks at the dog. The dog looks at the plate.

A little later, Logan hears the front door click. He goes to the sitting room to open her laptop and Achilles follows him in. *I'm not prying*, he tells the dog, *I'm investigating*. He doesn't know Jules's passwords, but the machine does. So, without fuss, here is her TwitFace profile, here are her 'friends', and a quick scroll down, a click, give him Merriweather's shaving-advert face. With, it's true, a woman's adoring face beside it. *This is shit*, he tells the dog as he pages through the photos, *but I have to be sure*. And after a few seconds, no question, *the man's in love*. And not with Logan's wife, but with a brunette called Sam Rollinson.

But there's something up. *Sam and I, Sam and I, Sam and I* say the updates, driving inexorably towards a boutique wedding until they hit an invisible wall. Five months since Cunty has posted a word. *Something's up*, he tells the dog. *Something's definitely up.*

Back at his own laptop – not wanting the search to surface like a lewd suggestion in his wife's browser's bar – he enters 'Simon Merriweather'. Nothing unusual. Place-holder stuff, a small biographical puff on the Freedom from Fistula website, an interview for some charity magazine, and nothing in News. He enters the woman's name. A model called Sam Rollinson has digitally obliterated less celebrated Sam Rollinsons. He selects 'images' and scrolls past her remarkable cheekbones for several pages, waiting to see the face that looked adoringly into Cunty's. But then something comes up that isn't a face.

It is the fuselage, the wing, of a small white plane which has crashed into an African landscape.

When he has read more than he needs to, Logan closes the lid of his laptop. Cunty's woman is five months dead. How grief might drive a man over the cliff of reasonable behaviour he understands acutely. Repeatedly, Flora's death has nudged him into the thin membrane that divides a sad man from a madman. And Flora, for all her perfection, was not the only good thing in his life.

What if Cunty's woman was? What if her loss clanged the huge unsounded bell of Jules's loss a decade before? And what if the unrecoverable loss of his second fiancée provoked him to consider the recoverable loss of his first? He counted forward from the day of Sam's death to the week he had received the article. The timing was perfect. A week for shock plus a month for grief. Another month for the cogs that grind towards revenge.

Logan sifts his first meetings with Dr Salmon for grit; for signs of complicity in his deception. Is she pawn or puppet? Plant or mole? All he knows is this: he is out of his depth. And if she is a charlatan, he has put his most high-profile client to date in her care.

Peace

It is odd, not to know who you are. In the early hours of the morning, April sits on her bed, fully dressed, and listens to the silence. Not just the ordinary silence of the building. The extraordinary silence of her head. Before the pool party cracked through her defences, before she had to muffle it under hymns and nursery rhymes, she'd used bees. Beneath the buzzing, not only Dr Logan's voice. Beneath the buzzing, the secret enemy of her peace: the relentless chatter of her brain. For years she has been harangued from troubled waking to exhausted sleep by a self-generated critical commentary over which she has only minimal control. Emerging into consciousness, recalling perhaps some strands of some *bloody awful dream* and it would be off.

But now, this morning, nothing.

At first she doesn't move. Protecting the fragile peace, her body stalls. As if moving might wake the beast. Kick the voice into speech. Automatic, to minimize her breathing, like a child hiding when someone is coming, someone is looking. But no one is coming. And no one, so far as she knows, is looking. She's alone on the bed, fully dressed, cross-legged, and her head is as still as a pond. Not one ripple.

All her fears gather up into something that needs expelling: she sneezes. Nothing else happens. The voice remains quelled. Not just silent: not there. No praise, no damnation.

She is renewed. Her brain was an attic room, full of mouldering toys, too-small dresses, things you can neither bear to look at, nor let go. Now it is swept clean, junk-free, stripped down to sanded wood floors that almost snug up to your feet as you ballet across them. Yes, unweighted by self-blame, unhampered by fear, she could dance.

So she breathes, and she is, and the dawn light grows in the window, and after some time, a shaft of it falls through and across the floor like a gift. Like God unfurling His palm and saying, *Look*.

She unfolds her legs, gets up, walks into sunlight. The floor is cold beneath her feet, but her face receives the magnified warmth of the late year, the sun touching her skin as tentatively as a new lover. It is beautiful. It is miraculous.

She tests the limits of her peace. She finds she can pad about her room without tripping her inner alarms. No thought intrudes besides the observation, *This is beautiful* as she runs her hand over walls. So smooth. So carefully built. There is so little in her room. Nothing one might damage oneself with, if one had a mind to, so no mirror, no pictures, no sharp-cornered furniture. But what does one need besides a quiet cube of air, white walls, a bed to lie upon? And a window. Secured it may be, coated and unsmashable, but it gives her the world.

The wide-armed cedar has seen so many drugged-up people, taking a turn in their plain white pyjamas, staring at a grass blade as though it might cut them, or the sky as though it will fall on their heads. And all these years the tree has reached out to embrace them.

Birds. A flight of starlings on their way to somewhere warmer, more generous with insects, finer for breeding; all of them magnetized, each to the other. When she was at university, there was a place they would gather in the evenings, over the old pier.

They would swoop and curve, iron filings drawn by a magnet in the hands of an invisible artist: no sense to their movement but beauty. Nothing in its purpose but joy, a ballet of birds practising their flow and connection, as the sun sank towards the horizon satisfied that nothing it could illuminate would surpass this miraculous dance.

And hinted in the window, people. A road that will soon bear cars, its tarmac laid over the hill like a discarded necktie, marker of desire. Its route determined centuries ago by communal long-ing; scored into the earth by the tramping of feet that chose this one same way to go. Later, rutted by the wheels of carts, and later still, when mud clagged business and ruts damaged profits, laid with stones. Finally, soothed with tarmac. And a thought surfaces. Human beings are astonishing. They are not thought-less apes. Nothing like. Apes are still collecting leaves to make nests in their jungles. Using sticks to winkle termites from tree bark. But humans have invented cities, cars, fridges, aeroplanes, laptops; they've sent submarines down to the ocean floor and rockets into space. Made something you can carry in your pocket that lets you access the infinitely expanding knowledge of the entire world – or call your mother and say you'll be late for tea.

April cannot call her mother. There would be paperwork to do. And she doesn't want to. Words ran out between them long before April blew up the bus. She learned her silence under the carpet-bombing campaign of her mother's tongue.

We never bonded, her mother had said to the latest set of Liquid Supper friends, nine-year-old April gangling in the door-way. *Did we, Mischief?*

I wasn't there.

You were there! Her mother hooted. *You were there! Only in an incubator.* And to her temporary friends, conspiratorially, *Got tangled in the cord. Not breathing, see? So they took her away. Put her in an incubator. So how was we supposed to bond?*

They couldn't have bonded if she was dead, either. But April said nothing.

And ruined my figure, didn't you, Trouble? To the Liquid Supper friends, *Her father ran a mile. Ran a mile! I thought a sprog would bring us together, turned out she did for us.*

That was a cue for the strangulation mime, the big eyes, *I could kill you!* and the friends cackling and pouring themselves ungainly splooshes of wine. Predictably in the months to come, April's mother would turn on each of them for spurious offences. Would find new confederates, closer to dissolution. Would start swearing about *this bloody place*, move herself and her underfed daughter to the next cheap town, and start again. *Just you an' me, Monster.* Until the new Jeans and Joans and Janets arrived.

April imagines herself in her mother's belly, listening to the cackles and hoots, looping the cord around her own neck to the words of her mother's favourite refrain. *I could kill you.* Without friends, it came with teeth.

But she is not with her mother. The silence of a made-safe room hums around her. Sunlight a sheet of gold on the floor, the wonder of human achievement framed in the window.

She breathes once, twice, and her mother dissolves.

Panini

There is a thought at the back of Logan's mind that he's struggling not to notice. All morning as he tries to work it is gnawing just behind his ears, a pernicious beetle whose mandibular motions are boring increasingly joined-up tunnels of air into the structure of his reality. Again and again between the hours of nine and eleven he finds himself stationary, eyes frozen halfway through a page of text or hand paralysed in mid-motion as the effort to shut out the gnawing shuts down everything else. Again, and again, Logan heaves his mind back to the new case on his desk, but it is unengaging: a woman has brained her spouse with his own guitar after decades of assault in the other direction. Far from being unbalanced, it may well be her first act of sanity. The effort to spin out this simple opinion to the required minimum of a hundred words feels beyond him.

He wrongly diagnoses himself as needing lunch. A professional, he is certain he has ring-fenced his investigation into Simon Merriweather's private vendetta into his personal hours and that his lack of focus is symptomatic only of the fact that he has consumed nothing but coffee since he woke. But as he surveys the flattened shoe-print of his panini, a shiver breaks out at the top of his cervical spine and sets off a chain of neural explosions all the way to his sacrum. The gnawing grub is suddenly launched into air; the thought is set loose, word by word.

Did…

No, no, no, no, no.

Did the cunt…

No!

Did the cunt…

He is pushing the words away but they are coming, they are coming, and now something is happening to the panini. It is crawling with insects. No, not insects, for as he peers at the platter he realizes what is crawling is the surface itself. The molecules that rendered the panini solid to his eyes are separating and moving across and around each other like disorganized conga chains or cross-purposed ant colonies. And for a moment he is almost saved by his brain's brilliant tactic, the old-TV-show get-out-clause, *create a diversion*. But then the words muscle in.

kill…

No! His fist slams down on the ant panini. But it's coming anyway. Like the TV-show criminal pressed to a confession, no longer able to outwit the relentless detective or contain for another second the brain-bursting pressure of the murderously unsaid, he roars out loud, *Did the cunt kill Flora?*

Air savaged into a ringing silence. The café and its lunchtime occupants inked back into Logan's momentarily erased surroundings in open-mouthed detail. Only the youngster who knows no better is staring at him, her pupils like goldfish frozen in their globular bowls. Everyone else is studying the menu, their shoes, their fingernails, though he can feel their souls staring at him as intently as the ululating pod-people of *Invasion of the Body Snatchers* stare at the living.

Oh, Christ.

He has to get out of there. Leaves on the table the panini, a broken plate, enough money to replace it.

There are cameras, of course. Even the corner café has CCTV. Back at his desk, his fingers are scurrying through papers. Telling himself the café is busy, the staff turnover rapid, and even though he eats there once or twice a week, they don't know his name. What did he do, anyway? Nothing illegal. Broke a plate. Scared people. Caused a woman to choke on her rocket. And nobody followed him. He checks at the window. But just in case someone knows who he is, God forbid, better dig out—

The panic is a more effective distraction than the ant panini illusion and for more than forty minutes his brain can congratulate itself on its brilliance. With the primary function of protection rooted so deeply in the amygdala, it is only fulfilling its evolutionary purpose in side-stepping the larger problem. Which finally downs him, as a lion's paw-swipe will down a wildebeest some considerable time after claws slice flesh.

Is it possible?

Flora was jumping for Merriweather's charity. He didn't question the coincidence at the time, only winced at the surgical accuracy with which the universe administers guilt. But what if it wasn't coincidence? What if it was meaningful? What if Merriweather recruited Flora, through her friend, recruited the friend first with the singular purpose of—

No, he tells himself, ridiculous. The instructor was killed too. Doctor her parachute, maybe, but doctor his? Unless—

His mind is running around him in circles, barking. There are any number of scenarios. What if the parachute instructor had also crossed Merriweather? Then again, someone who will murder an innocent girl for her father's crimes would hardly baulk at inflicting collateral damage—

For Christ's sake, snap out of it, Logan! On the so-called evidence of the common letter S and a bereavement, you'd make your old squash partner, charitable do-gooder and CBE-awardee a murderer?

Something is going badly wrong with Logan's eyesight and it takes some moments for him to locate the problem in his rapid, irregular breathing. He tries to slow his breath but his lungs are panicking independently of the notional adult in charge. Jules, he thinks, Jules will soothe him.

But Jules is not answering her phone. Hard to believe: she always answers him. He tries The Brockenhurst House. The mobile. Brockenhurst again. The mobile again, and this time a message, *Jules, please… just please. Ring me back. Something terrible… please.* Incoherent enough to get her attention. But minutes pass and Jules doesn't respond.

He is in free fall. The accident report gave the heights at which the main and reserve parachutes were deployed and failed. Cause of failure for both chutes undetermined. Sometimes these things happen and no one knows why. Logan is at two thousand six hundred feet, and the main canopy has failed to open. He is cutting it loose. What might be the rest of his life is whistling past his ears, and the Surrey Hills are greener than he has ever seen them, a wide grinning expanse of cemetery green. He is at nineteen hundred feet and tugging the cord for the reserve.

And then his phone rings.

Jules, he says, *thank God*.

Logan? It isn't Jules, it's—

Gabrielle Salmon. Not long now until he's swallowed into Surrey turf, the wide eyes of daisies gazing at him impassively as he travels past them into burrows and wormholes.

Are you—?

No.

Whatever she was going to ask – are you okay, are you free to speak, are you in your right mind? – the answer is the same.

She says, *Your breathing...*

I am, he answers, mishearing punctuation.

Breathe with me, she says, and her breath becomes a cliff wind on the mouthpiece, a noisy bluster, slow inhale… slow exhale… again… again… And much as he wants to resist her, the white noise washes over his ears and smothers his brain's misfires with calming static, until eventually all in his head is steady and still. For a moment or two he is genuinely thoughtless.

What was it? she asks.

He considers. Should he tell her?

I had a thought, he says.

He can hear her considering whether or not to ask him.

A powerful one, then. Not a good one by the sounds of it.

No, he says.

He feels naked. But no language he can access would serve as a snatched towel.

Are you okay now?

She has nursed him, assisted him through some kind of climax.

I think so.

Yes, he realizes, he is as naked, deflated and powerless as if they have just made love.

I hope your phone's not tapped, she says. *Wouldn't want anyone to think we were, you know, heavy breathing together or something.*

Not for the first time he is discomfited by the sense she has read his mind.

Why would my phone be tapped?

Isn't everyone's? she says. *Basic Government protocol, surely. Potential terrorist threats, the lot of us. Logan, I'm guessing this is a bad time.*

The worst, he thinks, the worst yet. *I'm okay*, he says. *What did you want to speak to me about?*

She hesitates. *April Smith.*

I don't want to go ahead with that, he says hurriedly.

There is a pause.

It's... gone ahead. As scheduled.

Ah.

I wanted to speak to you about the results.

Ah.

I think you should see her.

Really?

Yes. The second hand on his desk clock takes three more bites out of the day. *Logan—*

Everything's fine, he says, cutting across her puzzlement. *Everything's fine.* He clicks her into silence.

This time, the reserve parachute opened. This time, he floats down to earth, bends his knees, rolls, recovers, stands. Nothing is broken.

He leaves another message on Jules's voicemail.

Sorry about the message earlier. Had a bit of a panic attack. Nothing to worry about. Everything's fine.

Beastly

April is now allowed paper and pen. Dr Logan will not see her until the end of the week, but has given his permission. He would like to see what she writes. April writes with that in mind, knowing full well he will not understand it. She sits at her small table and positions the paper to be entirely in sunshine.

I breathe my mother's 'kill you' into nothing.
My mother, too, dissolves inside my lungs
and carbons out, dioxide-dies, reborn
as air for leaves. What used to hurt, I breathe.

As she finishes the poem, another piece of mother-hurt surfaces. She scratches it onto the paper.

> *Trouble, Mischief, Monster, Squirt.*
> *Other girls were Darling, Love,*
> *Precious, Angel, Sweetie-Pie.*
> *I was Beastly. I was Dirt.*

A tear arrives, and another. Ever since her mother's carpet slipper stung her six-year-old head *for making that bloody racket*, she has squeezed tears back into her skull. Over time, pressure and heat turned them to steam: to a powerful, cog-turning, piston-thumping rage. Never tears. Now, a Tuesday afternoon in November, she can cry. Enough tears to fill an hour.

Dusk begins. A blackbird chooks alarm across the lawn. The cedar hugs an intake of shadows. April is flooded with tears. The water wets her face, but she cries and breathes. Cries like a wave breaking; breathes like the same wave's water drawn back through the beach, washing it clean. A beach of pebbles, each pebble both a name and its ripples: the distorting effects of her mother's dark rechristenings. Trouble. Monster. She'd thought she rebelled, yet how obedient she was. Each label her mother set round her neck, she became.

She cries and breathes. The curses slake off, the names lose their power. Soon they are nothing to do with the pale young woman ghosting in the window.

She presses the staff bell to ask for a mirror. She wants to see herself clearly. They bring her the kind she can't smash. When they are gone, she sits cross-legged on the bed, placing the circular, plastic-handled device on the bed in front of her. Leans gingerly forward, a forest animal meeting its reflection for the first time in a glade's dark pool. A stranger looks back. Her face is open and smooth as a clean cotton sheet. She searches her eyes for herself. For who she is, beyond the history that has so recently melted: the mother who regretted her, the boys who raped her, the students she killed.

Yes, she killed them. Or maybe not she, but her: that other self, the one with the names. Who is she now? She drills the question into the depths of her own reflected eyes.

Been looking into that mirror all evening.

April glances up: two faces in the observation window vanish, like pond-fish, disturbed. She returns to the mirror. What she has found in the mirror, she dare not say. But there is a word for it.

Epiphany

Insane?

Logan is following a harried, keycard-clutching member of the nursing staff down the corridor. *You wouldn't say she was any better?*

She's talking. If that's better.

Flip-flap, flip-flap: comfortable soles on linoleum.

But insane? Logan presses.

The nurse speaks in time with her steps.

It's not a clinical assessment, obviously. Not my job.

Logan is struggling to keep up. He hasn't been sleeping well.

She's still singing? Rocking?

No, none of that. She's lucid. Calm.

So, why do you say insane?

A shush, a finger to the lips. They stop at a small scratched window set in a door. The nurse leans towards him and whispers, *It's the things she says, Dr Logan. Very disturbing.*

Disturbing, or disturbed?

She swipes her card over the reader and the bolts clunk into their casings.

You'll see, she says, ushering him in and staying on the hall side of the door as it closes.

April is gazing out of the window. A notebook lies in front of her. He waits to see if she will acknowledge his presence. He cannot tell whether she is aware of him or in a state of reverie. Something has undoubtedly been occurring in the room. Against regulations, and against good sense for a mental patient on remand, April has decorated the wall beside her bed. In pencil, in large hollowed-out capitals, she has written:

LUKE
17:21

For the first time in his life he wishes his knowledge of the Bible stretched further than how many different crayons you needed to colour in a picture of Jesus entering Jerusalem on a donkey. Once out of April's room he will look it up, but how to remember the numbers? It comes to him savagely: Tom and Flora's ages when she died. Blessedly, before he can be snagged into tears or mis-breathing, April says, *Is it not beautiful, Dr Logan?*

He follows her gaze. The low, grubby buildings of the adjoining wing shed their paint eczematically. A disorder of bins cluster around the kitchen door like hungry pets. A large rectangle of lawn in need of mowing and worn away in patches, shaded by an unruly, gangling tree. A sky glowering with undropped rain. Unkempt flowerbeds where a doolally lady in a pale blue nightie is squatting to urinate.

Isn't what beautiful, April?

She swivels to face him, her eyes full of light.

Everything. Her eyes travel over his face, as though scanning him to include him in her assessment.

Everything?

Yes. Everything.

Nodding as if to say, Yes, even you, Dr Logan, even you are beautiful.

What you've written on the wall—

That's especially beautiful, she says. *Especially beautiful.* And turns back to the window.

Can I?

Make yourself comfortable, she says, without taking her eyes off the view.

Glancing up at the camera's fish eye in the corner, he sits primly on the edge of the bed.

Our conversation is being recorded, he says for the sake of legality.

Of course. Everything here is recorded. Going for a shit is recorded.

Can you tell me what happened during the process? he asks.

No, she says simply.

No?

It's beyond words, Dr Logan. Nodding to herself, confirming with herself. *Beyond words.*

But you're feeling – different.

Different. Yes.

There is something different about her, for certain, but Logan cannot place it. Something is missing from her face, but in its absence, he cannot name it. He continues uneasily.

Dr Salmon says the process creates the sensation of being connected to – he reaches for a substitute for the word that makes him squirm – *a higher power.*

His sense she is about to speak dissolves into a soft curve at the corner of her mouth and Logan realizes she won't answer a statement.

Well? he asks. *What do you think?*

April turns to face him.

That's the question, isn't it? she says.

What's the question?

Again, like a head of wheat in an eddy of air, she is nodding.

He has the feeling that, even as he is assessing her, she is conducting her own assessment of him.

What I think, she says. *What you think.*

In what way?

Space is made for him, as though she is the teacher, he the pupil, and he might come up with his own answer given time. But when he fails to so much as chuck a spadeful of conversational earth at the hole, the teenager informs him, *Our thoughts are very powerful, Dr Logan. Very powerful.*

Our thoughts?

Everything that happens, everything around us, we create with our thoughts.

Logan doesn't like the direction of her conversation. But at least she is talking.

Not me, April. You didn't create me with your thoughts. My parents created me, in the usual mechanical way that humans do.

April is having none of it.

But they thought about it first, didn't they? Thought, Let's have a baby. Even if you were an accident, Dr Logan.

'Accident' triggers Flora's face in the car, mutating catastrophically into hatred. A muscle just under Logan's left eye begins to twitch in rebellion.

Someone thinks the thoughts that lead to a child, April continues. *One only has to think Sex without thinking Contraception.* She skewers him with an intense green eye, as if she knows.

The twitch has spread to his cheek, suggestive of some electrical circuit shorting out. Logan rubs his face, the hard needling of stubble just under the skin, engaging some emergency procedure of masculinity. The steel of emotional control returns to him: the cheek ceases its rebellion.

However it happened, he says, *they created me. Not you. You didn't think me into being, April. I'm real. I exist.*

I thought you into my life, she says simply.

Meaning?

She lifts her right foot off the floor and tucks it under her left thigh. *Meaning, I thought a whole series of thoughts that have led to my being here in this place. You weren't in my life, and then you were. I magicked you out of nowhere.*

Out of Hampshire.

Out of nowhere, from my perspective. And you brought me Dr Salmon, and Dr Salmon brought me – this! She indicates a sphere of nothing around her head.

What?

The understanding that I created everything in my life. Everything. Just with my thoughts.

Okay, he says, *what about this? You didn't create everything in your life because you didn't create you. Your mother did.*

Indeed. With her thoughts. Though she'd deny that. She'd say I was foisted on her by circumstance, but on some level she wanted a daughter. Maybe to put all her self-loathing outside herself, onto another. A little hateful external her, something she could blame instead of looking in the mirror. But it was a co-creation. On some level I was willing to be born to her, Dr Logan. Had to be. One in four pregnancies end in miscarriage, don't they? One in four bail out. I didn't. And yet I knew her from the inside. I would have felt her, heard her, known what I was in for. And I stuck with her all the same.

For what?

Eyes roll up in her head like a blind to let the light in. Then, two cannonballs, drop back down with an answer.

For this! For the experience. To go through what I did, do what I did, until it leads me to finally getting it.

Logan isn't getting it.

To wake up, Dr Logan! You can get to Heaven through Hell. Through the valley of the shadow of death. How else can a person wake up? Meditate up a mountain maybe? My roots are Catford, not Kathmandu.

He is lost. His whole quest was to get her talking, yet now he is mentally flicking through a rack of medications that would render her speechless. He could rope in someone with expertise in post-process behaviour, but the thought of calling Dr Salmon is unappealing. He presses on.

Are you telling me, April, that you think mass murder is part of some spiritual path?

The eyes lift again, taking his suggestion to her brain, retrieving the answer with gun-dog efficiency.

For me it was, Dr Logan. For me it was.

He is distracted by a disturbance of his visual field in the patch of light behind April's left shoulder: a bee banging itself against the window. Though rendered noiseless by the security glass, it batters its furry body repeatedly against it as though April were a nectar-drenched flower. Then it is off again, rebuffed, but rapidly forgetting.

He says, *More than thoughts brought you here. Any of us might have murderous thoughts. You had the thoughts. But you also did the deeds.*

She nods at her foot.

The thoughts led to the deeds. I couldn't do the deeds without having the thoughts, Dr Logan. And gazing up at him, *I am meant to be here.*

How do you mean?

Every fragment of my life from my conception forwards has led me to this single moment of existence.

The more he looks at her, the more like a child she becomes.

Are you suggesting you were destined to be a murderer?

She is back to her foot.

Murderer is a judgemental term. It has bad associations, Dr Logan. I can no longer relate to them. I think of the whole business differently now.

How do you think of 'the whole business'? He cannot veil his sarcasm.

I understand you won't get this, Dr Logan. I'm saying it for the record anyway. Some day, people will get it.

He doesn't like how often she says his name. As though she's nailing him to darkness, chanting a curse.

Get what?

Her eyes rise like twin moons over the surface of some alien planet. And it is he, planet Logan, whose craters and dried-up lakes are thrown into relief. April's gaze is steady.

I was the means by which some people left this life. That's certain. But on another level it was all agreed between us.

What are you saying?

What I said. Those people on some level wanted to die. Co-opted me as the means as much as I co-opted them to bring me to this moment of epiphany.

Epiphany?

Epiphany, Dr Logan. The falling into place of profound understanding. I have seen the light, Dr Logan.

She smiles, and the smile is so unnerving that he doesn't know how to respond. Not because it is threatening, or evil, or deranged, but because it is purely, innocently happy. The smile of his six-year-old daughter on a beach with a bucket and spade in her hands. He shakes the memory out of his head.

The young people who died in the bomb, he says. *The bomb you placed on the bus.*

Yes.

You were angry with them?

Isn't that a leading question? She glances at the camera, smiles. Again, innocent. Amused at him. *Yes, I was angry with them. The way I saw it, they were turning their backs on God, who had created them. And they made fun of anyone who did believe in God. They saw faith as a sign of stupidity. When you assume the soul is an illusion, Dr Logan, there's no limit to how badly you can treat people.*

But when you assume the soul is real, it's a kindness to blow people up?

In a way, that's truer than you know.

How so?

If you assume the soul is real, death isn't the end, is it, Dr Logan. Death is an illusion.

Logan is on his feet, surprised upright by a rush of anger.

He is determined to cut through her grandstanding, crack her certainty, dynamite a hole in the new line of defence that Dr Salmon's process appears to have gifted her. Forensically minded, he has, on a sheet of A4, arranged the victims in the order of their demise. Ending with the girl unplugged from her coma by a tearful mother and sister after a fortnight, it begins with the boy plugged into his headphones directly below the shelf where April's backpack was stowed, killed at the instant of detonation.

Luke Fisher, he begins, *massive head wounds, time of death 17.21.*

Oh Jesus! she says, joining him on her feet, hand over her mouth to catch the oath. The effect is more instantaneous than he was expecting. Heartened, he continues.

Richard Abbot, catastrophic blood loss, time of death—

Stop! she says. *Go back! Read the first one! Read the first one again!*

Her hand removed from her mouth, he can see she is not in shock. She is grinning.

Luke Fisher—

17.21, she interrupts. *Luke 17:21! Luke 17:21! Dr Logan—!* Her eyes are shining, tears streaming down her face as she wags her finger at the wall.

He turns slowly, steps backs and takes in her pencil-work. April is rising on the balls of her feet, bobbing up and down like a child watching someone unwrap the perfect present.

This is… this is a miracle, isn't it? You were here, she says. *You saw! You know!*

It's… odd.

It's not odd, she says, *it's perfection! It means – everything, everything, every part of it—*

She doesn't finish. Whatever conclusions she's drawing, she is drawing them only for herself.

April—

You know what it says, Dr Logan? Luke 17:21? Why it's on my wall?

No.

Because it's the central truth. I woke up and I finally knew what it meant. Some translations say 'in the midst', but it's not that at all.

What are you saying? What's the central truth?

Luke 17:21!

Irritated almost beyond professionalism, *I don't know the Bible, April. What is the text of Luke 17:21?*

She looks about to burst out of her skin with excitement.

The Kingdom of God is within you, Dr Logan. The Kingdom of God is within you!

Acts

Logan probes his rearmost molar with his tongue. It's been giving him trouble for a couple of days now. Just here and there, an icy jab, like a tiny climber's axe getting purchase on his jaw. Under the stalactite root, perhaps, in some unseen crevasse.

I must ring the dentist, he says, and only when the next thing happens does he realize he has said it aloud.

Knuckles rap on his window. It is the lay-by's mobile snack vendor. Logan clicks a button and the glass slides down.

You want a coffee, Guv? Saw you sat there and figured you might want a coffee.

A ridged cup is being fed into his hand. He acquiesces like a trauma victim.

Milk? Sugar?

Little cartons, packets, a stirrer dropped into his other hand.

That'll be a fiver, Guv.

Logan, imagining the man was committing a random act of kindness, is taken aback at the request for money. Ashamed of his naivety, he digs into a front pocket, lifting his buttocks for better access. The man waits with his hand out, smiling until he is paid. The loss is swallowed and the window sighs back to its shut position, deadening the air. Logan watches the bandit tramp back to his van. He is looking to detect a dance step, a heel click.

The coffee tastes foul. Or maybe there's just a bad taste in his mouth, thinks Logan. The foul cake of deceit topped with the sickly icing of evangelism. What has she done, this Salmon woman?

Though he was hoping to save April from prison by proving her mad, he fears his efforts to break her silence have now made matters worse. Her cheerfulness, her lack of contrition, will not play well with a jury. A lifetime's incarceration is hovering over her ecstatic head. His tooth twinges again.

And there is something even more disturbing about all this. When they lock her up – which they surely will – they will not be locking up the same person who committed the crime. The young woman he first met was a chrysalis: silent, defended, and a mess inside. But something has cracked and a whole other creature has emerged. The jury will say, 'This is she who committed a crime', and they will be wrong.

How he knows, he cannot tell. He has no proof, and he cannot trust himself. His sense of certainty is falling away. He knows less than he knew this morning, and even less than he knew a week ago. Indeed, when he tries to untangle his thoughts, they become less like strings and more like mush, melting into each other, formless and endless. This is the secret he must hide from the rest of the world. He has had to pull over because he, like April before her hatching, is now a mess inside. Whether he will crack and emerge as some certain (but perhaps certifiable) creation he doesn't know. He might just as easily fail to progress, the essence of him rotting quietly away until he is just a casing, grown dry and hollow, swinging from a windowsill by a thread.

¤   ¤   ¤

The dining table is set for two. The room is lit by a religious profusion of candles, the wax-polished wood dark and brooding. Yet Jules can't help noticing how like an operating table it is with its air of expectation and risk, its sharp, gleaming instruments laid out with precision. She would like to be nonchalant. But the more disordered her heart, the more ordered her surfaces. The more silence infests the gap between her and her husband, the more time stretches to make room for the snipping of flower stems, the ironing of napkins. The Venetian regulator wall-clock inherited from her uncle bongs eight, the vegetables sweat under foil, the meat bubbles quietly in its sauce, teetering on the brink of perfection, and Logan is absent. No call. No text.

Where is he, her husband? In the sinewy arms of the woman he refers to only as Salmon? (Not as one addressing a classmate or colleague, but as one attempting to hide the tenderness inherent in speaking her forename.) Being picked off a train track by vis-vested workers with plastic gloves, his identity not yet matched to the wallet in the glovebox of the car parked by the level cross-ing? Both thoughts make her shiver, but were she empowered to choose, by wish or by prayer, she'd plump for the second. Cleaner, no arguments. She, who has felt widowed in all but name for a year and a half, would be allowed to wear hair scraped back from an unmade face, no apologies. Would allow herself public tears: a quiet cry in the meat aisle, glistening eyes over a friend's thought-ful risotto. And she would automatically keep the house; this house of old trees sawn true, this house of shelter and forgetful-ness. More than keep it, she would own it, every joist and tie of it, every timber and cleat of it, every rafter and tile of it transferred to her sole name as a solace for widowhood. The son has no use for it; Logan has a policy for Tom. So it comes to her. She imagi-nes receiving the knock: two officers at the door, one of them a woman; how she would take it calmly, spring tears, but feel relief.

She has waited a long time for her husband to return to her. Not minutes, but months. Never once did she imagine that when he resurfaced from his daughter's grave, he would fall into another woman's arms. Now she fears she has been tricked into holding on to a shadow. Like an illusionist's assistant, she has played the game of gripping the thing that, time and again, changes shape, but she has been fooled. It will never turn back into the magician. Any moment, he will appear, to a gasp, at the back of the audience. All she will have in her hands is a flown dove; an empty cage.

Yet she cannot challenge him. Divorce: the house sawn in two, both halves swung open to reveal – nothing. The magician's glamorous assistant dropped through a trapdoor into her elderly parents' kitchen, and from there to a charmless flat in Swindon that never seems to be the right temperature. Buying a cat. Taking up the cello.

A bong for half past. She will not ask him where he's been. Why whisk off the black cloth before the reveal? No, if he comes home, she will help him off with his coat. She will ask about his day with the tone of someone fishing for a lie. Neither of them will make any comment about the crusty edges of the dish that has waited far, far too long for his return.

Stalk

Logan is neither tonguing Gabrielle Salmon, nor being tonged from cinder track into evidence bags in filleted lumps. He is staring at the smoke-stained teeth of a woman called Maureen, whom he has bought a half of bitter shandy in the Goldsmith on the corner of Sawyer Street and Southwark Bridge Road. If he left now, he would be home before midnight, and yet he cannot tear himself away from the compelling idiocy of her monologue, her worn yellow incisors.

And then my husband upped and left…

Three hours ago he had been parked on the corner of Loman and Risborough streets, wondering at the provenance of the street's solitary tree – why plant only one? – and watching a door. The door fronted a converted warehouse, squatter than its modern neighbours and arranged end-on to the pavement, a circular Cyclops-eye window in its apex. A warehouse that in the 1960s had been the storage facility of a respected furrier and was now glass-blocked and plate-glass-windowed into the contemporary-feel headquarters of the UK's only fistula repair charity.

What compelled him to stalk his wife's ex in this manner he could not formulate, beyond the sense that the fabric of his life was unravelling, and that by catching a glimpse of this man, logging his visage and gait, he might better assess the mental state of both of them, and light the match that would bond the frayed ends of his thoughts into blobs of reality. Observe, assess, coalesce. Had he hoped this simple transaction would end his unravelling, he was to be disappointed.

First the orb of light around the street lamp began to separate into haloes. Then each halo began shedding light in fizzing particles, like sparklers. Then someone who wasn't there began to speak to him from the passenger seat.

What are you doing, Daddy?

The voice was six, seven.

I'm watching that door over there.

Why?

To see who comes out of it.

Why?

I'm waiting for someone in particular.

Ju-Ju?

This is Flora from the days when he used to pick Jules up from work.

Ju-Ju's old boyfriend.

Why?

He remembered that phase: tireless questions. He'd loved her so much it almost taught him patience.

Because I think he might have done something... bad.

Why?

> *Because he doesn't like me.*
>
> *Why?*
>
> *Because I took Ju-Ju away from him.*
>
> *Why?*
>
> *Because...*

Logan turned to look at his interrogator. She was there and not there, flickering in and out like a faulty signal. Something in her mouth was pushing her cheek out like a small molehill. A wine gum, he guessed. She'd had a passion for them.

Why? she asked again. *Why did you take Ju-Ju away from him?*

Because...

Not simple. He remembered a desire for her that felt like love. But conjuring that distant Jules in his head, he saw her standing in Merriweather's kitchen, looking at her fiancé, and it was how she looked at him that Logan craved. With a little work on his part she had diverted her love to Logan and, for a time, gifted him a look she had poured herself into. But never the same look. Never quite the same look that had once been Merriweather's.

This was not an answer he could give Flora.

Because I thought it would make me feel better, he said. *I thought if she chose me over him, that would mean I was better.*

Were you sick? she asked, not looking at him, playing a game with her fingers. The sucking had given way to chewing.

What do you mean?

Did you want to get better because you were sick? she repeated.

He supposed he was. He supposed he always had been. But this is not what you say to your daughter.

Are you sick now? she persisted.

He considered her question. He had been sleeping badly. He had been drinking too much coffee. He had been parked for two hours outside the headquarters of a fistula repair charity, waiting to watch a man he had wronged walk down the road.

Very likely, he said.

Will you get better when you see Ju-Ju's boyfriend?

Old *boyfriend*, he said. *Maybe.*

He turned to her.

Flora?

But she'd crackled out of existence. The minute he was ready to ask her something, she was gone.

She would know, would she not? *On the other side.* She would know if she'd been murdered. Maybe not wine gum Flora, to whom he was Ju-Ju's boyfriend. Nor the pigtailed nine year old, nor any of the other child or teenage echoes that had scissored his peace into ribbons. But grown Flora. The one Gabrielle Salmon claimed to have spoken to. She would know.

The warehouse door opened. Though winter's early dark concealed Logan from his prey, he slid lower into his seat as Merriweather emerged, coat collar turned up, a red scarf draped uselessly over his shoulders like a priest's stole. Nothing in his face or walk betrayed an emotional state. Signally neutral, he walked – for it was certainly that dullest of perambulatory verbs, rather than a stride, saunter, traipse or trudge – past Logan's occupied car.

Five seconds after Merriweather turned south onto Sawyer Street, Logan was locking his car and following. Locating his target only twenty yards ahead, he felt foolish, too old for this Boy's Own Adventure. His caffeine-fuelled heart was hammering at the thought that the man might turn at any moment and notice him. But workers from other small businesses and offices were emptying themselves onto the pavements. The two men were not alone as they walked southeast across the Southwark Bridge Road and left into a quieter street that had clearly been three-quarters bombed in the Blitz. The buildings in this street were largely box-ugly utilitarian affairs, but the far end was dominated by a reassuringly solid and handsome Victorian institution: yellow-bricked, cream windowsilled, and set back from the street behind black-speared railings. It was up the steps of this building that Merriweather sprang before being swallowed by the double doors. Logan stopped to fumble for cigarettes he hadn't smoked in twenty years, and so convincingly that a young woman, roll-up already pinched between her lips, asked him for a light.

Sorry, he said, squinting past her head to read a poster pinned to a noticeboard on the railings.

Life After Death, it said, 6–8.

You know what that building is? he asked, for there was neither name nor identifying features.

Sorry, she said, and left him there, now patting himself down for his phone. Then he remembered: not wishing to be traced, he had turned it off. Had tucked it into the glovebox of the car, now some streets away.

It must be, he reasoned, almost six. A handful of other people converged on the building and entered. He would wait.

His reward for the two-hour wait was yellow-toothed Maureen, now nearing the end of her shandy and still babbling the breathless monologue of someone who has no one to speak to at home. She and Merriweather had emerged as a pair, seemingly deep in conversation (probably one-sided, he now realized) until the corner where Maureen had made a play for both of them to enter the pub, but he had stalled, made excuses with his hands as Logan crouched to fiddle with a perfectly done-up shoelace. Maureen had hugged Merriweather on parting, smoothing his scarf, making some comment that had caused her to laugh and him to nod a polite smile before raising a palm for goodbye.

What Logan needed was information. And so, at a safe distance, he had followed Maureen into the Goldsmith, struck up a conversation at the bar, offered to buy her a drink, and was now watching small strings of saliva in their constantly doomed attempt to darn her mouth shut. She was certainly a fount of information, but not necessarily the right sort. He already knew more about her ex-husband than her own children did, and had been taken through her dysfunctional childhood the way an unconscious body might be dragged down the stairs, head thumping on one hard fact after another. Twenty minutes without giving quarter: not a gap large enough for anything more than an agreement, and certainly no opportunity to divert her stream of words with any subtlety onto the subject that interested him. But the story was heading his way in any case.

And then my mother died.

Oh?

Yes, the last person on earth who was on my side. Can you believe it?

Yes—

I know, these things happen, but still. I was out of my mind for a while, I can tell you. Bereavement? Nothing like it for taking you right down to what matters. Strange things happened after she died. Strange things.

Like?

Like I was watching telly one night, only about a fortnight after they pulled out her tubes, and one of her piggy banks – she used to collect piggy banks – flew off the top of the bookcase, right across the room, and smashed on the floor. It didn't fall off, I'm telling you, it flew off. And I thought, That's Mum, and she's angry. Every reason to be, too, she wasn't ready to go. It was euthanasia really, though they didn't say that. But they stopped the fluids, upped the painkillers, one more off the books, isn't it? So it got me thinking, this life after death lark, maybe there's something to it. That's why I'm here in fact.

Really?

Been to a meeting round the corner. It's a regular thing, been going for a few months now. Friend of a friend told me about it. We get together and talk about it. Our own experiences. Stuff we've read. A couple of times we've had speakers.

Speakers?

Oh yes. Last month someone from the Fortean Society. Not very useful, to be honest. And a lady from Sussex University. Talking about studies and whatnot. Interesting actually. She was looking for people to experiment on. Two of the group signed up, I was a bit scared, to be honest. Thought I'd let the others try it first. She was a good speaker, though.

You remember her name?

No. Oh, hang on. It was an animal or something. No, no, a fish.

Salmon?

Yes! That was it, Salmon! Maureen's eyes gleam with wonder. *How did you guess?*

Logan taps his temple.

Psychic, he says.

Observation

He is under the bed. Six years old, and under the bed. The carpet, rough on his face, smells of the Hoover bag, itches his legs below knees pulled up tight, so tight he can taste them: saltiness. A tang of the playground. School shorts cut into his groin. Not much room here, between the two suitcases Mummy keeps *for emergencies*. But good for hiding.

Thump! goes something downstairs, and his mother's voice squeezes out of the mess like an eel from a shipwreck, squealing, *Please, please…*

Suitcases *for emergencies*. This might be an emergency. He will be ready. With the suitcases.

Roar, goes his father. *Roar Roar Roar* like a lion. But this is no game.

Under the bed, are there spiders? There are probably spiders. He's frightened of spiders, but shouting is worse, bigger. If he could see a spider, right now, he would stare at its legs doing their horrible finger-crawly thing but not move, because the noise in the kitchen is scarier.

Another *Thump!* A wail. His mother's voice rising like a siren, but this time there's more wail than words. His father's is clear, though.

That fucking child! it says, and that's him, he's the fucking child. No brother, no sister: it has to be him. What did he do? Dozens of things. Stroked the cat with fleas. Sweet-wrappers down the side of the sofa. Sucked his thumb at school. He begins to cry. Mummy's voice comes in waves, high and low and high again. One of the waves shouts *Don't* and one *fucking* and one *Finlay*, but the rest go under like small boats in a storm. When the shouting started it wasn't about him. It is now. *Fucking... Finlay!* And both of them are saying that word, the word they shush if someone else says it, like Uncle Fergus. They cover up Finlay's ears too late. They never say that word when he can hear them, but he can hear them now and they are saying it anyway, as if he isn't there.

Maybe they've forgotten. Maybe they don't know. Nanna dropped him off early, Dad was sleeping, Mummy wasn't back yet. He was making Lego models in his room, trying to make birds, but they were too square, and their wings dropped off. He heard Mummy come in from work and straight away start making tea, and he knew how she'd say he was under her feet if he went down, so he didn't, because anyway, he hadn't got the birds right yet, to show her. So maybe they don't know he's there.

Or maybe they're too angry to think about anyone hearing them. Because normally if one of them is too loud, Mummy says, *Neighbours!* and now she's not thinking about the neighbours at all. And they will certainly be hearing this, because everyone in the street can hear the people next door when they turn their telly on, or cough, or even, Dad says, rustle their newspaper, though Finlay thinks that's probably a joke.

But this isn't a joke. This is very bad. And now it's getting worse, because it's coming up the stairs.

His mother first, screaming, *That's it, that's it!* Finlay hears her stumble halfway up, but she keeps going, and she's already on the landing.

His father bellows from the bottom step, *That's what?* and now he's following, and Finlay can feel the anger coming towards him like a fireball. Tears are hot in his eyes.

His parents crash through his bedroom door like one out-of-control animal; one of them hits the wall. *Mummy*, he thinks. A really angry noise comes out of his dad and the next thing he sees is his mother's bare feet, just above the carpet. She is making a tight sound, like she can't breathe.

Then she's dropped like a sack.

Down comes her hand with its pearl-coloured fingernails, one of them snapped. It's fishing for something, a handle. Finlay shrinks back.

What are you doing?

I'm leaving!

The hand disappears.

The twelve inches of world he has made for himself don't show him what happens, but the noises make pictures in his head: animals scuffling in the undergrowth, something giving way, a thick branch snapping.

Her face arrives on the carpet, one eye closed up like a vandalized shop. The other eye stares straight at him, growing wide as a gasp and staring, staring.

Static

The car sits in the drive.

The driver sits in the car.

For twenty minutes, Logan hasn't moved.

Inside: his armchair, his whisky.

Inside: his wife, her questions.

Each cancels the other: the pull, the push. So he remains frozen. Even the eyes in a fixed position drilling the house for answers. The lights are on randomized timers to hoodwink burglars. She might be sleeping. Yet he senses her wakeful presence: the restlessness of a cat that hasn't been fed.

Logan paints a scene: a parallel world where Flora isn't dead and his marriage hasn't cracked into two empty halves of a nutless shell. In this world he has entered his home with a surge of relief: purged himself of his day, let his sweet wife wash out its strangeness with comforting words. Even now, in that twinned night, the good couple are sleeping, stripped of their clothes and their burdens, spooned in a snugness of contact, their breathing in sync and in tune.

But Logan is trapped in a different strand: the one where his daughter introduced herself to an Area of Outstanding Natural Beauty at terminal velocity. Two failed canopies, and the distance between ground and small aircraft rushes into the marriage in a cathedral of air, pushing the husband to the altar, the wife to the cloisters. Remoteness rebrands the wife's comforts as platitudes, her devotions, mechanical duties. Passion is reduced to moving lips whose words are dredged from the Book of Common Prayer.

If he wanted to bridge that distance, he wouldn't know how.

He is not who he was.

She is not who she is.

So he stays, paralysed, in the car.

And why does it visit him now, the suitcase day? The sharp sting of wee, the underbed smell and his mother's white eye?

He would like to discuss: these things, this day. His client shining with wonder, shrugging off her damage like a coat. The impossible collision of the murderer's new favourite nugget of Bible with her first victim's time of death. The all-too-easiness of a stranger's yellow-toothed mouth feeding him exactly what he sought. For how could a single stake-out produce such a catch?

Ask and it shall be given you. Seek, and ye shall find. Now that he sifts it, every detail seems unlikely, as though he were making it up, just as April insists. And now this.

Footsteps on gravel. Jules approaching him through the dark.

The window slides down to his touch; she hands him a coffee in his favourite mug.

I thought if you're going to sit out here all night, you might appreciate something hot, she says.

They look at each other. For a moment he wonders if she'll ask him for money. His mind cranks through possible responses, each more inadequate than the last. If laughter had survived in their practised repertoire, he could say, *You've added a new layer of implausibility to my last fifteen hours*. But with no humour to wash down his words the thought remains a sticky lump of failing to speak, and his wife turns, clay-faced, to re-enter the house.

It gets worse: these patterns and parallels, these unlikely synchronicities.

Thank you, he says to the closed door.

Interpretations

Logan has tiptoed into his study. The subject of this dawn assessment is himself. Logan makes notes:

SYMPTOMS
- Insomnia.
- Feelings of unreality.
- Sporadic hallucinations.

He pauses before the next one:

- Paranoia?

Or is he genuinely on to something? How does one tell? Weigh up the evidence, Logan. Study yourself. He pours a whisky and heads a new list:

QUESTIONS
· Did Merriweather recruit Flora?
· Was Merriweather one of Dr Salmon's volunteers?
· Did Merriweather eradicate guilt with the process?

Stop. Does Merriweather even have guilt? Logan has imagined him guilty until the shimmering suspicion has hardened into a reality the man would need to shed. The bigger question:

· Am I making all this up?

Whisky both cool and hot in his throat. The last question must be answered first. The answer cannot be mined out of the unstable geography of his own head, but from the focused seam of a book.

To arm himself against Dr Salmon, Logan has been ordering popular science books. Human consciousness. Quantum mechanics. They have been arriving like orderly turds, squished through the letterbox in their brown padded bags, their corrugated cardboard wraps. Now is the time to start reading. Logan arranges the comfortable chair, the specialist reading light.

When he understands this stuff, when he has hammered it flat with his intellect, reality will stop bucking like an unbroken horse. Outrageous coincidence will once again be banished to Quiz-and-Tell magazines, and the final pages of bad detective novels. This is what he needs to believe, in any case. This is his hope and his prayer.

But something sluggish in his brain, some resistance, keeps the words pushed away from his understanding. Lack of sleep, lack of nutrition, have worn his synapses into duds, spatterers, misfirers. His answer: coffee, and tinned sardines on toast. Half a slice chewed slowly as he ponders.

THE BOX PAIR EXPERIMENT

The waveform of a single atom is split by a semi-transparent film – as light will both pass through, and reflect off, a window – and the two halves are captured in two boxes. Look in one of the boxes: half the time, there is the whole atom, acting like a particle. The other half of the time it is in the other box. Another mouthful of sardine.

They repeat the experiment, but don't look in the boxes. Simultaneously cut slits in them, so whatever's inside gets out and hits a film, making marks which build into stripes. The stripes of two waves hitting each other, their peaks and troughs colliding. A classic wave interference pattern. A pattern which says, *I am a wave, and in both boxes at once.*

Outside the door, slippers, uncertainty: Jules hovering on the edge of her own interference pattern. A moment while she decides whether to make her observation. But she doesn't open the door, doesn't make anything true or untrue, and Logan returns his attention to the strange behaviour of the universe's fundaments. These building blocks that freeze when you look at them, like they are playing a game of Grandmother's Footsteps, but the minute you avert your eyes, they become, again, a blur of possibilities.

Both particle and wave: a wavicle. Treat an atom like a particle: it's a particle. Treat it like a wave: it's a wave. Tom, he thinks, his tired mind staggering gratefully into a human association. Treats him like an arsehole; he's an arsehole. Every atom of him collapses to arsehole. An inescapable destiny once viewed through that particular observer's eyes; for it is the first observer who determines reality. Subsequent observers all see the same thing. So Tom sees, and then Tom's friends see: Logan the arsehole. When in fact Logan is a collection of wavicles. A blending of contradictory, oppositional, mutually exclusive characteristics which settle into fixed polarity only in the eye of the beholder. More sardine.

Strange things have been done with ones and zeros, sealed cassettes and time delays. Logan drifts, finds his head lolling and dropping, and moves to the couch for a nap. Within minutes, he is on a game show, opening paired boxes. Son, no son. Wife, no wife. Confronted with the pair of boxes marked 'daughter' he asks, *Can we leave them unopened?* The game show host is his old Physics teacher, Mr Wife, a man who delighted in setting his students tests on topics he hadn't taught so they would score zero and he (with the answers) would feel bigger than his five feet two inches. Mr Wife says the choice must be made, one box or the other. Logan asks, can they instead cut slits in the back? Mr Wife, who would never have agreed to such a thing, morphs into the amiable Jules, brandishing a knife she uses for filleting fish. Slits are cut in the boxes and the sky shines through them, its light tearing them open to reveal nothing but the blue and cloudless emptiness a daughter might have passed through.

Logan wakes like a man saved from drowning: shocked into sitting, his lungs rasping for air. He recovers himself slowly. Here is reality: scuffed leather Chesterfield, walls insulated with books, the titles as comforting as childhood prayers. Then coffee. Toast. Back to the page he had folded down. The sun swings a quarter arc, pulling the shadows like taffy.

Logan learns there are many responses to the uncomfortable implications of quantum mechanics, and most try to put the genie back in the bottle. Here are the four he will later remember.

1. INFINITE PARALLEL UNIVERSES

It's an idea so embedded in the Western imagination that it leaks from science fiction films into daily thought and conversation. In a parallel universe Elvis is an octogenarian, Oswald missed Kennedy, Hitler won the war. When we chose this over that, a version of us chose otherwise, splitting off to exist as successful, fulfilled and adored. Logan now discovers this theory is no more than an attempt to reassert the certainties of Newtonian physics on a quantum universe. Since quantum theory threatens to destroy the safe cage of a mechanistic worldview, simply multiply the cages, ad infinitum. Multiverse theory keeps our decisions unimportant, since the other choice is always simultaneously made. The observer opens both boxes, slits them, burns them, destroys them with a hammer. The waveform never really collapses; all realities exist.

2. THE HIDDEN VARIABLE THEORY

This theory has the air of someone struggling with their homework. The indeterminacy of quantum physics is an illusion due to our ignorance. There are probably some hidden variables. If we could uncover these variables, and knew their values, all the insecure feelings that quantum mechanics invokes would instantly vanish.

3. THE COPENHAGEN INTERPRETATION

This one needs extra coffee. The wave function of matter is a theoretical concept, not a reality; it's the probability distribution of all possible states. The collapse of possibilities into a single state occurs when a machine takes a measurement. So, say the Copenhagenists, we can't say anything about quantum realities, because all we have are our observations. They throw up their hands and shrug. Blanket life's mysteries as 'beyond our ken'. The Copenhagen Interpretation gives quantum mechanics the flavour of God in the mouth of a newly appointed vicar, who nods at tragedy with homilies.

4. THE VON NEUMANN INTERPRETATION

Logan likes how it sounds like a thriller, rather than a mathematician's chain of logic. Von Neumann asked what it is about measuring something that causes the waveform to collapse. He envisages this:

A box pair experiment set-up is linked to a measuring device. It exists in an indeterminate state – as a waveform of probabilities – until it is measured, at which point the wave collapses into a particular state. What collapses the wave function? Not the measuring device. Being physical, it too is subject to quantum mechanics and exists (until the wave function collapses) in an indeterminate state. Not the photons of light in the room, not the eyes, the nerve cells, the brain of the observer, nor the electrical signals that pass between them, for all are part of the physical world, and thus subject to quantum laws. Since the entire physical world is quantum mechanical, the process that collapses the waveform cannot be a physical one. There is only one non-physical link in the chain: the observer's consciousness. On the quantum level, according to Von Neumann, consciousness does indeed create reality.

The house has become very loud in its silence. Logan goes to his door, pulls it open, and listens to the nothing of the hallway.

Jules? he calls.

Hours since he heard her moving around, but he never heard her leave.

Jules?

No question, she isn't there. Unobserved, her position cannot be determined.

Wisdoms

The camera stirs, its eye widening to accommodate Logan, who has entered the room and adopted the chair opposite April's bed. The film will show this to the court: their places reversed between the two visits. Its pixels will demonstrate that the accused stares for the first five minutes at the ceiling, but fail to pick out the sardine oil on Logan's tie, the slept-in creases of his jacket.

I have some further questions, he says.

Go ahead.

I gather you're pleading guilty to planting the bomb that killed your fellow students.

Dr Logan, I think you'll find that's a statement, not a question. Though her eyes are still on the ceiling, her smile is for him.

Logan is also split: what he logged on the system as a second pre-trial assessment is much more for his sake than hers.

Do you feel guilty about their deaths? he asks.

She hesitates, checking with herself. *Strange*, she says, still the science student, nodding at another small but vital discovery. *I'm pleading guilty. But I don't feel guilty.*

You don't feel guilty about killing fifteen people?

Oddly, no. Responsible, but not guilty.

Did you feel guilty before the process?

No. I felt they deserved it.

They deserved it?

An eye for an eye. I'm afraid I was rather Old Testament about it.

An eye for an eye? he says. Flora's rebuke in the car: *Dad, if you're just going to play Dr Psychoparrot—*

But Logan pushes on. *They didn't kill anyone.*

No, says April. *But they made someone want to die.*

Fortunately, before his tongue can vandalize any rapport by asking who, he clicks.

Didn't you already want to die?

She pauses, tasting her own lip.

Yes.

She seems very calm but he notes – and the camera notes – that her foot is jiggling, ever so slightly. Logan continues.

So you had nothing to lose. You decided to kill yourself, and take them with you.

It's always on the news, isn't it? Suicide bombers. I was in a bad place. It seemed like a plan. A gift, even.

A gift?

Second term. I'd just done an option on the chemistry of explosives. Thought it was… you know.

I don't know.

Divine guidance.

The foot slows and stills, like a trout on a riverbank finally succumbing to the air.

So you pretended to be a convert to atheism.

Yes.

And signed up for their trip to the Richard Dawkins Memorial Lecture?

Yes.

What was your thinking that morning?

Somewhere down the corridor, an alarm sounds.

'I'll show them there's a God. We can all go and meet Him together.'

The sound of running. The alarm turned off mid-whoop like a shot bird.

And you don't regret it now? asks Logan.

What would be the point of regret?

For the first time, her eyes swivel from the ceiling to meet his own.

If I hadn't done what I did I wouldn't have met your friend Dr Salmon. I'd still be locked in a world of pain, Dr Logan. Trying not to go mad.

They drift back to the ceiling. He must have them again.

Was it not the bombing that made you a little mad?

She spikes him with a look.

You've read the diary.

Yes.

Then you know that's not true. I was in a bad way. For so long, I didn't even know I was in a bad way. I thought that was just me. My personality. But this is me.

April is matter-of-fact. He recognizes the same quality that disturbed him during his meetings with Gabrielle Salmon: the absence of emotional reactions to calamitous events. The only person being triggered is him. He feels a tide of anger rising. He wants to provoke her into reaction.

Even if it has helped you in some way, is this – he struggles to locate some neutral terminology – *experience you're having now worth the deaths of fifteen innocent people?*

Still, she is conversing chiefly with the ceiling.

Apparently, that's what it took. Could fewer people have died and I get the same treatment? Maybe. But fewer people didn't die. Fifteen people died. That's just how it worked out.

And to you their deaths were worth it? A boyhood memory: crouched by the back door, poking ants with a stick.

April – finally! – swings her legs off the end of the bed and sits up.

Let me ask you, Dr Logan, why you think death is such a bad thing. She stares at him. *I mean you, all of us, start from the assumption that death is bad.*

There is a sound in Logan's ears like rushing air. As surreptitiously as he can, he pinches himself.

You're telling me it isn't? he says.

Half of him is in the London kitchen, eating cereal.

What if it isn't? she says. *What if we have it completely wrong? What if we're in some giant illusion, some giant dream, and the people who have died have just – woken up? And when we die – that is, wake up – we'll join them.*

He imagines joining Flora. She's ruffling his hair as though he is the child, saying, *Miserable old scrote!* The image of her melts away into a taped-off area of hillside. April hasn't finished.

People say of the dead, 'She's here in spirit.' Why do they say that?

They're in denial, he says. *They refuse to accept death.*

What if they say it because it's true? Have you ever felt it, Dr Logan? Have you ever felt someone who was dead was right here with you?

In the pub, ash on the carpet and Flora in pigtails. Wine-gum Flora waiting with him in the dark car in Sawyer Street. All the other ghost echoes of Flora, categorized as after-shocks and hallucinations. But he can't give April any kind of hold over him. And is conscious of the camera, in danger of recording him irrational.

No, he says.

A corkscrew look; she knows he's lying. She shakes her head. *You're too scared to say it's true, but we've all felt it. We've all felt it, Dr Logan. Yet we make this big deal out of death. Even Christians treat death like the end, and they're supposed to believe in Heaven. What if death's a beginning, Dr Logan? Or a renewal? A chance to go back to your essence? What if, in this life, we stretch ourselves out like rubber bands and death just releases the tension? Snaps us back to ourselves?*

What if? he asks.

Then killing them wouldn't be a bad thing, would it?

He hopes the camera is catching her smile. He no longer wants to save her.

But what about the Bible?

What about the Bible?

Thou shalt not kill.

You think God wrote the commandments?

I thought you thought He did.

She shakes her head. Draws her knees up to her chest, not in a protective move, but to pick a patch of dry skin from her feet.

And so the hour, minutely observed, goes by. The Old Testament, she says, was written by a bunch of prehistoric near-savages trying to control other prehistoric near-savages, and only in parts is it a true reflection of God. Thou shalt not kill, she says, is not one of these parts. *How would we live, if that were true? We kill every day, Dr Logan. We kill mammals and fish for meat and leather, we kill plants to make way for homes and agriculture, we kill insects to protect ourselves and our crops, we kill each other.* God, she says, doesn't give orders. God doesn't judge; Judgement Day is a human invention, a millennia-old instrument of social control. She is luminous with clarity. When he tugs her conscience back to the bus, like an owner collar-dragging their dog to the carpet-staining its nose must be rubbed in, she insists that they couldn't have died had they not, on some level, concurred.

Every event, she says, is a co-creation. Murderer and victim agree on the level of their souls; one is ready to kill, one is ready to pass back into the ether. *Every death's a suicide.* He repeats the words back to her, the idea smeared across his tongue so foul he wants to gag.

He drives to his dentist knowing this: she's not right in the head. She is, as true lunatics are, free of her troubles. She is *Hamlet*'s Ophelia at the flower-bestowing stage, smiling sweetly as she dances towards her oblivion.

The dentist, a Mrs Akbar – he seems to have been allocated a different dentist every time he visits – is equally clear on the source of his molar pain.

It's your wisdoms trying to push through, she says.

At my age? he says, uncomprehending. *Why now?*

One of the mysteries of the universe, says Mrs Akbar, snapping off her disposable gloves. *Like volcanoes, they can remain dormant for years. They might push through in your teens, or sit quietly in your jaw your whole life.* She washes her hands in the small sink. Logan wonders if she has a rubber allergy.

What next? he asks.

Mrs Akbar's assistant – a mousy young man with painted fingernails – removes his bib and presses a button. The chair hums back into an upright position.

Who knows? says Mrs Akbar. *What will life throw at us next, eh? That is the bigger mystery.*

I mean for the teeth, says Logan. *Are you going to extract them?*

Mrs Akbar sits on the small stool beside him.

Tell me about the pain, she says, and for a moment he thinks he will tell her everything: how his daughter threw herself out of an aircraft and hurtled to the earth, how her death severed him from normality, time, his wife, how everyday things like supermarkets and train journeys and city parks have become dangerous, how paninis dissolve into ants and his dead daughter sits chewing wine gums next to him in the car, how he is vomiting in front of neuroscientists, how he is hanging on to his sanity by the skin of his teeth… oh. *The skin of his teeth*. She only wants to know about his teeth. The pain of his teeth.

It started off just aching, he says. *Now there's throbbing. And the last couple of days I'm getting this shooting pain.*

Yes, says Mrs Akbar. *Unfortunately you have a major nerve involved. For that reason, I wouldn't want to do an extraction. There is a risk of nerve damage. You wouldn't want to lose your jaw function, would you?*

Something about her serious brown eyes makes the question sound almost like an invitation to consider it.

No, he says. *But can you give me something for the pain?*

Determined

Jules has gone to stay with her sister. This fact is easily determined by a note on the kitchen table.

Gone to Prissy's, it says, as though Prissy's were round the corner, when Prissy now lives in Dubai. The moniker itself is duplicitous, for isn't it always Priscilla Jules uses with him, the formality marking like urine the mistrust and rivalry of her sibling relationship? Prissy to the sister so as not to make waves, but to him Priscilla, the A-star pain in the coccyx who beat her to Daddy's affections and every school prize. She might have given him notice or flight numbers, dates to score through on the calendar, but could not have said more than she said with those three words. This is what my distance has done, he observes. It has abbreviated Priscilla, cut her from insufferable to tender. It has made them close.

The immediate problem is the dog. He cannot always be there

for the dog. It is Jules who is always there, and her absence is causing the beast to whine at unpredictable intervals. Though he has only just brought the creature in from a plod through the forest, it remains by the doormat. It has read the future out of his creased forehead, already foreseeing the long dark hours when Logan's legs marinate in the stew of the motorway, and a walk, though only inches from its nose, remains the other side of seasoned oak.

Enough! he says to the dog. *Achilles, enough!* And it slinks away to the basket he designated *a waste of money*, the floor being good enough, why spoil the beast?

For some reason he cannot explain, Logan continues to sleep in the car. He buys a four-seasons sleeping bag for the purpose. The bed has become hers, and the thought of occupying it in her absence is like sleeping in the enemy's trenches. Truth be told, excepting his study, the whole house has become hers. In the living room, her plumped-up cushions eye him ruefully. In the kitchen, the colour-labelled cabals of the spice rack wait to be plucked up by her fingers; the table yearns to be set. He takes blankets to his study and lies on the sofa like a sick child, but the growing disease of silence ticks through the house until he is wide awake with it. So Logan continues to sleep in the car. There, he can witness Jules's pre-programmed lights flicking through their rituals, can pretend she is moving through the house, tucking and tidying while he is watching over her. The dog – whose howl is an insufferable blackmail – sleeps in the car beside him.

Noodles

Logan is hiding behind the noodles. Merriweather is idling at the sprouting mung beans. For the second time in three years they are close both to each other and to pasta, but this time it is no accident. The independent health food shop has angled aisles and backless shelves, perfect for peeping. Logan has two client reports to prepare, but yet another sleepless night in his driveway has wired him for only one task. He will confront Merriweather. The timing will be perfect. It is not yet perfect.

He spotted Merriweather on Sawyer Street. To avoid being seen, he slipped into a vaping outlet; watching his target, sideways, through the window. He placed his thumb on the sensor below the picture of the latest model and a black-and-silver e-cig dropped out of the chute. There was no one to ask how to operate the thing; a ten-second video instruction played on the wall. Logan took his first drag in the doorway, savouring the hit. He watched Merriweather enter the health food shop.

Now they are yards apart, and the moment is almost upon him. He must be calm. He must prepare what he's going to say. He's still rehearsing it under his breath when a woman asks him where the falafel is.

I don't work here, he says, offended.

The woman considers his dishevelment, the crushed suit.

No, she says, *all right, but you were moving things around*.

They were in the wrong place, he says, staring at her in a deliberately unhinged way until she shakes her head and moves off. He peers again through the hole he made, which no longer frames the indecisive Merriweather. Where is the man? Logan shifts the rice noodles and the egg noodles and the thread noodles, slinking the hole along the row like the gap in a nine-square puzzle. Not a Merriweather in sight.

Finlay.

The voice is behind him. Logan startles, straightens himself, and turns around slowly.

Simon.

Merriweather's face is troubled. Whether guilt is a component of that trouble, Logan cannot tell. The creased forehead could simply be a reaction to Logan's dishevelment, the coffee-pumped eyes which Logan spots over his old friend's shoulder as ghostly reflections on the organic ice-cream cabinet. Logan feels panic fluttering in his chest.

What are you doing here? he asks. (Good thinking, he tells himself. Challenge him before he can challenge you.)

Shopping? says Merriweather, his uncertainty about Logan's motives transferred onto himself with habitual politeness.

Good, good, says Logan, struggling to find solid ground. *Find anything nutritious?*

Rye soda bread, says Merriweather, lifting it in his basket as proof. *Look, Finlay, are you...*

What?

Are you spying on me?

Logan fluffs up indignantly.

What can you mean?

You were peering through the shelves.

I was peering at the shelves. Logan pats non-existent glasses in his breast pocket. Where are they, actually? *Eyesight not what it was. Why would I be spying on you?*

I don't know, says Merriweather. *What are you doing here, then?*

Same as you. Shopping. Unlike Merriweather, he has no basket.

I see no shopping, says Merriweather.

Logan grabs two packets and holds them either side of his ears. *What do you say?* he asks. *Teriyaki? Or Medium Egg?*

Logan has never before played silly buggers in public. All his clowning has been saved for the bathroom mirror. Merriweather is thrown.

Depends what they're for, he says. *Look, Finlay, a lot has happened in the last couple of years, and—*

To me too.

Obviously. Merriweather's eyes alight on the pinstripe shirt which, looking down now, Logan can see is stained with the ketchup from yesterday's hotdog. *But whatever's going on with you, I'd appreciate it if you'd leave me alone.*

Why come and accost me, then? says Logan, replacing the noodles among the Italian wholewheat pastas and turning his body in a confrontational manner.

Accost you?

Yes. You didn't need to speak to me. I was minding my own business.

Something comes over Merriweather in that moment. Logan sees it arrive on his face like the wake of a tanker. Merriweather steps forward, Logan steps backwards, and all at once they are doing a disconnected tango down the aisle, until Logan is backed into the bakery shelves.

I rather think you were minding mine, says Merriweather, grabbing a wrist and hooking it by its cuff onto a hook made for paper bags He grabs the other wrist, presses it against the other wooden upright. *I don't know what's got into you, but I'm asking you to leave me alone.* He looks around wildly; nothing to hook it upon. But as if summoned by the Old Testament God, an acned member of staff attempts to pass them with a pile of posters and a staple gun.

Excuse me, says Merriweather, snatching the gun and pressing it hard against Logan's palm.

Do something! says Logan, and the youth does something. He runs back into the storeroom.

I should crucify you, says Merriweather, and Logan unwisely embraces the word *should* with relief, for when Merriweather sees it, he presses the trigger. Pain zings through Logan's palm. The staple is too shallow to meet the wood, so Merriweather staples again, violently and repeatedly through the shirt-cuff. He leaves Logan hooked and nailed to the bread shelves, abandoning both weapon and basket of shopping at the till.

Did you kill Flora? Logan shouts after him. *Did you kill Flora?*

There is fuss made of him. The police are called. Two witnesses are kept from their offices for nearly an hour, but will face their bosses' disapproval with tales of good citizenry and the delicious, repeatable tale of a man stapled to a rack of flatbreads. The police, when they arrive, take his answers with professional detachment. Yes, he knows the man. No, he does not want to press charges.

He goes back to his car, where the dog is waiting for him.

I'm going mad, Achilles, he says. *I'm afraid I am properly going mad.*

Compassion

April has a dream. Dr Logan is sleeping in his car and there is a dog beside him. A liver-and-white coloured dog with long furry ears. The ether of April slides through the solid roof of the car and coalesces into the shape of herself in the back seat.

Where are you taking me? she asks. Dr Logan, still asleep, says nothing. The dog wakes up, muzzle still on its paws, and raises an eyebrow in her direction. She asks again, uses his name, *Dr Logan*, but he is solidly asleep. Under his eyelids, dreaming eye-balls jiggle like wakeful children mucking about under blankets.

She ghosts through the car and floats across a wide gravel drive to a house. She's not sure whose house it is; it doesn't feel like Dr Logan's. No one answers the front door but the back door to the kitchen is open and there are people sitting down to breakfast. She knows them. Rick, her annoying former house-mate, eating porridge. Luke Fisher, telling a joke to Naomi Bell. Other faces familiar from campus. Now she understands. It is everyone she killed on the bus. She goes to sit down among them, and they make space for her. Listening in to the joke, she realizes it is that one about God, about the man on the roof of his flooded house who is sent boats and helicopters, but refuses them all, saying, 'God will save me.' The waters rise, he dies, and when he gets to Heaven he says, 'God, why didn't you save me?' and God says, 'I sent you boats, I sent you helicopters...'

If God isn't real, she says, why are they so many jokes about Him? But nobody hears her. They pass a teapot around the circle, anointing each cup. No one is angry with her. Even though they know she blew them up, they offer her toast, pass her the marmalade.

Professional

This time, he has no appointment. This time the woman on reception calls Dr Salmon and apologizes for the intrusion *but there is a gentleman here, a Dr Logan*, his name hitched like a trailer to the indefinite article as if she doesn't recognize him, even the name of him. Perhaps he is unrecognizable. Perhaps three nights spent mostly in his car, as though on some interminable but motionless journey, are enough to rub off even a distinguished man's distinguishing features.

The result of last night's gravel drive contemplations was this: he must see Dr Salmon. For Dr Salmon's past actions must be read out of her head as a future is read out of tea leaves, and Logan cannot read a person of her complexity down the phone. In matters of high importance, he is dependent on subtleties of facial expressions and body language: those barely perceptible giveaways on which his reputation for accurate assessment rests.

The receptionist's *Sit*, even with its embroidered *Please*, he ignores even more markedly than before. This time he stands not at the information boards but at the plate-glass windows of the entrance, the better to watch the rain that once again accompanies his visit. His face is arranged to hold no more expression than an unaddressed envelope. Behind his back, his hands clasp one another in firm and supportive brotherhood. He is on business, and here is the stance of a man on business: focused, formal, controlled.

The awareness, nevertheless, like an itch: the last time they spoke, Logan was hyperventilating. She had caught him in free fall, floated him down to the ground. This time, his feet would be pillars planted on the earth; he, the unshakeable edifice. So he had determined through three hours of self-talk on the journey here, and so it would be. Thus, when a voice behind him says,

Logan!

he is able to reply with a cool nod,

Dr Salmon.

And when her next remark is,

Goodness, this is out of the blue,

he fishes effortlessly for the sour comedy of

Out of the grey, surely?

without so much as gifting her a smile. He will not be hooked into friendship. He says,

I'm here to talk about Ms Smith.

His subject made opaque under the formality of address, for, since the bombing, no one has referred to the young woman as Ms Smith, who might be anyone, but always April Smith, with its inappropriate crack of sunshine. Dr Salmon's face becomes blank for a moment until her train of thought reaches the logical station.

Of course. April,

and her brows twist up and release in their own silent conversation (*What's up with him? – Say nothing!*).

Come along then, she says, *come to my lair*, and leads him through double doors into the heart of her department. No student-infested coffeeshop this time, he notes: she has slept in his house, eaten his wife's preserves. Thus he follows her shapely calves into a maze of grey-carpeted corridors where the doors to professors' offices can be distinguished from store cupboards and toilets only by a subdued level of personalization. On the door of one Professor Andy Spinoza, a Blu-tacked postcard reads 'To Save Time, Let's Just Assume I Know Everything'. On the door of one Dr Ali Fanshaw, an A4 poster advertises a one-day seminar on 'The Holographic Body'. Gabrielle Salmon's door is decorated with a snipped-out cartoon of two scientists by a blackboard. Two sections of complex formulations separate the phrase '… then a miracle occurs…' and one scientist is saying to the other, 'I think you should be more explicit here in Step 2.'

It's not much, but it's home, she says, recycling the phrase with a half-American accent as she ushers him in.

The room offers shelter to a desk, three chairs, a small coffee-maker and a single, half-empty bookcase.

I thought you university types had rooms full of books, he says.

All online these days, she says. *Why kill trees?* She motions to one of the chairs. *Park yer bum.*

The slangy familiarity: an attempted antidote, he thinks, to his newly stiffened frontage. Two adoptions of alien vernacular in less than a minute. He is determined not to descend into mateyness.

Dr Salmon—

She laughs disconcertingly.

You've really got your hackles up, she says.

I don't know what you mean.

You do, Logan, you do. But okay, not a problem. Adopting a dash of Received Pronunciation, *Do carry on.*

Perhaps, he thinks, I am making a mistake. What he really wants to know is whether Merriweather was one of her guinea pigs: information she may be more likely to share with a friend than a prickly professional.

I'm sorry, Gabrielle, he says, *I just feel a little awkward about*—

How should he phrase it?

She: *Your panic attack?*

He, rapidly papering over the top of her suggestion: *Our last conversation.* He adjusts the knot of his tie distractedly, saying, *Being here on a professional matter, I wanted to establish a more professional tone. I apologize if it seems*—

Arsey?

Stiff.

Look, she says, leaning forward and placing her hand on his knee, entirely out of line with his stated wishes, *none of it really matters. We're all human. Relax, you'll live longer.*

I suppose you'll tell me you have figures, he says.

What?

That relaxed people live longer.

She withdraws her hand.

There's a fascinating study on baseball players— she begins, but Logan cuts her short.

Dr Salmon, Gabrielle, sorry, but we have to talk about April Smith.

They talk in turns. Logan speaks of amorality, the absence of guilt, the dissolution of conscience. Gabrielle Salmon speaks of insight, peace and clarity. Logan launches into a deconstruction of the psychotic personality, peppered with technical language, though so impassioned that towards the end he inadvertently uses the word *loon*. April is now free of distress, says his opponent, adding *as any psychiatrist – or psychologist – would surely want for their client*. They butt against each other, but so unalike in their substance that where Logan comes away feeling fragmented, his opponent simply subsides, unharmed as a tide.

Rain applauds at the window. He has lost. But even in the knowledge of his loss, a salient point floats like a fragment of wreckage to the top of his mind, and Logan attempts one last stab at his argument. (Though won't water simply part for a blade and lighten the arm that wields it?) His eight-year-old self, once told off for tearing a boy's shirt in a fight he didn't start, and not believed, stares at the floor and divests himself of what feels most abhorrent:

April said all deaths are suicides.

Gabrielle Salmon has been swinging in her chair, one way, then the other. Now she stops, and, without looking up, Logan feels her stillness. It is the stillness of a hawk hovering over a field mouse. Then the rapid descent.

This is about your daughter, she says.

Times folds over the room once, twice.

He wants to look up but can't now, for the tears in his eyes.

Logan, she says, *for God's sake, do the process. How can you function under this burden?*

And it's true, it feels like a burden, so suddenly heavy it is hard to breathe beneath its weight. Not only Flora's death but other losses: his boyhood dog Sandy, who slept in his bed as a puppy, whom he taught to balance a biscuit on her nose before she was crushed beneath the wheels of the island's only police car; his mother, who said, *I will always be here for you*, but slipped the emergency suitcase from under his bed without waking him and was gone by breakfast, only a letter to his dad marking her place at the table. Breath-sucking vacuums triggered briefly by every subsequent loss, yet he had successfully contained and sealed every absence, large and small, stored his losses in the dark behind a door he couldn't even remember how to open. Now time has fermented them. Flora's loss is too big to contain. And now, all together, they are bursting their lids, and their contents descend upon him, and he dissolves in the office of a woman who already knows too much.

Do the process! she says again, taking his hand in hers with so much tenderness that he finds himself fighting an inappropriate urge to kiss her. No, no, not that, but what? Under the wash of emotion he cannot think, only feel. And what he now feels is that Gabrielle Salmon, against the fatal tide of his losses, is somehow pumping, through the portal of his hand, love. Love that, like a blood transfusion, races up his arm, pours into his heart. An overloaded heart which beats harder, faster, distributing the anti-dote through his blood vessels until every cell, every atom of his body, is suffused with her warmth. Breathing slows. Heart slows.

What did you do? he asks, not daring to look up at her.

Held an intention, she says.

That's twice, he says. *That's twice you've brought me out of—*

He cannot name it.

Yes, she says.

Now his hand, awkward again, wants to withdraw into a pocket, so excuses itself to go hunting for his e-cig.

Do you mind? he asks.

Propylene glycol, she says. *Why should I mind?* She, too, needs to move, leaving her seat to set the coffee-maker to its business. *I didn't know you smoked*, she says with her back turned.

Not for years, he says. *Not since smokes were tobacco. Bought this last week. Find it calming.*

It's mostly the breathing, she says. *The calming effect. Studies show—*

Not now, he says. *Please.*

They listen to the rain, and again their intimacy feels, to him, post-coital.

Gabrielle, he ventures. *I think you may have met an old friend of mine. Simon Merriweather.*

How so?

She is shepherding black liquid into mugs decorated with the word SHINE and the explanatory small print: Stop Harmful International Newt Experiments.

You spoke to a group he attends. Life After Death. In Southwark.

Yes, I remember. The group, I mean. Not your friend, particularly. Not great at names.

Really? But he would have come here. He signed up as an experimental subject, I believe. A leading question, he knew. Not the kind that would stand up in court. But this wasn't for any court. This was for him. And if he was mistaken, she could correct him. She comes to him bearing their coffees; places his down slightly away from the table's edge, as though he is a toddler and might scald himself.

I've no idea, she says. *That was a double-blind randomized control job. Sign-ups went through my postgrad, Alice. And the processing too. I just crunched the data.*

So you don't know if he signed up?

Even if he signed up, I wouldn't know which group he belonged to. Might have been in one of the control groups. In the control groups we stick the jellyfish on their head, press the right buttons, but either they get no electrical pulses at all, or the electrical pulses are random, not controlled by biofeedback. She blows on her coffee. *Why do you ask?*

Logan stares at her face; nothing he can hook into, nothing he can read.

Does the process eradicate guilt? he asks.

Yes, she says. *Yes, it does.*

And you think that's a good thing?

She smiles.

Do you have any guilt, Logan?

He is on the verge of saying no when the faces begin to crowd in. The truth: there is barely anyone he has known he doesn't feel guilty about. Rachel, whom he had both failed to read and failed to leave, only to abandon her eventually to single motherhood and now, like him, the isolation of bereavement. Poor Johanna, with whom he had repeated the pattern so disastrously that she had cursed their son with the memory of walking in on her corpse. Yes, Tom – Tom, who rightly despised him. Jules. Even the dog—

Logan, she says softly, *would you feel better without it?*

How can I feel better when I can't behave better? How would any of us stop hurting others, if we didn't feel guilt?

What if we can't behave better until we feel better?

Sorry?

You've been feeling guilty for a long time, she says. *Has it stopped you hurting people?*

He turns his mug around. *Experiments,* it says. Still too hot.

But people should feel guilty. For doing bad things. It would be inhuman not to.

What good does it do? she asks.

Images loom in his mind, April's beatific smile, Merriweather, remorseless, and *What if someone's killed someone?*

Does guilt bring the dead back?

But they should suffer! People should suffer for the wrong they do!

She scoots her chair forward on its wheels and takes his hand. *Say you could start afresh*, she says. *Shake off your past. As though you were almost* – her gaze dances briefly to the ceiling as she stretches for the words – *a brand-new person inhabiting the same body. Like – like the person you would have been had you grown up with perfect, loving parents in a perfect, loving world. Would you have ever hurt anyone, if you'd never been hurt?*

He doesn't know. How could he know?

Your friend, she says. *What makes you think he's undergone the process?*

No guilt, says Logan. *No remorse.*

That's not the same thing, she says. *Guilt and remorse. What should he feel guilty about or remorseful for?*

And Logan is about to begin, *Killing my daughter*, until he realizes that isn't established fact, that's only suspicion, and for a moment he's not even sure why he's here, as though a small crack has appeared in this bubble of gloom and confusion through which the bright light of reality is winking. And then he remembers: the Post-it note from 'S', the article, this fishy Salmon and her neural net, the spectre of professional ruin, the revenge of his wife's thwarted fiancé – and look at yourself, Logan, you have walked right into the trap, you are sitting in her room crying, your hand in her lap!

Jesus! he says, jumping up. *I can't believe you! I can't believe I'm falling for this shit!*

What? she says. He can't read her face. Look, she's perplexed. No, she's pretending. Two parts of his brain, at odds with each other, wrestle for control of his perceptions, and he can no longer tell, can no longer trust anything. *Christ!* he says.

She's out of her chair, coming towards him – *Logan?* – reaching out to touch him, and he cannot bear it, pushes her away, harder than he meant to. Her body slams into the bookcase. She crumples, slides down to the floor.

Oh, Christ! he says. *I'm sorry.*

Crouches beside her. Mummy's one wide eye staring, and this time it's him playing Daddy.

Ow, she says. *Fuck.*

So sorry.

She nods slowly, even as she's rubbing the pain out of her hip bone.

God, he says.

Stop it! Stop Godding and Christing!

I'm sorry.

Ah, bugger it. Poor call on my part. Should have let you rant. But it broke the moment, I suppose.

I didn't mean to—

No, she says, standing with some difficulty. *I understand.*

He takes her elbow, helps her back into her seat. Sits down in front of her, contrite.

How far are you going to let this go? she asks, picking up a pen and tapping it on her notepad.

I don't know what you mean.

Logan, come on. It's plain as day. You're under a lot of stress. If you're not careful, you're going to mess up in a big way. You could lose your career.

He tries to read her eyes.

What are you saying?

Is she threatening him? Will she call it assault, hold it over his head? But no, here's her voice again, brown-sugar-soft.

You've got to do something, Logan. Before you push the wrong person into a bookcase. She's smiling. *At the very least, rest. Stop work completely, go away somewhere.*

Then I really would *go mad*, he says, and feels the fear of it, inaction, grinding like a rat into the nerves behind his eyeballs. There would be nothing to save him, nothing to keep him from drowning in his own grief.

Then you've two choices, she says. *See your GP and get some drugs. Or try the process.*

The process, he echoes.

Yes.

Didn't help Merriweather, he says, and she's instantly curious.

How was he when you last saw him? Calm? Peaceful?

No. Not really, no.

Was there anything unusual about his behaviour?

He stapled me to some shelves, says Logan, rubbing his palm. But there's nothing there. No injury.

Sorry, she says, *what? He did* what?

No, thinks Logan. Wasn't that a dream? He remembers the figure that walked past his car; the figure he followed.

He seemed upset, anyway.

Then he hasn't done the process, she says. *I can't check the records, you understand, but I'd stake my life on it.*

Or mine, says Logan.

Nothing bad has come out of this yet, she says. *No abnormal reactions. You have to sign the usual disclaimers as a legal precaution, but honestly, Logan, we've had over five hundred people don the jellyfish and not a single one is worse off.*

I don't know about that. April Smith is ranting about death being some kind of blessing.

But is she worse off, Logan? Is she in a worse position than she was before? Legally speaking? Or in terms of sanity?

He considers.

No. I suppose not.

And does she seem happier?

He compares the hard-eyed, withdrawn April he worked so fruitlessly to crack open with her new garrulous, rhapsodic incarnation.

Yes, I guess so.

He doesn't understand what happens when he's with Dr Salmon. How as he moves into her sphere he is altered, his whole course diverted from its intentions. His very thinking reversed. Some magic she does, some hold she has over him. As though, in her immediate proximity, he slips from his track and into hers. A small part of him is tapping out Morse.

I need to think this through, he says.

Go for a walk, she suggests.

I'll go for a walk, he agrees.

Semi-transparent

Dusk is falling. Inside the building, lights are coming on automatically in occupied rooms. As Logan walks through the Alterman complex, tonguing the twinge of his wisdom tooth, the corridors light up ahead of his footsteps like a pinball's high-score totalizer. Whether he is illuminating them, or they him, he isn't sure. Nor is he sure where he might walk that would be roomy enough to lay out his thinking; away from Dr Salmon it feels tangled and chaotic. Preoccupied with unravelling pros from cons, he allows his unconscious mind to dictate his direction at junctions: left or right, straight on or turn. Now, directly in his path, a wall of glass, a glass door. Behind the glass is darkness: an internal oasis of shadow he can only make out dimly in the failing light. A ghostly reflection: half him, half darkness, one overlaying the other.

Pass through the glass or let himself be deflected? To go forward, he will have to walk through himself; push himself out of the way and enter the darkness. It will surely be cold. And who knows what's in there?

To his right, a corridor that seems to have life at the end of it: the bright illuminations of an eatery, people murmuring anonymous conversation. But he wants to be alone.

This isn't the choice he needs to make. It doesn't matter either way.

3A.

CHEMISTRY

Reflected

There is a moment of paralysis as the decision takes shape. Behind him, the Alterman Centre's bright corridors hum patiently. Here I am, he thinks, at one of those semi-transparent surfaces scientists use to split the wave of a single atom in the box pair experiment. If I were pure light, I would both bounce off and pass through.

The face that stares back at him solidifies, and the darkness disappears. Look at yourself, Logan. He tugs the creases out of his jacket, straightens his tie, and turns down the corridor.

In the brightly lit, chattering room, a gaggle of students hovers by the 3D printers, waiting for objects to be sprayed into existence. Whether these are shoes they have ordered on the internet or models of bridges for their engineering coursework, Logan isn't concerned to discover. The rest of the room is livelier. At glass-screened tables, more students sit nursing coffees, gaming or swiping their e-mails. There is a sign on the wall that says 'Cafeteria', but the room boasts nothing besides drink vending machines and another bank of 3D printers devoted to printing food. Though Logan is hungry, he is not hungry for replicated protein, and plumps for a simple coffee – real granules! genuine hot water! – before taking the only unoccupied table.

Is he thinking straight? He can't tell. Not enough sleep, not enough food, too much coffee, and this terrifying magma-chamber of emotion that threatens to blow him open at any moment. How can he make any rational decision? The last decision he made resulted in a low-grade re-enactment of the cru-cifixion. Perhaps he should resign himself to losing the lot – his mind, his career, Jules, the house. For what did any of it matter without Flora? Flora was gone, gone, and there was no bringing her back, no talking to the dead, no matter what nonsense Dr Salmon had visited upon him; it was all just shades of his own madness. Was he not better off surrendering to it, descending into it? He had lost everything already. What else mattered?

And yet if nothing mattered, why not surrender to Dr Salmon's process, and wipe out the pain? *LOL*, says a young man behind him. *ROFLMAO*, says the young man's friend. Words he knows thanks to Flora. And they're right. The idea is laughable. Especially when you consider the possibility that Dr Salmon is a trap that Merriweather set, and on the other side of her process lurks professional ruin and a different form of insanity: Logan the medium.

If only he could make no decision at all and yet hold himself together. If only he could stay exactly as he is and pass through this crisis, unbroken. For that is all he wants, now that he thinks about it: for the world to stop changing and pressing in on him; for the future to stop unfolding and overlaying Flora, pushing her further and further into the past; for Jules and Tom to accept him as he is.

Coming through the door now, as though Logan's thoughts are warping his eyesight, there's someone who looks a little like Tom, who could even be Tom if he wasn't laughing with a woman on his arm. This almost-Tom spots Logan staring, changes direction and comes to a stop (with his woman) right in front of his table.

Finlay.

Logan, taken aback, recalibrates.

Tom.

This is my father, he explains to his companion. To him, *What are you doing here?*

A meeting, says Logan. *You?*

Nodding at the wall of printers, *Mei Mei's got something to pick up.*

Good, says Logan, feeling the meaninglessness of his response.

Yet somehow, because they were unprepared for each other, he has not fallen directly into Arsehole. *You're looking well*, he says, and means it. So well that he didn't even recognize his own son.

The pills I guess, says Tom. Well-groomed, happy-looking Tom. Clothes-and-a-smile-that-fit Tom.

The Anesthine.

Yep.

He's wearing the glasses again. So is Mei Mei. The real-spectacle frames imbue an aura of intelligence and the inward focus of the wearer's pupils augment the illusion of deep thinking. An alert must have popped up on Mei Mei's. She nods brightly, says, *Excuse me, Mr Logan, nice to meet you*, and heads off towards the printer bank.

You have a moment? asks Logan, nodding at the spare chair.

I guess. Tom sits down, but his eyes are on something more interesting, close to his face.

You can say I'm your sponsor, says Logan.

What?

If any of your friends see me. If you don't want them to know I'm your father.

Oh, says Tom, focusing on him now. *I don't care.*

The nonchalance seems genuine. The words are suffused with disinterest rather than spite.

You don't care? asks Logan.

If people know who you are. Why should I? I'm done with all that. What happened happened. The past is the past.

It is hard for Logan to credit he is talking to the same person who eviscerated him in the Battle of Trafalgar only six weeks ago. Or the same person from *any* part of Tom's fury-fuelled existence. This version of Tom has never previously existed, to his knowledge. Little wonder he didn't recognize this son whose face, free of the tensions of unexpressed rage, has arranged itself differently.

This is the Anesthine talking?

Tom is undoubtedly watching something else.

I don't know. Is it?

You were different before, Logan persists. *Angry.*

Okay. If you say so.

Strange not to touch on his anger. Like stepping on the grass at the edge of a pond and discovering it's duckweed that gives beneath your feet.

You don't remember?

Tom gifts him a few seconds of eye contact.

Kind of. It just doesn't feel important. Only now is important.

Like mindfulness, thinks Logan. Like that Zen claptrap.

Only now? he says.

His son nods vaguely.

The past is like a dream or something.

So you're not – Logan hesitates. This is a dangerous test – *still blaming me for the death of your mother?*

His son looks at him blankly.

Why would I do that?

Logan looks for tension in Tom's hands, shoulders; for small acts of destruction. But his son's fingers are untroubled. The sweetener packets that Logan placed on the table remain unmolested.

You remember what happened, right?

I don't remember you leaving. I was two.

But your mum? You remember what happened with your mum?

He watches his son's eyes blinking, a cat in the sunlight.

I remember finding her on her bed, covered in vomit. But that was, what, when I was— I don't know, much later, wasn't it?

You were eight.

So six years after you left. Not really connected.

No?

I don't think so. Do you?

Mei Mei reappears as though beamed in.

Look. She grins, opening the mouth of her bag so that Tom can see whatever it was she picked up.

Very nice, says Tom. Their look shares a secret as she closes it again. *We should go*, Tom says to his father. *Stuff to do. See you.*

Logan gets up for their leaving – clasped hands from her, no more than a nod from Tom – and for a while after they have vanished he remains standing, watching after the effect of them, the way one might watch a rainbow fade until not a trace of it remains. *Anesthine, then.* A fortuitous meeting at exactly the moment he was stuck with a question has given him the answer. Anesthine.

Though he left his scarf in Dr Salmon's office, he cannot return for it. He cannot risk re-exposing himself to her influence, being diverted from his path. The scarf was a dull thing in any case; a practical present from Jules. He texts Dr Salmon from the cafeteria. Safer than a phone call, for he knows she can work her voodoo on him with her voice alone. *I've decided the process isn't for me*, he types. *Off home now. I'll be in touch*. That last sentence – the casual reassurance of future contact – is to stop her running after him with the scarf. He already knows it's a lie.

Clinical

Within a week of starting his prescription, Logan feels able to Skype Jules in Dubai. Even Prissy's hovering presence doesn't faze him. He shakes the small brown bottle at the screen.

Got these, he says. *They're working.*

His wife looks drawn. Middle Eastern sunshine is too harsh for her to go out in. Perhaps the sister is a little wearing, too. Too hasty a leap from pan to fire.

What is that? she says. *Turn it around.*

He holds it up to the webcam. As she leans in to scrutinize the label he can see high-definition crinkles in the neck he used to nuzzle.

Ah, she says. *Okay.*

They sit staring at each other. The inset picture of him looks dark and green-tinted in the study's low light; a glow-worm in a wine bottle. Her backdrop is clinical white, as though Prissy has her contained in some high-class correctional facility.

So will you come home? he asks.

She looks down at her fingernails.

Maybe.

He waits for her to say something else, but nothing else is coming.

I'm really feeling better now, he says.

Good, she says.

He is waiting for her as she emerges from Customs into Arrivals. There is an awkwardness about them, neither sure if they are on hugging terms. The hug attempt is confused in any case by who should put down, or pick up, or hand over, this or that item of luggage. They settle on a half-missed kiss on the cheek, and Logan piling everything onto a nearby trolley.

The drive home feels like an extension of their call: stilted, halting, each of them editing a tangle of thoughts into silence for fear of stepping upon some terrible wound. What little conversation passes between them is the safe sort: the flight, the weather. Even these trifles are soon rubbed out by the motorway's numbing miles. The silence is heavy with the unsaid, so Logan clicks on the radio, but every station the unit locates is out of tune with them. Music that jars with its youth and vigour, or with its optimism, or whose failed-romance soundtrack risks scripting them into a tragedy. Talk shows and phone-ins are no better, flaming from irritation into antagonism. Logan returns them to the hush of passing miles.

On smaller roads, the nearness of human habitations provides them with the relief of conversational fodder, largely on the subject of Christmas lights. How charming the lights in that hedge, or the raindrop animations in that tree; how garish the dreadful competitive display on that row of former council houses. How surely there are fewer visible Christmas trees in windows every year, as though more and more people are counting their pennies, giving up decoration, giving in to the gloom. It is mostly Jules talking; Logan is simply agreeing. He weighs the gaps between his responses, ensuring his murmurs of assent are both warmly toned and sufficiently regular for his reticence not to be mistaken for a symptom of morose contemplation. *Or perhaps it's just that more and more people have other religions*, Jules says. *Or no religion. Not everyone celebrates Christmas, do they?*

Once they are home, the awkwardness of going to bed begins to loom. It feels too soon to sleep together. They are strangers again and must get to know each other, flirt and date for a time before allowing each other the sight or touch of naked skin. Except they are too wary to flirt, too hurt to date. So they stay downstairs awake, though both are tired, and prepare a light supper side by side, though neither is hungry. Logan senses his wife's words, only seconds after they are uttered, draining through a grating and disappearing from his awareness, as if washed into the sewer of the past; not for him to process. The medication, he supposes. He stays focused on the bright present; her hands spooning his coffee into the coffee-maker, her waist in that sweet blue dress cinched by a bout of food poisoning at her sister's. Now she is polishing a teaspoon and putting it back in the drawer and he says, *I'm very glad you're back*.

I'm glad you're back too, she says, and drops the tea towel to put her arms around him, very lightly, resting her head on his chest. He wonders if he is back, really. Or whether he seems a different Logan altogether, as Tom seemed a different Tom. If she has noticed this, she isn't letting on.

¤　　¤　　¤

She wants him to be back, so he is back. She holds him for almost a minute, to be sure of it. But holds him very lightly, so he won't vanish.

Come on upstairs, she says, leading him by the hand. But by the time they reach the bedroom door she has let go of him, and undresses herself matter-of-factly, turned away, as if for a doctor. And of course, I am a doctor, he thinks, but the thought is like a dead vole at the roadside. He follows her lead and undresses more carefully than usual; folding things onto chairs, dropping things into the linen basket, leaving nothing on the floor but the forlorn twins of his shoes.

Turkey

Christmas crashes in on him like an unexpected guest. All along it was there in the calendar, disguising itself as dates among the other dates, and suddenly it is descending upon him, demanding attention. Logan feels ambushed, although now he can recognize it as the small unreachable itch in his skull, words that wouldn't quite form into thoughts, shy children who were waiting for him to notice them. Only when Jules assembles their realistically fake Christmas tree (looking worn now, its LEDs blinking without conviction) does he register with some urgency that he must lift his head out of his case reports and go out to find presents for Jules and Tom. He senses a gust of annoyance but the feeling is brief as a dog's bark. *Pointless hiatus, meaningless exchange of gifts* slips very quietly out of his mouth as he is crossing the driveway, but the wind rattles the hawthorn bush and he is back to feeling nothing again.

He drives himself into Brockenhurst to poke around in the shops. The problem with shopping on Anesthine is he can hold no ideas in his head. By the end of the High Street's short and tasteful parade any small inspirations have blown away like that crisp packet skittering along the gutter, and he must make his way back again, this time tapping possibilities into his phone's notepad. The owner of the tiny gallery says, *Hello again*, and he explains, *Can't make up my mind*, when the truth is closer to, *Can't hold on to it*, but he knows he mustn't scare her, or himself. Mostly the drug is good, and allows him to focus. His work has become easier, for so long as there's no emotion involved, his brain functions near-normally. Only when emotion is present do words and thoughts disappear as though flushed down a lavatory.

He sits in the award-winning teashop to consider his list, his forgetfulness; there must be emotion in this task, though he cannot detect it. The Anesthine can. He reads through the list again and again, but he might as well be reading the Cyrillic alphabet. When the young man comes over to clean his table, flourishing his cloth like a toreador, Logan engages him in his dilemma, shows him the list for Tom.

What do you think? For my son? He's about the same age as you. Which one of these?

The young man reads through the list, makes a noise like sucking through a flattened straw.

Just give him money, he says, handing back the phone.

You're sure? asks Logan.

Whipping a tea towel over his shoulder, where it rests like an epaulet, *Money is always best*, he says. *Better than making a mistake. He can get what he wants.*

He leaves Logan's table with a cockle-shell pattern of wipes. Logan considers the pattern as it dries. The old Tom would be as hurt by money as by any present Logan would care to buy: the former translated into *my father doesn't care* just as swiftly as the latter would be read as *my father doesn't know me*. But Tom is on Anesthine, so can't be hurt; money will be fine. It is Jules he needs to worry about it. But the drug precludes worry. Worry is a temporary swelling no sooner discovered than dissolved into the white noise of *hush, hush, all's well.* He sits for some time, his tea going cold, staring at the list he has made for Jules and repeatedly forgetting the reason for his reading it. A story without a plot.

He can't ask the young man again, for what could he know about wives? What, for that matter, does Logan know, even about his own, given his inability to choose between an ice-cream maker, a book featuring arty photographs of lost shoes, and a picture from the gallery. Then it strikes him: all three! No choice required. Buy them all, wrap them all up, let her have them all and decide for herself what she likes best.

Ten minutes later, an ice-cream maker and a book of haunting shoes dangle in their bags from his fist, and he is back in the tiny gallery. Unfortunately he is again paralysed by choice. Which picture?

Can't keep away? says the woman with amusement. She is tweezering small pieces of coloured glass onto a canvas, creating – he can already discern – the throat of a kingfisher.

Ah, he says. *I'm just not sure. I want a picture for my wife.*

She puts down the tweezers, gets up from her stool and comes to stand beside him.

What sort of thing does she like?

He looks at her blankly.

This is terrible…

The more he tries to remember what his wife likes, the blanker he goes.

It's okay, she says. *What about animals? Does she like animals?*

Achilles comes wagging to his mind. *Animals*, he says, *yes.* But does she like pictures of animals?

The woman has guided him to stand in front of a landscape where the sheep are constructed from the shavings of recycled fizzy drink bottle tops. She is talking him through its symbolism but Logan is conscious in his peripheral vision of a cyclist in a mustard-yellow coat. *That's her*, he says. *That's my wife.*

The gallery owner laughs. *Aha. You're Finlay!*

Indeed, he says. Of course. Jules knows everyone in the village. Jules cycles past the gallery, oblivious that she is being observed and talked about.

We're in the same book group together, the woman explains.

Ah, he says. What he wants now is a polite way to leave the shop as quickly as possible. Goodness only knows what Jules has said about him, for his name to stick so in this stranger's mind.

Oh, I know exactly what you should get for Jules, says the woman. *This one.* She leads Logan over to a landscape in the corner. *She dropped in to see me last week, couldn't keep her eyes off it.*

The landscape – a peaceful enough depiction of a forest glade in acrylics – is dominated by a foreground of real barbed wire. He should feel grateful, he thinks, as he watches the woman swaddle the picture in several layers of bubble wrap. But he feels nothing.

On Christmas Eve a storm rattles in out of Russia; a bitter wind in the mood for breaking things. Logan is sleeping well now, thanks to his prescription, but the gale's howl keeps his wife wide-eyed and worrying that tiles will blow off the roof or worse, that some trick of the wind down the flue will snuff out the Rayburn. In the morning, she finds it cold. An oil-filled monstrosity that she insisted upon, it cannot be relit except by an expert; an expert who cannot be called out on Christmas Day. Jules is standing at the fridge in tears, staring at the clammy, featherless breast of the Gressingham duck she had planned to roast with thyme and cranberries. A comforting touch on the shoulder only makes her shake him off angrily. *Christmas is ruined.* Later, calmer, she is ringing around her village friends trying to borrow a microwave. *No chance*, Tom says, overhearing. *Cancer scare, remember?* When she finally embraces defeat,

Logan breaks out the alcohol. This is how they will jolly themselves along and make the best of it.

At least you won't have to cook, he says, filling her glass.

I wanted to cook, she says.

Their gift-giving is haunted by the spirit of an uncookable
dinner. Tom opens his envelope and nods. *Nom*, he says. When
Jules unwraps her final present she stares at it for a long time.

She said you couldn't keep your eyes off it, Logan explains.

Marjory?

Yes. I guess. If that's the woman's name.

She is certainly staring and staring at it.

What's that? Tom asks her.

A picture, she says.

Of?

She hands it over, like she doesn't have words for it.

Barbed wire, says Tom. *Nom*.

Things

There are things to be done. Words to be dispatched to the
battlefronts.

There is no further need to see April; his experiment with
nonsense is over. He writes his report; unambiguous. The girl
is a religious fanatic, and she is, indeed, insane. At least her
incarceration will be gentle, he thinks. Being housed among
lunatics is surely better than living with murderers. If the judge
directs the jury to trust his testimony, she will be getting away
very lightly. And if a law follows as predicted, the world will
be a safer place. He is doing good. Overly passionate religious
orators, who could never be arrested, will instead be sectioned,
as can anyone they infect with their *my God is better than your
God* shenanigans. How many humans have died in these fights
over who has the best imaginary friend? And to think grief

almost sucked him into the same insanity. He signs the report in three places, files it, and feels a sudden blankness that can only be what used to be emotion. The Anesthine, still policing him like a rogue state.

He is glad of the drug's protection. Sometimes he tests it in the quiet of his study: says *Flora*, and the name bounces back to him like a squash ball off a wall, with a surge of nothing. He knows the emotion is there because of the blankness. He says, *My daughter is dead*, and such a whoosh of it responds that he forgets a few minutes at once, and finds himself emerging out of a frozen position like a brought-to-life statue. He has no wish to return to imbalance. Has not yet dared ask his doctor about the safety of long-term – or permanent – use. If my father could have had it, he thinks, none of that need have happened. His mother's one staring eye frightening her little boy under the bed. The following morning, the first of many mornings where there was no porridge on the stove and he had to fetch his own cold cereal. What kind of Logan would have grown out of a boy whose father was peaceful; whose mother had stayed? Logan unpeels the pithy skin of this question curiously, but only with his intellect.

What he needs to do – what feels pressing, even without emotion – is to report Gabrielle Salmon. To whom, he is not sure, but he feels certain some Government department should know what the country's scientists are up to. And though he wishes her no personal ill will, he feels a civic duty has fallen upon him to prevent her recruiting further guinea pigs into her experiments. If religious observance drops off in subjects who have undergone her process, it is not because they are cured of religious belief, but because they now believe they *are* God. Naturally Gods have no need to go to a church or a synagogue to worship themselves. They will not be found on their knees, praying.

He arranges to have a Friday night drink, somewhere off the Old Kent Road, with an old school friend who is, quite usefully, a civil servant. On the second pint he floats the question. If there were a scientist whose experiments had in some way derailed her, psychologically; had induced her to think she was talking to the dead...? She has not, he stresses, come to him as a client; he has met her in the course of his work; he is simply concerned. The old friend is reassuring. He will have a word. Someone will be in touch.

The response is surprisingly rapid. A phone call on Monday afternoon is followed, the very next morning, by two suited men being shown to his study. They stay for an hour and a half; refuse tea, make notes. Or one of them does, typing rapidly into the laptop, precarious as a cliff-top beach-house on his knees. The other asks questions that he reads from a form on a clipboard, his seriousness so disconcerting that Logan feels obliged to make small talk – to say *how reassuring these last-century props, paper and clipboard* – in the moments of silence between them. The other man gives him a switched-on-switched-off smile; Logan's words clatter to the ground. Very quickly, he knows he is making a statement; the kind that will be catalogued. Never to be read to a court, be pored over by lawyers, but nevertheless it will be passed higher up for a judgement, sent down for execution. Should a Freedom of Information Request ever require the giving up of this hostage, it will emerge into the sunlight blindfolded with redactions.

After ninety minutes, the suited men leave with a brief flurry of handshakes. Jules sees them out. Logan stands in the sunlight of his upstairs window to watch the black car pulling out of the drive; right, to London. The note-taker, in the passenger seat, glances up as they round the gatepost, and Logan wonders if the man can see his face, or only the sunlight glinting from the pane.

Bonds

At first, she was sure he was back. He was calm and rational. He was ordered and detached. My Finlay, she thought, my Finlay is back in himself. No more Brian. But it only took a few days to understand: not all of him. Something of him was missing, and what was wandering around in her kitchen was more like the inadequate clone of a husband you would find in a sci-fi horror movie: same body, same memories, but something indefinably wrong. Anesthine obligingly obliterated grief, but the whole of him, all of his fire, was dampened down. Like a twentieth-century cancer drug that made no distinction between diseased cells and healthy ones, Anesthine could not tell bereavement from love; perhaps because bereavement *is* love, or the end result of it. Jules thought of her brother in the final fortnight of his life, struggling to get up the stairs by himself; skeletal not through the cancer itself but the drugs meant to kill it. And that was her marriage: weakened, poisoned and bald. Who knew how long she could keep looking at it?

Nevertheless, it limped the six weeks from New Year to Valentine's Day. They agreed it was too much bother to go out, so they had food delivered, exchanged cards like legal contracts, and sat opposite each other, swapping reassuring smiles through the wax bars of a triple candelabrum. Jules had laid the table with her usual care, but with a Valentine's theme, stooking red napkins with small bows of pink ribbon, and scattering crêpe paper hearts around their plates. But the symbolism of the day was immaterial. Finlay stripped the napkin of its ribbon as though he were filleting a fish, and spoke mostly about his caseload, salting this unappetizing plateful of psychopaths with new train diversions due to engineering works. The heart-shaped pink-foiled chocolates she'd arranged by his serving of cheesecake could have been any shape at all – Christian crosses, Satanic pentagrams, bloody parallelograms, he wouldn't have noticed. What's to notice? Peel, chew, swallow. It was pointless. Pointless. She cursed herself. She should have known that love cannot be fabricated with any amount of ribbon and crêpe paper. Jules went to bed early and numb. Finlay stayed up – *do you mind?* – to watch a film about a miscarriage of justice.

¤   ¤   ¤

Is there something about yearning that sets a beacon blinking across the human wilderness? Two mornings later, Fate delivered to Jules a belated Valentine's gift. Disguised in the plain brown wrapping of a practical nuisance, it was nevertheless recognized and devoured. She was on her way to Fordingbridge to assess a family whose child had been missing a lot of school. Halfway across the common north of Lyndhurst, in an area entirely devoid of mobile signal, the car made an alarming noise and lost all power. Jules coasted to the side of the road, watched by a motley collection of ponies. Yanking on the handbrake, she began to cry.

Everything is wrong, she said to the sky that watched her from the other side of the closed sunroof. *Nothing is working.* Not knowing what else to do, she got out, opened the bonnet, and stood staring hopelessly at the engine.

But something was working. Some grand puppeteer was staging a mystery play. For she hadn't been there five minutes when a swisher, more frequently serviced car slowed down and crunched to a halt in front of her, nose to nose. A man got out. A man in a long tan coat.

Now she is lying in bed thinking about him. Finlay is asleep beside her, snoring lightly, but Jules is wide awake. Her chest is buzzing like someone has passed electricity through it. Someone has. His name is Donal O'Connell, and he has just started working in the area as a locum. A few hours ago he got out of his car to offer assistance and now she is imagining running her hand over his jawline. He was friendly, not flirty. He had a lanky sixth-former-ness about him: a volunteer for any useful expedition, and too polite to make a pass. How practical he was, with his tow rope in the boot and his warning triangle: all the right safety equipment. How comfortable he was in himself, delivering his fairy-tale rhyming name without apology. When he said he would take her anywhere she wanted, she believed him. When he dropped her and the car at the garage, she knew everything would be fine: he made sure of it. He gave her his number, *just in case you need a lift later*, scrawled on the back of a leaflet for Hot Yoga. She would like to see him doing Hot Yoga. In the plough position, tipped onto broad shoulders, loose shorts and a black T-shirt sticking to his skin, sweat running down his thighs. Oh Jules, what are you doing? She scolds herself, and then, without meaning to, she is conjuring his lips. He has inviting lips. What has got into her? The devil, perhaps. Hunger, certainly. She imagines him kissing her. Imagines he, too, has hunger. Imagines his tongue filling her mouth. Guilt, guilt, yet she cannot stop herself. The thought is too delicious. Even the guilt seems delicious.

But why feel guilty? She hasn't kissed him. What's the harm in imagining? She's committed no sin.

But tomorrow she will ring the number on the Hot Yoga leaflet. She will ask if she can buy him a drink to say thank you, and on Thursday they will meet in The Cartwheel in Fordingbridge, and she will drink a little more than she intended. She will blurt out a sentence or two of unhappiness. Not enough to haunt their friendly drink with her husband's ghost, but enough for her eyes to well, and for the locum, in an act of compassion, to reach for her hand. Achilles will be curled up at her feet, as if to guard her mistress from intruders. But Achilles will be the opposite of protection. Achilles will be the reason Jules and the locum will walk into the forest; *the dog could do with the exercise*. The locum is all for exercise. And soon they will be deep, deep in the forest, deep in the pockets of their coats, deep in the intoxicating possibilities of something neither of them dare imagine. He is married. She is married. But all the trees have gathered around them; their leaves are shushing and no one is listening. The alcohol will soften her fear: *Go on*, it will say, *go on*. She will feel his eyes reading her. She will watch her own feet with a smile, like a girl, and every time she looks up she will see those eyes brightly upon her, both asking and knowing. When will the game mutate from playful to serious? When his hand knocks against hers and she snags his fingers. That will be her sign to him. Then he will stop her with a locked arm, as though he has captured a burglar. She will think he could capture a burglar. He is capable and fearless. Capable and fearless, he will kiss her. It will feel like a game. But for the first time in a decade, she will know the taste of another man's mouth, bitter with hops. Lips softer and wider than she is used to. His tongue unpredictable, probing for hers, asking, *More? More?*

Medication

Are you going to stay on it? she asks.

She means the medication.

The thought of coming off it is— interrupted by the chemical eraser she wishes to discuss. She is filling a pan of water from the filter. Logan wonders why she is still in her coat.

Sorry, what was the question?

She sighs, stops, puts the pan on the counter top.

How long will you stay on the Anesthine, do you think?

He knows she wants him to come off. How would that feel? Again, the blank. This time he registers its presence. Must be fear, he thinks. Fear, washed into forgetfulness. This drug is like a creature evolved for its own survival.

Are you cold? he asks.

What?

You're still in your coat.

Just got in, she says. *A referral meeting overran. Thought I'd better get dinner on the go.*

Something is different about her hair. She has put it up, like she used to do, in the old days, but the wind has been at it. Ruffled it.

Well? she says.

He hasn't looked at her legs for a very long time, but there they are, sticking out of the bottom of her coat. There is dirt on her tights.

I don't know, says Logan. *I'll have to see. Did you fall over or something?*

She looks where he is looking. Brushes her knees, *Yes. Tripped in the car park. Stupid really.*

She changes before they eat. She has brushed her teeth too: he catches a whiff of the arctic coldness of mint. He watches her eyelashes fluttering at the food, at the salt cellar, at the tablecloth; landing repeatedly on her environment but never on him. Now that she has mentioned it, he is having trouble with the Anesthine. He looks at her; something registers in him, and whatever he was about to think is washed away. He is constantly blanked by her presence. Whatever document his brain is trying to write, Anesthine is holding down the backspace key.

After dinner, he excuses himself from a romantic comedy she wants to stream, and takes himself to his study. Tucked behind his small run of Jung, the journal he has kept, from time to time, ever since his training. Some problems need talking out, and those that cannot be spoken aloud will sometimes submit to a page. He begins.

> *The drug is doing its work. But what is underneath? I cannot approach it.*
> *Jules—*

The sentence won't finish. The words won't come.

After an hour he rejoins his wife for the end of the movie. He cannot tell if he might have enjoyed it, even against his critical judgement, because he feels nothing. The film ends and she drifts upstairs. He drifts after her.

I think I may cut down the dose, he says to her back, as she is cleaning her teeth again. *Of the Anesthine.*

His wife is intensely focused on the enamel gleam of the sink. She makes an *okay* noise through a mouthful of foam.

Jules lies in the dark and imagines the sleeping body beside her is Donal's. She turns Logan's desert chest into Donal's unruly forest; Logan's too-sad-to-eat waist into Donal's pulpy white belly. Yes, she knows something of his body.

She cannot blame herself. She blames the time of year. It is still dark in the early evenings, and a few hours ago, tempted by the dusky light, she fell to her knees in the pub car park. She blames the blue van. Enough to be kissing him goodbye, but behind the blue van obscured from anyone's view, she was possessed by an urge to astonish him. In her action, these thoughts: she had planted desire in him and he was going home to his wife, a wife who might prove a willing receptacle for her husband's desire, a desire that might rekindle something between them. Better to strip him of it, right there, than give it away. And how else might Jules haunt the locum through the handful of days that connect this goodbye to the next arranged hello? So she dropped to her knees.

What was most delicious? His gasp as she dropped. What delight to harvest that gasp, the collision of surprise and certainty.

She is deliberate at his belt, at his button, undoing him. Undoing him, she knows, in every way, for kissing one can excuse, but this, this— Yes, he will be haunted. Anticipation scrunches his fingers into her hair. Inevitable now. Barring the sudden reappearance of the blue van's driver, she will push him gently over the cliff of his desire. And there is the added thrill; any moment, discovery. So unsafe, to do it like this, in the open air. Now, the unholy act. Yet it can't be a sin if she doesn't believe. And she doesn't. God hasn't been there for her. Unless. Unless you count this, this answer to her prayers. First touch of tongue on tip.

Jesus, woman, he says, and she thrills to hear that again in her head, its intimate brogue: *Jesus, woman*. She can still feel his hands in her hair. So responsive when Finlay is so—

Behind the blue van, Finlay didn't enter her mind. Briefly, the thought came: *I'm married*. But only as a fact, something currently true. A simple thought, limping in with its baggage of wrongness, giving this act the frisson of an atheist's sin rather than the dragging weight of betrayal. For hadn't her husband betrayed her by running away in his mind and heart, and now so completely behind the bulletproof glass of this drug that he doesn't even know he is gone? If Flora's death had a message, was it not that, out of a clear blue sky, any of us could die at any moment? *Live!* was the call that Jules was now hearing above the quiet organization of cruet set and place mat. *Live, live!* From the flowers she jollied into pointless displays on the coffee table and the sideboard. You have asked for passion, and passion has come for you. Not in the shape of your husband, no, but *live!*

So she lies beside her husband in bed, and puts herself back in the car park. Donal's breath quickening. How powerful she is, every tiny movement of her tongue controlling the flow of his breathing. Powerful too, to be playful with him, when he is so suddenly serious. And the danger, the exquisite danger. Any moment, someone could come.

Without

The painkillers Mrs Akbar prescribed are no longer working. Either the pain has grown to such intensity that it overpowers them, or there is a conflict with the Anesthine. Whatever the reason, Logan can no longer live with his buried teeth. Several times a day, he is jarred by such a fierce bolt of electricity that he cries out, spilling his coffee, startling the dog. The throbbing in his jaw colours his work with distraction and his dreams with the black cartoons of nightmare: stairs dissolve into lift shafts; familiar faces morph into hideous corpses. There is no question: the wisdoms must be surgically removed.

You must read the forms properly before you sign them, says the girl on reception.

Logan skips over the legalese until his eye snags on Risks and Contraindications. But the phrases 'permanent nerve damage' and 'mild to severe impairment of jaw function' trigger the Anesthine; his brain is washed into blankness. The receptionist clicks her tongue on the roof of her mouth in an impatient percussion. After four attempts to read the paragraph, Logan is shocked by another jolt from the nerve in his jawbone, and recognizes that the forgetfulness it provokes is irrelevant. Torture must work this way, he thinks, as he surrenders and signs.

The wisdoms are extracted. A needle full of anaesthetic; the stinging jab and the numbness he finds hard to trust. Wait, he thinks, wait. Has it taken? But the woman is sure of herself. She takes up her tools and digs deep into his gums. A terrible tugging and cracking – he can feel everything but the pain – and a running tide of blankness as wave after wave of Anesthine knocks the spikes of fear down flat.

Afterwards, though his face is numb and his tongue lies in his mouth like a paralysed caterpillar, he can nevertheless move his jaw; rinse and spit, mumble the vowel-sounds of *thank you* to Mrs Akbar. Nothing bad has happened, and when the deep wounds in his gum have healed, and the stitches have melted, he will be free of pain.

He takes more than the recommended dose of Ibuprofen and retreats to his study, reading the file on a new referral and lightly sipping a whisky he tells himself is medicinal. Outside, the weather is turning nasty. Though it is barely four, the sky has darkened sufficiently for him to need his desk lamp, and rain is clattering against the window like random bursts of gunfire. The phone rings and he ignores it. His lips and tongue are only partially revived and he is afraid he will sound disabled, or drunk. But the ringing doesn't stop.

Mmm? he says. He doesn't want to say *hello*. He is hoping the other person will speak and he will be able to say very little.

Hello? says a woman's voice.

Shit! he thinks, and goes to put the phone down, but the drug kicks in. Unsure whether the emotion-fuelled action was the right one, he lifts the receiver, tentatively, back to his ear.

Logan, is that you?

Without question, it's Gabrielle Salmon.

Yesh, he says.

The line is quiet for a moment. Perhaps she is trying to work out if it really is him.

Been on the whisky? she asks.

The still half-asleep tongue, like a teenager on a weekend, raises itself with difficulty. It touches the roof of his mouth softly.

Gno, it says.

What's wrong with you?

How to tell her about the dental work in the least words, with the fewest consonants? But it turns out that she doesn't mean his speech. She continues, with barely a pause, *I've had my grant cut. I've had police turn up at the centre, confiscate my computer, all my research data… what the fuck is going on? What have you done?*

Numb, numb. The swear word tells him she's angry, but her tirade has washed him into a place of absolute peace, absolute wordlessness.

Logan! I'm talking to you! Whatever you've done, undo it. Seriously. I've been charged under the Prevention of Terrorism Act. This is insane.

He listens to her. He doesn't mind listening to her. Indeed, the angrier she gets, the more peaceful he feels. Something very beautiful is happening. Whatever she is saying – and the words are as meaningful as bright washes of colour – it is taking him to an extraordinary place in his head. It feels as if the external world has dissolved and everything that is him, the conscious thinking centre of him, is floating deep inside his own mind, bathed in a warm white light. The more she speaks, the more beautiful the sensation. Now she is shouting, and even though he must hold the receiver slightly away from his ear, because of the jarring sensation on his eardrum, she invokes in him such a powerful sense of peace, such a beautiful nothing, that he hopes she might go on swearing at him forever, for he has never, even after sex, felt so deliciously satiated…

And then she is gone, the line buzzing. The intensity subsides. It is followed by a pulsing afterglow which he imagines might be guilt, or some other muffled emotion, failing to assert itself.

He replaces the receiver and tips back in his chair, overcome by the experience. He is still not quite in his own body, and observes himself breathing. There is something about phone conversations with Gabrielle Salmon that are always – always! – like sex. Now he supposes there will be no more of them. Yet he wonders if he might find a way to experience that sensation again. It is hard to provoke Jules. The things that would make another woman angry tend to make her quiet. But there is a whole world of people out there who might shout at him, given the opportunity. People right on the edge of themselves, ready to explode at an aggravating stranger. *But you told her you'd wean yourself off, cut down the dose.*

Yes, if you lie to her, and she finds out, maybe she'll be angry.

For some reason he can't understand, he is getting an erection.

Julesh! he calls. It was so spontaneous, he is shocked at the sound of her name on the air. But her footsteps are coming up the stairs. She pushes the door open.

What is it? she asks. *Are you all right?*

Now, of course, he doesn't know how to broach it.

I've been finking, he says, dumbed by the deadness of his tongue. *I dough gno if I can come off fer Anersheen.*

He notices how different she looks, standing there in the doorway. She doesn't look like his wife. She is lit from within.

Ish that a gnew top? he asks.

No, she says, and something in her reply washes him blank again. He wishes he knew what it was. *You're going to stay on it, then?* she asks.

He struggles to recapture the thread of his thought.

The Anesthine, she says. *You're going to stay on it?*

Yesh, he says. *Maybe.*

Okay, she says. *Your choice, I guess.*

Not angry, not anything he can understand, she pulls the door shut behind her and leaves him to himself. And that is when he knows something important is happening that he cannot access from this side of his medication. No matter how difficult, he will have to come off. And in any case, his appearance at April Smith's trial is looming. With the media hungry for every detail of her mental state, he cannot risk going blank in the witness box. It is time to face whatever is underneath.

Off

The doctor is off with stress. Either a euphemism, Logan thinks, or he's wary of his own prescriptions; some cooks lose their appetites. The locum, Logan detects, is somewhat nervous, perhaps because he knows his patient, too, goes by the professional title of Dr. They discuss the local cricket team before settling on a schedule for reducing the dose. Stopping cold is not an option.

Over the following week, Logan cuts down by degrees, splintering his pills into quartered crumbs, removing only a fraction of the dose at a time. The more he cuts down, the more his blankness grows. The doctor had warned him: Anesthine patients taking the drug for anxiety called it fear of the fear. As the masked emotion rises, fear of that emotion also rises and the Anesthine still in the system is constantly tripped. In Logan's case, it's not fear of the fear, but fear of the grief. The result is alarming: for whole sections of the day, he simply can't function. He returns to the doctor, who signs him off sick for a fortnight and suggests he go away for a while. Staying at home, he says, you're more likely to be surrounded by things that could trigger emotion.

Like the wife, Logan jokes, and the doctor smiles.

Very good, he says. *Exactly. Like the wife.*

But Logan doesn't go away. The thought of going away makes him blanker than anything. It's as if a part of him believes that leaving his house is the most dangerous thing he could do. He is loath even to walk Achilles, and takes her out for the most perfunctory of marches through the growing inches of mud. Because it is raining; *the wettest March for a decade*, says Jules. As he waits for his own tears to surface, the sky is obliging with its own, as if demonstrating How To: *Just let it fall, Logan.* Water courses over the tiles outside his study window. The drops play musical notes on the jam jars Jules hung in the trees to catch wasps in the summer. And now the emotions are surfacing. He stands at the window, hoping for distraction. But observing the driveway, all he can think is how empty it is. Why does no one ever visit them? He was never very comfortable with people, but what few friendships he enjoyed were dissolved by bereavement. The wives sent cards but the men didn't know what to say. Invitations were floated, but Logan was too out of shape for squash, had no appetite for beers and blokiness. Nor could he stomach suppers skating over what mattered, heading off platitudes, listening to someone or other's opinion of a film that couldn't interest him less when his own drama had destroyed all normality. Then they moved. Now he is important to no one but Jules. Perhaps not even important to her, any more. The first sting of sadness. He retreats to the sofa, crunches his knees up under a blanket. He writes in his journal

Coming off Anesthine is like peeling off layers of skin

but the words don't transmit the pain to the page, and the pain doesn't lessen. Now he understands why April wrote poetry, reached for expression, putting something outside of herself that she couldn't contain any longer. Perhaps if she'd been a better poet, she wouldn't have needed to explode people. But it is too late. Logan has never practised writing consistently, and now the words come tumbling out and he knows they are the only words that matter, the only words worth writing, and he must write them out, over and over, tears wetting the page as he howls.

Flora is dead and I miss her so much.
Flora is dead and I miss her so much.
Flora is dead and I miss her so much.

Frozen

Jules has never heard her husband cry. On that Saturday when the police arrived – is there anything more ominous than opening the door to that strong/sympathetic pairing, policeman and policewoman? – he had made no sound at all. Listening to those dreadful yet ordinary words, the sorry that made nothing better, the lies undoubtedly invented for his ears ('died instantly and would have felt no pain' – how could anyone know?), he had sat very still and silent. It was she who was the source of the terrible noise that began to fill the room, a noise she didn't at first even recognize as her own. It was she who had sobbed and caused the policewoman's arm to snake around her shoulders in consolation. Finlay had remained silent, though in response to her noise he had begun to shake like a naked man in the snow. Since then, a handful of times, she had seen him tear up and leave the room, but she had never heard him cry. If he cried elsewhere, he was silent, as his childhood had taught him to be. Because what father wants to hear a son wailing the loss of the woman he himself drove out of the house, the woman he also wants to wail for?

So when the noise first rises out of an upstairs room, Jules freezes. It is a terrible animal noise, inconsolable and bottom- less, the kind of noise that might crack a wall, fell birds from the sky. It is a dark drowning noise, an anguished and muscular noise, a toddler's despair expressed with a grown man's lungs.

Her first instinct is to leave the house. If she goes out she can pretend she hasn't heard it; there is no obligation to go to him. But even as she collects her coat from the hall closet like a thief, and holds down the handle of the back door to close it without the latch clicking, she realizes she cannot start the car, or even open the garage door to retrieve her bicycle, without him hearing. Hoping the noise in his head will at least drown out her feet on the gravel tramping away from him, she lets Achilles lead her into the forest. When she returns, the house is silent. She tiptoes upstairs in her walking socks and cocks her head to one side, the better to strain for some auditory proof of his existence. There: a sudden collection of ragged in-breaths, the aftermath familiar from her own memories of childhood sobbing bouts.

With her fingertips, she pushes the door open, letting it venture into the space ahead of her, while she keeps her feet planted on the landing carpet. She can just see the top of his head, a muss of hair on the arm of the sofa.

Finlay? she enquires.

He doesn't respond. Taking a deep breath, she circles round the sofa and hovers awkwardly a few feet from him. Better that, she thinks, than stand over him like a parent, or a priest. His face is hidden under the crook of his arm.

You okay?

A sharp expulsion of air through his nose, almost like a laugh, but no words.

I'm really sorry, she says. She is frightened he will be angry with her. Will say something hurtful. It feels like a huge risk even to be in his presence. She is doing this because somehow, despite everything that has gone wrong between them, and despite the fact that she has – three times now – had oral sex with Donal, she does care about her husband. She is still a good wife, she tells herself, and it is not just place settings and bedspread-folding.

Please go away, Jules, her husband says, his voice muffled.

A tightness rises in her throat. Whatever she cannot say, its containment is painful, though in truth she doesn't have words for it, and might have to speak many barely coherent sentences before finding out what it is. But he has said *go away*, which also means *don't speak*, and now she will never find out what words were compressed to form the lump in her throat.

His wife has not gone away. He can sense her still in front of him. Still under the shield of his arm, he opens one eye and can see her knees. Ordinary knees in black slacks. His head is getting hot. He would like to emerge from under his arm. But he doesn't want her to see him like this: red-eyed, vulnerable. That is not how they have been together. It could change – everything.

I don't mean to be rude, he says, still under his arm. *I just need to be alone for a bit.*

For a bit? The voice comes back quiet and tremulous.

Maybe a few days. Until the drug is out of my system. 'The drug' she will understand. But the drug is already out of his system. What he needs to get out of his system is grief. And how to get it out of him when it feels endless? Like the dark opposite of the little Dutch boy in the story from his childhood, he has pulled his finger out of the crack in the dyke and now a relentless flow of grief is running through him. This respite is only exhaustion. He knows when he has slept and woken, he will weep again.

He feels Jules shuffling in front of him. She is searching for something more to say. But at last the hum of her anxiety moves away, and after a defeated click he knows she is on the other side of the door.

Over the next days, Logan lives and sleeps in his study. Discreet knocks at the door signal the leaving of sandwiches, cups of tea, glasses of water; tokens of filial love, he thinks, for the prisoner in solitary confinement. He fills the rest of his journal with the same three words. *Flora is dead. Flora is dead.* He must write them until they have no impact. He must write them until they are as meaningless as a brand name. He must strip them of their power.

May 2nd is looming, and May 2nd, he has been formally notified, is the day he must turn up at the Old Bailey, push through a press of cameras and boom microphones, take the stand fully in control of his mind and emotions, and swear a Bibleless affirmation before expressing his expert opinion that April is mad. He must say it sane. But grief is in his way, and the more he hacks through its thorns, the more he comes to understand it is he who is planting the brambles, making the rescue of himself an impossible task. Only part of him wants to stop grieving: the practical part that is tired of being in pain and incapacitated. Another more powerful part wants to grieve for her forever.

Because to stop grieving for Flora, he must finally let go of her, and that feels like betrayal. Shouldn't the loss of a beloved child destroy a loving father forever? A love easily surrendered is a love less than total. To lose himself in grief for his daughter has been his shout to the world: *This mattered! Flora mattered!* His refusal to get on with his life like she never existed has been his badge of fealty. Out there in the world, hardly anyone knew her. The world is wide, and preoccupied, and she was only a name on a funeral notice. Having moved away from where she grew up, he meets no one who knew her. But even for the months he remained in their neighbourhood, those who did know her avoided her name like a curse. When she was all he could think about, all he desired to talk about, they would rattle on about weather, and celebrities, and the news. Here, in the forest, not a soul seems to know she existed. *Move on*, says the world. *She's gone.*

His grief is a tribute to Flora; the only tribute he can make; his life laid down like a wreath. The last time he spoke to Rachel, she said she had *come to terms* with the loss of their daughter. Tom has forgotten his sister in a mist of Anesthine and Mei Mei. Even at her wake, he saw some of Flora's friends *laughing*.

He feels like he is the last person on earth holding on to her; that if he lets go she will be lost for all time. It is as though she slipped under the ice and drowned, and he is holding on to the tips of her frozen blue fingers, unable to let go, even though he knows she is dead, because if he lets go, her frozen body will drift down to the bottom of the lake and she will be truly and utterly gone.

Floored

She has lain down for the locum on the forest floor. In a den of twigs and ferns left by weekend survivalists, with Achilles guarding the entrance, she has pulled the substitute doctor inside her. For weeks she has imagined how it might feel; the different flesh of this different man. Imagination has cooked her into such a state of desire that now she cannot have enough of him, and as she feels him getting close to the brink of release she says *no, no*, holds him still, goes dead beneath him, so it will not be over just yet.

But reality is bothering her. She imagined his stubble sand-papering her cheek and that full-up feeling of a man inside you. But she didn't imagine the damp leaves sticking coldly to her thighs or Achilles panting very loudly close by, as though she is drawing their breathlessness with a cartoonish marker.

She has helped the locum tug down her underwear and pulled him into her. Now it is done. She has completed the circle of unfaithfulness. Should Finlay ever ask her, she will not be able to lie. And if he asks why, she will seek these words. *He is bright when you are gloomy. He is attentive when you are neglectful.* But the true answer will be *I am empty and will never feel full.* Empty of what? *Of love, of love, of love.*

Slowly, then, she says, loosening her arms, allowing movement again. She knows the urge is possession. The excitement, the ancient and animal one of claiming another male's mate. His thrusts are about obliteration. He is obliterating her husband. She is almost not there. But then, as if he had sensed her thoughts, he remembers her, and is furiously kissing her mouth, like he must resuscitate her, bring her back to him. As though he understood her mind had drifted off from its mooring, and instead of being moved by her lover's thrusts, had sensed their annihilation of her husband. Tugged back inside herself by his kisses, she finds what is waiting for her is not desire, but sadness. She is full, she is empty. She is full, she is empty. She is full, she is empty. And she has failed.

The wife of Tam Lin has dropped the bewitched husband. Not when he was a snake or a white-hot poker, but when he was nothing but a pail of water. That's when she couldn't recognize him as her husband.

Full, empty, full, empty.

Say she'd married this locum instead. Would she not have ordered things in their house with equal perfection? Would they not, she and Donal, just with their daily rubbing against each other, have scuffed each other's flaws to the surface? Would not one of them, now, be here in this forest, lying down with a lover? How could she think she'd be happier with Donal, when she can't be happier with herself? Empty, full, empty, full.

She is crying now, and he notices.

Oh Jules, he says, kissing her tears, *what's wrong?*

I'm so lonely, she says, weeping properly now that she's heard her own words.

Her tears excite him.

I'm here, he says, rhythmically, *I'm here*.

And for one shuddering moment, he is.

Deer

Finally, the words grow blunt. His daughter's name is no longer a blade. The severed artery of his life is stitched back together. His tongue staggers but does not trip over the past tense. For hour upon hour, he endured emotion thundering through him like an endless goods train. Now it is clanging its ghost down the distant track. Inside him, at last, it feels still and silent. Not like peace, but like a warehouse that has been emptied.

He responds to a muffled sound on the landing. A tray outside his door; Jules sock-footing away from it down the stairs.

Jules, he says, and she looks up, bright as a deer. *It's kind of you. Shall we eat together?*

She is awkward with him. Over-talkative. Apologetic. Her conversation is like a person painting an unstable plaster wall, over and over, though flaws keep appearing. There is a small purple smudge just beneath her right ear, like the burn of a rope.

No.

Like the suck of a man.

Where've you been today? he asks.

All over, she says. *Fordingbridge. Ringwood. New Milton.*

Family visits? he says.

That kind of thing.

Car behaving itself?

No problems, she says, and her hand slides up to rest on her neck, over that bruise. *It's a little bit funny when you accelerate, though. Sort of juddery. Maybe I should take it back in.*

Is that it? Something to do with the car? He struggles to imagine Jules with a mechanic. She isn't the sort to tolerate oily hands.

I'll give Ray a ring tomorrow, he says.

Okay.

Meek as a lamb. So not the mechanic.

Something has happened, though. While he has been under the Anesthine, his wife has slipped from his side. She has been unfaithful. This was the sentence his mind couldn't write. This was the hurt he couldn't access, and now it is rising in his throat like acid. He thinks of her tights that evening, dirty at the knees.

I'm going to get an early night.

Puts his plate in the dishwasher, kisses her on the forehead, starts up the stairs.

My birthday is coming, she calls after him. *You haven't forgotten, have you? I thought we might go to Carluccio's on that Friday.*

Friday, he confirms, and goes upstairs to puke.

Brushing the bile and acid from his teeth, he stares into his own eyes in the mirror. They are the eyes of an explorer who has been on a long trek into the jungle and come back to find his wife in the arms of a stranger. Can he blame her? He has been pushing her away for almost two years. He spits. Frankly, Logan, it's a miracle she hasn't left you.

He climbs into the cold bed and sits upright, bolstered by pillows. Her nervousness at dinner tells him all is not lost. It suggests the guilt of a transgressor. Perhaps she is already having second thoughts. Maybe there is still time to entice her back. If so, best to do it without letting on that he knows: that way lies argument, recrimination, the risk of their splintering. The images coming into his mind are bad enough. If he has to hear her admit it, he is liable to get angry, and he has no wish to give her an excuse to leave. Plus, if he doesn't appear to know, she won't ask him to forgive her. The birthday is his chance to court her anew. Did she not remind him for that very purpose? His challenge is to win her from her lover, just as he first had to win her from Cunty. The thought stirs him to an ancient but familiar excitement. He is back.

Perfume

There are so few department stores left, they are almost museums. Once every small town had its own: a Victorian family business set up to sell every available thing, in the days when every available thing was a smaller ambition. In his boyhood, there was Benzie & Miller, Benzies to locals, whose maze of departments – dispensing everything from dining tables to corsetry, from kittens to haircuts – were, even then, closing one by one. The few London survivors are visitor attractions, for there is now nothing like them, and they will surely survive only on the footfalls of Chinese tourists, who buy from the display racks products manufactured in their homeland. He is here, in Chase and Munroe's, because he doesn't know what he is looking for, and hopes an idea might arise from the juxtaposition of meat hook and mannequin.

He is handling the headscarves, not because Jules would ever wear a headscarf, but because they remind him of his mother. He is wondering, if she were alive and he knew where she was, which one he would buy her. Then he is looking at fountain pens. How do these places survive? Who buys fountain pens? Who even writes any more? Flora was punished once, he remembers, for submitting a piece of school homework handwritten. She had made a toy theatre, decorated it beautifully, and accompanied it with boiled-down scripts, carefully inked in a cursive hand. He had thought it all utterly charming. Indeed, had imagined it would garner extra points for handcrafted beauty. But schools had moved on. She was told it was wrong, was marked down for not word-processing and printing out the scripts. Came home crying, the first casualty of his Ludditery. His insistence she learn the principles first, word before Word, pen before PenTaGram, cost her a grade.

He is just about to wander into the dining-ware section when something brings him to a standstill. Devotion. Flora's scent. Memory is triggered so strongly that his first instinct is to whirl round, genuinely expectant that he will find her grinning behind him, perhaps wielding a fountain pen in gentle mockery. But there is no one behind him. Truly no one; not one human neck that might sport such a scent.

Logan's first fear is that he is, again, going mad. One thought of Flora and he smelt her. Is she about to appear? The Anesthine is out of his system. Are the hallucinations back? He plumbs his surroundings for symptoms of reality melting, but everything is still and sharp-edged, contained in its cabinets and boxes. There must be a rational explanation. His heart is thumping. The smell is already fading. Where is it coming from?

The answer lies just around the corner and three steps down: a perfume department. Two girls, just released from the local High School, are spraying testers on each other's wrists. Two retail assistants in white blouses and neck-scarves are staring at them disapprovingly. These are not the kind of girls, they have judged, that can afford to buy Devotion. If Devotion it is. The bottle they currently have in their hands is Jules's favourite, Eau de Tristesse. But presumably they are working their way along the counter; one scent on the left wrist, one scent on the right, two more under left and right ears as they smell each other and giggle.

There is always a rational explanation. He stands for a moment at the top of the three steps leading into the perfume department, holding on to the handrail, letting the feelings run through him. Relief. Disappointment. But how could he think otherwise? Dead is dead. At least the girls have given him an idea.

He exits Chase and Munroe's with a gift-wrapped bottle of Eau de Tristesse and a plan of romantic execution. It is old hat, of course, for a partner in a threatened relationship to take the other away on a long weekend in the hope of injecting a fillip of romance into the boredom. In general, the about-to-be-left spouse proves as deludedly optimistic as a doctor injecting a corpse with antibiotics. But this is because they are flinging the *idea* of romance in their once-lover's face: their destinations are Paris or Venice, Amsterdam or Prague. Such cities may forge new lovers and impel them to tangle themselves in rented sheets, but no on-the-edge couple can withstand the onslaught of beautiful architecture, overpriced beer, and the young people snogging on bridges. Logan's plan is more subtle; it's personal. For who but he knows his wife's attachment to a seaside house in Sussex, just outside Worthing, where she lived with her brother when they were students? This morning he googled the place, now a holiday let. The perfume will be appreciated, but its predictability will disarm her for the real gift, to which he will drive her, under a blindfold, the weekend after his court appearance. She will open her eyes. She will be surprised. But it's the key to Warbler's End that will make her cry.

Mad

The train into London feels interminable. It snakes slowly through the suburbs, as if to fill Logan with the deepest sense of pointlessness it can muster. The miserable houses whose gardens back onto the railway track are all in need of maintenance; soffits and barge boards green with neglect, tiles missing, an ancient conservatory coming to its knees to pray for its own demolition. He wonders what kind of people allow their homes to degrade so. Whether the general degradation is a symptom of insufficient funds or is simply not noticed, the residents so transfixed by their televisions that they are oblivious to the quiet collapse of their homes.

The succession of back gardens is mesmerizing. Most of these gardens, he notes, are given over wholly to children: littered with the bright-but-fading plastic of ride-on fire engines, cars, scooters, and the ubiquitous blue circles of trampolines. Unbelievable, thinks Logan, how people fill their whole garden up with these monstrosities. This garden they are passing now is so tiny you can barely get a good lungful of air out of it, yet even that has a six-foot trampoline whose safety netting touches the fences on either side. A few gardens on, there's an above-ground pool. What profound optimist imagined they would get more than a week's use of it? Like the trampolines, its chief colour is an unhealthy bright blue mouldered over with green. There are perhaps eight inches of brackish water in the bottom, sludged with a dark porridge of leaves. All this, he imagines, must be the result of parental competition. *Look how much I love my children*. And the children, no doubt, spend all of their time indoors, on screens.

Fewer than one in ten of these gardens show signs of being tended. Most are cluttered and unkempt. Sheds silver and rot. Unmown lawns are lumpy with tussocks. One or two have clumps of lonely, accidental-looking daffodils. All are edged with nettles and other out-of-control vegetation spilling over from the wild banks of the railway track. Nature outpaces owners who are too busy working to meet rents and mortgage payments to make time for mowing, weeding or, God forbid, relaxing.

This is what life has become, for most, he thinks. Mindlessly making ends meet till they croak. Thank God he is slightly removed from it all. Has the sort of career and reputation that bring him to spend a night in a decent hotel before giving expert testimony in a high-profile case at the Old Bailey. He will duck the cameras on the way in, but is prepared to be interviewed on the steps when he emerges. He has invested in a new suit. His hair has been cut, his sideburns trimmed. The pressure to have religious fundamentalism classified as a form of mental illness is growing daily. Logan is conscious that the words he chooses will be reported, and he has prepared them carefully. Has printed them off and folded them into his inside pocket, from which he now unfolds them to check, yet again, that they sound both clear and authoritative.

When the train finally limps into its terminus in the evening rush hour, Logan realizes something is wrong. Armed police stand in pairs at the barriers, semi-automatic rifles slung across their vis-vested chests. He spots the *Metro* in someone's fist, shouting: *RED ALERT!* Despite his general aversion to news, this could affect his safety. He snatches a paper from the evening pile and finds a place to stand, out of the way of the streams of commuters weaving through each other to and from the various platforms.

There has been a bomb at Victoria. Not inside the station, but planted in a cab in the taxi rank. No one has claimed responsibility, but a fundamentalist Christian group is suspected. Someone painted on the side of the taxi, 'NOT MAD, JUST ANGRY'. Dear God, thinks Logan, are these people idiots? Do they really think they can influence the outcome of April's trial, or public opinion, through sending innocent travellers to what they call Heaven? If anything, they are simply self-destructing.

He would normally take a cab, but something in his stomach says no. Nor does he fancy jamming himself into the underground's hurtling coffins. Instead, Logan taps the Temple Court Hotel into his phone's navigation app and sets off on foot, guided by the dot.

Waterloo Bridge is unpleasantly busy, overflowing with extra pedestrians thanks to the security alert. Londoners are ruder than usual when anxious, he notes, as he catches an elbow and is almost pushed into the road. The Thames below them is teeming too, with several police launches buzzing up and down the river. One pulls, slowing, beneath the bridge he is traversing. It doesn't emerge on the other side. Are they checking the undersides of bridges? At any moment, he supposes, he and his fellow travellers could be mashed into body parts. No wonder people needed to invent a deity and an afterlife, when this one falls so short of paradise.

Twenty-five minutes later, he is relieved to see the trumpeting elephant of the Temple Court Hotel. Tomorrow, he will deliver his testimony: April is insane. The girl will be hospitalized rather than imprisoned, and the move to have religious fundamentalism classified as a form of mental illness will be one step closer to becoming law.

It takes the efforts of dozens of people to put a religious nutcase behind bars. It takes only two signatures for a person to be sectioned. Those who, tonight, have triggered the denizens of London into a collective panic attack will, in the future, be stripped of their freedoms in advance. The words to begin this process are folded up in his pocket.

Remembered

On Thursday evening, he is back on the train home while another flattened, high definition version of himself is interviewed briefly on the national news. On Friday afternoon, he blindfolds his wife and drives her sixty miles east to a small crop of coastal villas. At the ten mile mark, she says *This is way past Carluccio's*. She is compliant and chatty. Logan is hopeful. But at a fuel stop, when he is queuing to pay, he glances across the forecourt to see she has lifted her blindfold a fraction to look down at her lap. As he approaches the car he is sure she is texting someone. He opens the door and her body twitches, but there is nothing in her hands.

On we go! she says in her jolliest Girl's Own Adventure voice.

On we go, he says. Dr Psychoparrot.

When they pull up outside Warbler's End he is momentarily afraid he has done the wrong thing. What if she *was* expecting Paris, or Venice, and is fully hoping to lift her blindfold to the sight of Gatwick's North Terminal? But then he reasons she must already know they are not at an airport. There is no jet engine roar in the skies above them. Local take-offs and landings are marked only by the cawing of gulls.

Can I? she asks, her fingers twitching on the sleep mask he has used to unsight her.

Yes, he says.

She pushes it up onto her forehead and gasps.

My God, she says. She stares at the house with her mouth open. *I haven't been here since – since Robert and I were students.*

It's ours for the weekend, he says. *The key is in the bin store.*

What about Achilles? she says, twisting her neck to take in the dog, who is looking longingly at the front gatepost.

Dogs allowed, he says. *I checked.*

He carries their bags from the boot to the bedroom while she wanders from room to room exclaiming, *Oh God, the Artex ceiling!* and *At least the bathroom's updated.* They have a cup of tea in the front room, perching awkwardly on a wine-coloured sofa. It's not as nice as their house. But Logan knew it would be basic. They are not here for the facilities. They are here for the memories. And Jules's are flowing out of her like honey from a broken jar.

He used to strut around that strange unit in the kitchen that looks like a hen coop and do his Foghorn Leghorn impression. You remember Foghorn Leghorn? From the old Warner Brothers cartoons? We loved that when we were kids. She smiles to herself. *And there used to be a battered old table right here, right in front of the window, where we'd have a takeaway curry on a Friday night with whoever was around. Usually a bunch of us. His friends, mostly. What are we going to eat, by the way?*

I don't know. Takeaway curry if you like.

Christ, I wonder if Shafiques is still open? Robert used to say that was as close to authentic Indian as you'll get in Worthing. He still feels like my big brother, you know. It's incredible to think I'm twice as old as he was when he died.

A surge of emotion temporarily halts the flow, but the sheer volume of memories ensures it soon starts up again. Minutes later she is on to *the night my brother came home drunk and climbed up the drainpipe because he thought it would be quieter.* It is years since his wife has been so open with him. Has not been tiptoeing around his stress or his grief, and keeping her thoughts to herself. It is like she has flung the doors of herself wide open, and is showing him everything that matters to her. Not long now, he's sure, until it feels safe to walk right in and reclaim her love for himself.

… that was before his diagnosis, of course…

Two years they lived here, brother and sister. For now she is running through their halcyon days, but the loss that immediately followed is likely to make her in need of a husbandly arm, the comfort of someone who knows her better than she knows herself.

Logan's plans, however, are derailed by a chain of events leading from his discovery that Shafiques is indeed still open, but no longer offers free delivery.

I'll collect it myself, he says, and Jules answers, *I'll warm the plates.* But when he returns – quicker than either of them expected – she has not warmed the plates. She is upstairs, in the bathroom. He can just make out the muffled notes of a one-sided conversation. He slips off his shoes, his fist still clutching the hot, pungent bag. Each stair moves a little under his weight but he is quiet as a cat stalking a sparrow. When he reaches the bathroom door he puts his ear against it.

No, he can hear her say, *come on, it's only a weekend… You can talk… I can't believe you're asking me that… Well, obviously… I know…No, I haven't forgotten… Listen, I have to go, he'll be back soon…*

He didn't want to hear. What possessed him to listen? Now unwanted knowledge is burning inside him and dropping down through him like an uncooled reactor core, melting through layer after layer of control until it hits the liquid heart of him, and all he wants to do is explode. His plan was to tiptoe back down the stairs, step into his shoes, and pretend to arrive again, opening and shutting the door with a bang and *Halloo*. But now he is too full of pain to want to keep it to himself. He stands very still, eyes fixed on the door at exactly the height where hers will be, so that when she opens it, she screeches and jumps back a step.

He can see her calculating what he might have heard; what lies she might try. *Don't bother*, he says.

What? she says.

And so begins a monumental row.

Breakers

Breakfast is a silent affair. They have said terrible things. The dog is sniffing restlessly at the door. The dog needs walking, and the sea is only a mile away. Logan dons his jacket and finds Jules beside him, doing up her boots. Nothing is said. The wind buffets the glass in the front door.

She puts the dog on the lead. Logan locks up. They turn onto Ilex Way. The road is divided by a wide central reservation lined by two rows of holm oaks. They cross halfway and turn onto the path. Jules unclips the lead from Achilles and wraps it around her neck.

This used to be the driveway for Goring Hall, she says. *You can just imagine the horse-drawn carriages, can't you?*

Logan doesn't answer.

The trees stretch for a good half mile. It's a bright morning, and they nod hello to other dog walkers coming in the opposite direction. Achilles scampers ahead, full of new smells, snuffling at the damp leaves. They pass the gates of Goring Hall – now a private hospital – and turn left onto farmland. The fields are already ploughed and planted with some kind of grass crop, perhaps early wheat. Sparse green blades poke through the soil at regular intervals, but have not yet taken; they have a fragility about them. The field runs all the way down to the sea, which is ahead of them now, a strip of blustery grey.

Alongside the field is a deep gully, for drainage or irrigation, he isn't sure. Jules and he traipse down the edge of the field one after the other, as the path won't allow them to walk side by side. As he forges ahead he senses she is falling behind, yet he doesn't want to vary his pace: he needs the briskness to work off his anger at thoughts surfacing out of last night's row. Achilles shuttles between them, darning the hole they have made, backwards and forwards like a needle through the stubby accidental plants seeded into the path. As though the dog is hoping to draw them tighter when in truth they are pulling apart.

When they reach a turn in the field, Achilles starts barking. She's found a stone, a raw heft of flint imbued with some unimaginable appeal. Bark, bark, bark. The noise is an assault, an affront. Logan paces back to the dog and picks up the flint. Unsure of where to throw it – not the field, clearly; he doesn't want to be accused of damaging the crop. So he throws it into the deep gully of the drainage ditch. A challenge, he thinks, for the dog to find it in the reeds.

The sploosh of the stone is followed by a larger splash as the spaniel vanishes over the edge of the field. Logan keeps walking. The dog will catch up, he thinks, just as his wife will. And then Achilles comes trotting past, tail furiously wagging, the whole of her snout entirely black with mud.

Logan can feel his wife's disapproval from twenty feet away. He can hear her criticisms in his head. She doesn't need to say anything. Now the dog will need to be coaxed into the sea.

On the beach Logan and Jules wander some distance from each other. No words are exchanged, but each of them searches for something that might tempt Achilles into the swell. And it is a swell. Achilles is a fair-weather swimmer, not keen on the kind of waves that break over an animal as it enters. The pebble beach might seem like a godsend for a dog that loves flints, but no matter what manner of stone Logan throws, the dog stands planted at the water's edge, only her paws in the brine. Separately, but at least united in their mission, he and Jules start to wander about, looking for something more tempting. Jules finds a spray of seaweed, not unlike the rag-rope toys one buys at pet shops. Achilles is there in an instant: bark, bark. Jules whips some half-enthused dog-love into her voice, *Achilles! Achilles! Look! What's this?* waving it above the dog's head, and flicking it out of reach when she stands on her back legs to snatch at it. Bark, bark. When Jules is sure she has wound the animal's enthusiasm up to a pitch, she swings the seaweed in a wide arc, like a fisherman's net, into the sea. The dog starts to run after it, reaches the waves, and stops, looking at her with puzzlement. *Go on!* she says. *Go get it!* But Achilles doesn't want it more than she wants to stay dry.

Logan finds a stick that isn't really a stick but a dried stalk of something like cow parsley. So light that when he throws it the onshore wind whisks it out of his hand and blows it further up the beach. Then Jules has the big find – a piece of wood from some DIY project, perhaps leftover decking, easily four feet of it. As soon as Logan lifts it into the air, the dog is all wag and bark and jump. Big wood, big wood. As Jules had done before, but without the commentary, Logan wobbles it over the dog's head, pretends to throw it twice, before lobbing it into the waves. Achilles follows without a thought, leaping through the surf like a launching battle craft until she reaches the smoother water beyond the breakers. She snatches it and turns around slowly, her tail an ineffective rudder. Her face is still black all the way to her eyes.

Logan throws the length of wood again and again, and Achilles retrieves it again and again, but her nose is still black.

She doesn't need to submerge her face to get the floating plank, only open her mouth. Somehow the top of her snout remains unwashed; the mud thick and sticky as tar.

It is clear Logan's efforts are pointless. A feeling of great heaviness descends on him. He has lost his daughter and now he is losing his wife. His attempts to correct his errors with Jules are as effective as this useless mission to clean the dog's snout. He may as well forget about trying to do anything, and just let things play out as they will. Hands in pockets, he turns his back on the horizon and starts clambering up the steep banks of pebbles to the grassy sward that runs along the coast road. He can hear Jules crunching after him. The dog follows too and then attempts to pass him, smacking him in the back of the knees with the piece of wood she wants to take home with them. He wrestles it out of her mouth. She barks and wags.

No! he says. *Leave it!*

He puts it on the ground with ceremony, warning the dog with a stern finger. The dog's hope is never crushed. She looks from the wood to his face and back to the wood, wagging her tail, but *No!* he says again, and she gets the message, turning away in the direction he is walking and connecting her nose to the current of the greensward, tail up like an aerial. Perhaps that is why we keep dogs, he thinks. They remain hopeful. They take disappointment well. They are a model for living in the present, and making the best of things, that we can never hope to match.

Jules catches up with him and they walk, side by side.

There's an outdoor tap, back at the house, she says.

He says nothing.

There's a route through the copse here that connects back to the Ilex grove, she says.

He says nothing, but they turn up into the copse, putting the sea behind them.

Look, I'm sorry, she says, *but you were gone. You weren't there for me—*

Don't start this again, he says. *Please.*

They walk a little further. The copse is crossed here and there by the quiet roads that link the housing estate. When she sees one ahead, Jules says in a warning voice, *Wait! Wait*, and the dog waits, her hindquarters trembling fractionally over the leaf mould as she waits for her mistress to check nothing is coming and give the command. *Over!* says Jules, and the dog bounds across with renewed energy.

Logan follows, eyes on the path ahead. The silence between them thickens. He knows she wants to speak. She is sure, as women often are, that things can be resolved by talking, whereas he is sure that talking will only make them worse. Something is bubbling up inside of him: an ancient fury that he's struggling to control. It feels like a monster that is poised to take him over. He can only imagine it comes from childhood, when he was powerless and the world was incomprehensible, and you weren't allowed to feel, but you felt – a murderous rage. Just the wrong words, and she'll prise off the lid.

Finlay, she says, *you have to understand I was lonely.*

I understand! It's all my fault!

There it is. Just the edge of it. Jules halts, stumped by the sudden bitterness, and he puts another small road between them. The dog stops with her. Jules shouts after him, *I'm not saying it's your fault. It's both our faults. But when a person gets lonely—*

He turns to face her across the cracked and weedy concrete.

You're telling me you were lonely yesterday? You were lonely in the five minutes when I went to pay for fuel? The ten minutes it took me to get the takeaway?

It's complicated now, she says. *It's like – he needs me.*

I need you! He has never said such a pathetic thing. He is furious with himself. Furious with her. *But I can't trust you any more. So you go and be with him. And good riddance to both of you.*

I don't want to be with him, it's over!

The dog leaps off the kerb.

Jules cries, *ACHILLES!* and the dog falters, looks back a split-second, and her skull thunks against metal, vanishing under the car whose whispering electric engine had gone undetected, which is braking but carries on going, ger-dunk, ger-dunk.

All the sound is sucked out of the air.

And then Jules is on her knees crying and cradling the dog's floppy head, with its tongue lolling out, and its crazy eyes, and the people from the car are running over saying, *Oh my God, Oh my God*, and all he can do is stand there.

3B.

PHYSICS

Through

There is a moment of paralysis as the decision takes shape. Behind him, the Alterman Centre's bright corridors hum patiently. Here I am, he thinks, at one of those semi-transparent surfaces scientists use to split the wave of a single atom in the box pair experiment. If I were pure light, I would both bounce off and pass through.

Logan puts his hand to the glass door and it admits him. He steps through into an engineered garden. At the core of the Alterman Centre is a beating green heart. He needs time to think. This looks like a good place to think.

Dusk is descending upon it like a kindness. The air in the garden is achingly mild, as though immune to the late year's weather. Nor is there sign of any rain in the air. For a moment Logan wonders if there might be a roof, but the warbling melody of a thrush suggests otherwise. If the space is protected from December's excesses, it is through some fluke or connivance of ventilation.

The garden's trees are sturdy-trunked specimens with generous canopies, as though the glass walls of the Centre were constructed around a pre-existing copse. Yet the space is undoubtedly only an imitation of nature: three silver birch, a substantial lilac and an unclipped laurel are arranged in a pre-meditated fashion. A mannerly path takes Logan to a bench by a soft-fountained water feature, and here he sits to watch the black water burbling, before tipping his head back to see dark clouds boil over the building's edge.

Commotion in the laurel bush, and a sneeze of sparrows tumbles out of it, reconfigures itself, and hops back in. The bickering continues until the bush has emptied and refilled twice more. After that, with only the thrush song to embroider a failing light, the garden holds an intoxicating peace. I could just stay here, thinks Logan, as the darkness envelops him. But he is disturbed.

A door, somewhere behind him, makes the smallest complaint to announce Someone Else in the garden. Logan's first instinct is to get up and return indoors, but his second is to wait, territorially, and claim this space for himself. Let the other person feel uncomfortable. Even though it is Logan who is measuring his breath, gauging whether his presence is detected. Feet along the path, and all paths converge at this bench.

A beautiful evening, says the stranger, gazing up at the square of near-night.

Hmmm, says Logan.

The stranger says nothing more, but sighs. And sighs again, this time shaking his head. As though there is a great deal of thought in him that entails the releasing of steam. As the end of the work day approaches, the movement around the building is enough to light all the corridors, and it is this light bleeding into the garden that allows Logan to see the trail of a tear on the man's face.

Are you okay? he asks.

Yes, says the man. *More than okay. I am... I hardly dare say it.* He nods at the bench. *Do you mind?*

Not at all, says Logan, who thinks he might mind extremely, but nevertheless scoots up to accommodate him.

They sit in silence for a few minutes. The silence itches Logan. He has half a mind to give up and go in, but is reluctant to surrender the peace of the garden to this interloper.

You work here? he asks.

Yes, says the man. *I'm a cell biologist. You?*

Just visiting, says Logan.

The silence sits between them like a third person, a demanding child that one of them must feed.

Something very beautiful just happened, says the cell biologist. *Do you mind if I share it with you?*

Not at all, says Logan, though, again, he thinks it likely he will mind very much. What man wishes to be larded with another's happiness?

I just realized— says the man, but goes no further. Logan is afraid he might be properly crying. Thankfully they are sitting side by side, so he can pretend nothing is happening.

Yes? he says after a polite interval.

People assume the nucleus is the brain of the cell, says his companion.

Logan is enormously relieved to hear they are discussing science. Real science. Petri dish and pipette science.

It isn't? says Logan.

No. It's the equivalent of the gonads. A denucleated cell can still function. It just can't reproduce.

Oh, says Logan. The water, he thinks, looks very thick, like a fountain of treacle.

You know what part of the cell is equivalent to the brain? his companion asks. Logan feels the shift of the man's attention onto him; those Elizabethan eye beams are most certainly directed at his face. *The cell membrane. The membrane is the brain. It receives input from the environment and sends signals to the rest of the cell. It controls gene activation.*

Okay, says Logan. *That's interesting.*

His companion shifts forward, elbows on his knees, so he is looking right into the treacle of the fountain.

Have you ever heard of those transplant cases where someone gets someone else's heart and they start behaving like the donor? A vegetarian hiker becomes a meat-eater and takes up motorbiking?

I guess, says Logan. *They're just stories, right?*

There's less light in the garden now. A few of the corridors around them have fallen into darkness.

I used to think that too, says the man. The silence clings to him until he continues. *There are receptors in the cell membrane called self-receptors. You know what I realized today? What they're receiving. They really are receiving the self. Like receiving a broadcast, the unique consciousness stream of an individual.*

Logan remembers where he is.

You've been speaking to Dr Salmon, he says.

Gabrielle? No. *But you're right, I must. I must!* And the cell biologist is off, catapulted out of his seat by the urgency of the thought, half-running down the path, and only just remembering to call back, *Goodbye, it was lovely talking to you*, as he darts through the door by which Logan had entered.

Logan wonders whether they are all mad. Then again, perhaps he is the mad one. He listens to the darkness: the shush of laurel leaves, a leaked ripple of laughter. If any of this is true, Flora's broadcast is all around him, passing invisibly through him like the radio stations he could pick up if only he had a tuneable receiver. If any of this is true, all that is stopping him from receiving Flora's broadcast is his emotional static. His persistent scepticism.

Yet what could matter more than knowing Flora wasn't obliterated by gravity, but continues to exist? What if she *is* a continuing stream of consciousness with which he might connect? Should he not do whatever it takes to find out?

Gabrielle is having a discussion with the cell biologist. Logan can see them through the small square of fireproof glass in her door; her grinning as she swings to and fro in her chair, him pacing and gesticulating, almost dancing, in front of her. The door softens their words into melody as Logan leans against the wall of the corridor, his heart noticeably beating in his chest.

When at last the door opens and the cell biologist spills out, he catches sight of Logan and beams, *You!* before trailing threads of farewell down the corridor. Gabrielle pokes her head around the corner.

Come on, then, she says. *Let's sort out a date.*

Particular

Logan can't discern what is left of the self he knew as Logan. His mind is an emptied carrier bag: spacious, near-weightless. He moves through the house like his own ghost, haunting his former routines, smiling at himself. The world, as if it knows, stays away. The phone sleeps. The front door chums up to its frame. Like bees behind glass, e-mails bounce soundlessly back to their business. He sits alone, perfectly content. Twice a day, he lets himself out of the back door with the dog close to his heels, who glances up often as if to make sure that her master won't be blown away.

Barely a thought passes through his mind. Or rather, the thoughts are so fleeting, so whispered, that it takes some days to recognize their existence. Everything loud – anguish, grief – is absent. Even the pain of his wisdom tooth, which had throbbed him awake for a week, has fled from Gabrielle's 'jellyfish'; vanished like some specious illusion, some sick note he'd invented to get out of lessons, leaving the jawbone quiet as an after-hours museum.

Seven days after undergoing the process, he is padding along with the dog under a canopy of leafless branches. Coming up over a rise, the low winter sun blinks at him through a stand of hazel. He stops and moves his head, this way and that, so that it flashes at him like smugglers' lanterns in the sea stories of his boyhood. He sucks in the long, long breath of a man who has been drowning and, when he lets the breath go, there are tears.

How miraculous it all is. This earth and everything that grows and grazes upon it. This planet, whose placement in relation to the sun could not be even fractionally closer to, or further away from, its perfectly sized star without life being impossible. The sun itself, feeding every living entity with light alone. The design of his perfectly adapted body, which breathes and digests and repairs itself without his direction or knowing. And more miraculous even than all of these, this sense of being, of being a being, inhabiting this peculiar island of conscious awareness.

And consciously aware of what? Suddenly, everything. A strange open buzz in the centre of his chest like the fist of his heart finally unfurled and plugged into some universal power source. At the sun's periphery, particles, he can see actual particles of energy, streaming down onto the grassy clearing, connecting with the grass. Instantly, all is particular; shaken out of its packets into a vast network of energetic charges. He can sense it all. He too is part of it: a vast and endless arrangement assisting itself, translating one form of energy into another. One giant organism that connects all living and non-living things, exchanging sunlight for heat, movement for sound, so that even the shush of the cars on the road that cuts through the forest half a mile beyond is the whispered transaction of energy into energy; nothing lost, only transformed, and now into his ears, forming thought. For is it not true, as Gabrielle said, that an electron can be part of your own eyeball one second and, in the next, jangle the bell of a child's bicycle in Holland, kiss a coffee cup in Boston, harden a crab claw in Australia? He looks down at Achilles. She too is knitted into the fabric of him, as he is knitted into the fabric of the forest and everything beyond. Somehow, the joy of his understanding has reached her tail and is thumping the leaves, every millipede and woodlouse in her wagging radius drummed into the same knowing.

Bursting with a power he cannot contain, more than the muscles of his legs can bear without striding him forward, he starts to laugh. Oh, laugh madly. He would surely be deemed insane could anyone see him. But he is alone. So he swings his arms like a six-year-old soldier, laughing and crying, and the dog runs around him, barking with joy as they ruffle the nap of the forest. The destination of his body is irrelevant, but his mind is travelling at pace, leaping hurdles of comprehension. It's all true. The essence of every major religion touches this truth. We are one. And what is the flow from thing to thing but love?

The earth, rotating at 1,037 miles per hour, offers the sun's miracle to New Yorkers on their lunch breaks and the New Forest falls into the peace of dusk, and Logan slows. He had no intention of walking home, but he recognizes by a fallen tree that he is only a few hundred yards from his starting point, and feels, for the first time, the cold of his toes in their boots, the pinch of hunger in his stomach. He holds out his hand in the half-light and watches in wonder as the edges of it bleed into the cool air, becoming the scent of wet leaves.

How long might he stay in this magnificent limbo, where nothing is defined or determined, nothing is separate or alone? A few steps later, the answer arrives. Crossing the road, he drops back into his separated self like a stone. For there, in the driveway, is Jules.

Peculiar

Without her, she thought, he'd go mad. She couldn't be responsible. She was surely the stopper in his bottle of insanity, and removing herself would leave him fountaining craziness into the vacuum. So she'd imagined. Now here he was, orbited by the dog, crossing the road on the prow of a smile like a priest bearing down on his congregation.

You got here just now? he asks, taking the handle of the largest suitcase as the taxi drives off. *You could have called.*

I would have picked you up. He hefts her luggage over the gravel and plants it triumphantly at the front door, reaching for his key. *How was Dubai?*

She stares at him as though she has lost all capacity to understand English.

Hot, she says, after a moment.

And Prissy?

She watches him insert his key into the lock as though she is watching a chimpanzee perform surgery.

Priscilla's fine, she says.

Not neurotic? he asks, dragging the cases into the hallway.

Neurotic but fine, she says. *Finlay?* She is watching him very carefully in his busyness; now hanging up his scarf and coat, now returning to help her out of hers.

Hmm? he says behind her, as she shrugs her mackintosh into his arms. Now he is slipping around the side of her, hanging it up beside his and striding into the kitchen.

Are you okay? she calls after him.

Just putting the kettle on, comes the reply.

She follows him into the kitchen. Nothing amiss. No pile-up of empty whisky bottles, no newspaper cuttings pinned to the wall; nothing to indicate a chaotic mental state.

You haven't been online at all? You didn't get my messages?

He is retrieving the special cups – the Paris cups – from their special box.

Ah, no. There were messages? I'm sorry. I didn't think we were talking.

Matter-of-factly. As though that were no more significant than the light being off in the downstairs toilet. It's true, they weren't talking. But there had been something awful in the silence. Something that after three weeks began to feel ominous. In the silence, she had imagined she could hear the creak of the canoe hook in the garage, and as the days passed, a humming: an ovation of flies, their lives hatched out of the cool December air by Death's magnetic pull.

I was worried when I didn't hear from you, she says.

Now he is spooning leaf tea into the teapot. Leaf tea! As though her coming home is a special occasion, not suited to tea bags.

Other things were going on, he says.

So carefully, he pours water into the pot! As though he is a god creating a permanent geographical feature.

Like what? she asks.

Now the whole shebang is coming over to the kitchen table on a tray. The Paris cups. The teapot cosied. Milk decanted into her mother's jug.

It's hard to explain, he says. *Later maybe. When you're settled.*

He sets the tea between them. Staring hard into his face, she finds nothing she can identify. No perimeter wall. Not a splinter of sarcasm.

He says, *I thought you were done with me, to be honest. I'm glad you're not.*

I didn't say that, she answers quickly. Surely, she thinks, that's like whisking the doormat from under his feet, he'll topple, he'll collapse into a Finlay she recognizes.

Ah, he says, and she sees something pass through him, clear as water. Then he nods and smiles. No, worse. He beams. *Ah well, I don't blame you. Have a cup of tea with me anyway.*

They have tea together. Despite his air of enthusiasm he says very little, and she finds herself prodding and poking him, as a child will take a stick to some mammal it finds lying by the side of the road. Any moment, she thinks, her poking will roll him over and she'll see his belly, the bloodied fur writhing with maggots. But instead, unwittingly triggered by some word she utters, he does what roadkill never does: he leaps up and springs away.

Finlay? she calls after him.

Sorry, he says from another floor. *Just had an idea.*

She presumes he has gone to get something to show her; will return any moment. She stares at the dog and the dog stares back. After five minutes, it is clear he's not coming.

She finds his feet on the top rungs of the aluminium loft ladder. The rest of him, invisible to her from the landing, is scuffling around in the boxes that crowd round the hatch.

What's up? she says.

Is it mania? This is more like the behaviour she was expecting. *Where did you put it?* he says. *The Christmas box.*

It was Christmas, then. Christmas was the word that had set him off.

You mean the decorations? she asks.

Yes, the decorations, he says. Now his head appears and he looks at her intently. *The Christmas decorations box.*

Oh, she says.

He doesn't need more than that syllable to tell him further searching will be fruitless. His head disappears back into the hatch. The light goes off. He is not searching now. He is just breathing.

It was all getting a bit tatty, she says. *There didn't seem any point keeping it.*

His body appears to be vibrating. The house is quiet. Downstairs, the refrigerator's motor has just come on, rattling the champagne flutes she stores on top. Finlay comes down the ladder slowly, deliberately.

There were a couple of things in there, he says, reaching for the hooked pole propped by their bedroom door. *Things the kids made when they were little. You remember them?* Pushing up the ladder so it folds back on itself. *That gold-foil angel that Flora made for the tree? Tom's Santa with the cotton-wool beard?*

She remembers the Santa. The angriest Santa she'd ever seen. His face the same colour as his suit, and a huge black hole of a mouth. Ho ho ho.

I didn't, um—

She didn't think. Preparing for the move, she'd opened the box and seen only what was on top: the Sellotaped foil garlands with snapped-off ends, the faded, crumpled paper chains that had served several years instead of a single season.

I didn't—

What? What's her excuse? This is it, now, isn't it? This is the point where he'll flip.

He closes the hatch with the pole and there are tears, real tears, running silent tracks down his cheeks. He places the pole in her left hand so she is standing there like a Nativity shepherd, and takes her other hand in both of his. He is looking at her with great warmth and sorrow.

Never mind, he says. *Never mind. We'll get some new decorations.*

Appreciation

He insists on visitors. *Everybody*, he says, *invite everybody. Anyone you know in the village. And what about old friends? They could stay. Who shall we ask? Pat and Phil? Frank and Sue?* And when she says, *Christmas is just for family, really, isn't it?* he says, *Sure, let's invite Tom*, artfully deaf to the word *just*. And when she starts fussing about numbers, he says, *I'll cook. I'll do the whole thing. How hard can it be?* and begins hunting down recipes. Is he simply shovelling people into the space between them, sandbagging in the face of a flood? She can't tell. She can't ask.

The new decorations come in packing cases. *Job lots*, he explains, *from a closed-down hotel.* A week up stepladders and every room is foil-garlanded back to the 1990s. He has never, she swears, hung so much as a bauble in his life.

Though the days keep them separately busy, at night they sleep side by side. He rests a hand on her thigh or her shoulder.

Friendship, it says, and she doesn't know how to respond. She is ready to reject him, but he makes no demands of her.

Finally the house is ready. The real Christmas tree that Finlay insisted upon is confusing Achilles; Jules must keep shooing her away from sniffing around its base. Finlay says the best defence is presents, and surrounds it with a ring of parcels criss-crossed with real ribbons and bows. Is he auditioning for the part of Santa Claus? On the morning of the twentieth, the morning Frank and Sue are arriving, she notices him looking at her as she poaches their eggs, and there is something so full about it, as though he needs nothing from her but the pleasure of watching her slide those yellow-pupilled eyeballs onto a bed of spinach.

What? she says.

You're a wonderful woman, he says.

Because I make you breakfast? she asks.

He laughs.

Because you make me breakfast. Because you came back from Dubai. Because you were the first woman who didn't make me feel like a heel. Because you draw little flowers on envelopes. Because you know how to operate the DVR. Because you feed the dog pieces of cheddar when you think I'm not looking. Because you tiptoed around my anger for a year and a half. Because you've kept that plastic tag I once pretended was a wedding ring. Because you looked after Tom like he was your own, and gave him stability. Because you never said a word, even when you thought I was having an affair with Dr Salmon.

She has paused over the breakfast plates like a priest about to bless them.

You weren't?

Only in my stupid teen-boy head, he says. *Not in reality.*

She brings the plates over and they sit opposite each other. She is scared to look him in the eye, though she knows he is still gazing at her. Best to grind the pepper moderately. Best to take a mouthful or two, and chew.

You don't have to love me, he says. *I quite understand if that's all over for you. Maybe you even want to leave. Or want me to leave. But whatever happens between us, I want you to know I love you anyway.*

She stares at him then. His pupils are wide and honest. She takes a sip of tea and pushes her eggs away.

Are you on drugs? she asks.

He laughs. *No, no.*

Then what's happened to you? What happened when I was in Dubai?

I don't know how to explain, he says. *Without scaring you.*

What would scare me? she asks, her hand twitching on the handle of the Paris cup, which along with its mate he is setting out onto the table every morning now, as if trying to give her the same present, again and again. But she knows what would scare her. Almost any version of reality where he is unpredictable. Like this one.

There is something – he reaches for the words – *something bigger than us.*

The Government? she offers.

He smiles at her protective attempt at derailment.

Something bigger than that.

God? she jokes, and watches his face slide into relief. *You found GOD?* she says, incredulous.

That's probably the wrong word—

What's the right word?

I don't know, he says. *Maybe there isn't a word. Maybe a word isn't sufficient. Look*, he says, *don't let it worry you. It doesn't have to concern you. It's just… you wanted an explanation. That's the best I can do at the moment.*

She stares at him over the cold eggs.

I was worried it was mania, she says.

Presence

People arrive and the revels begin. For the first day, Finlay ministers to his guests with a spectral attentiveness, mimicking the serving staff in high-class restaurants who refill your glass with such subtle frequency that you begin to believe it is a fairy-tale receptacle, refilling itself. But soon he is softly guiding his old friends to *top yourself up, won't you* and *please feel at home* and shortly Jules discovers them hovering in the kitchen, doing just that. She finds Phil staring into the open fridge like a forlorn teenager, wondering what he might snaffle. She nods and smiles but feels invaded. What does Finlay mean to achieve, visiting their old life upon them with such gusto? What can he expect from her, chopping her into the soup of their long-ago friends, stirring, heating, and adding alcohol? Though he, she notices, is barely drinking. The guests run through a case of Davenport Limney, a bottle of Laphroaig, while Finlay, without comment, makes himself another cup of tea.

He stays up with the menfolk till two and three a.m., nursing a tumbler of straw-coloured ginger cordial in a colour-match that keeps his guests comfortable. The other wives surrender to *beauty sleep*. Jules takes herself off to bed with a book, but lies there propped up on pillows, not reading a word. She listens to the gales of mannish laughter that blow up the stairs, straining to get the joke.

The effect of the alcohol is much like it is in school chemistry experiments: a drawing out of impurities. Or perhaps the alcohol is merely a catalyst, and her husband is the solvent? For where he was once a complexity of words and thoughts, there is now a neat-ethanol purity about him; an emotional clarity that has his guests dissolving into his arms one by one. On the very first day, Pat reveals to the assembled company that she is having tests. Something nameless is tiring her out, lowering her lymphocytes. It is Finlay she tells first, down at the end of the garden, coming in with her head on his chest, his arm round her shoulder.

The next day it's Sue – whose permanently manicured precision suggests she treats social occasions as interviews – who ends up ragged and red-eyed in Finlay's arms, sobbing with the grief of her infertility. An hour with Finlay in a quiet corner and she is at peace. She has also told him – and this he recounts with hilarity – that she is the 'S' who sent him the Post-it note about God in the brain that he got so worked up about. They'd had some conversation that touched on the subject, months and months ago. She was shocked he'd forgotten about it.

The men take longer to crack, but not much. Christmas Eve afternoon, when her friends from the village have joined them for an Open House, Jules comes upon the sound of a man weeping in one of the upstairs bathrooms over a musical murmur unmistakably her husband's. Frank was easy, though. Architects are essentially artists; drawing makes you vulnerable. She is sure he won't get Phil. Surgeons are emotionally immune, are they not? But a few hours later, Phil opts to accompany Logan on the late-night dog walk and returns undeniably altered. They help each other off with their coats, colluders in intimacy.

Jules, however, cannot be drawn out. There is nothing inside her to draw out. For how can you draw out an emptiness? She is all shell. Regrown inside her is the same gap Finlay identified when she was with Simon, the gap he had once filled with his exceptional attentions as an invading army will station battalions in the no man's land of an ungoverned neighbouring country. But now he cannot fill it, because he has caused it; by his nearness to some gentleness that has her feeling like a beast crashing through the undergrowth. Must all her men go this way? Turn into saints?

Overnight, a storm rattles in out of Russia; a bitter wind in the mood for breaking things. By some miracle the roof tiles cling to their battens and the kitchen range stays lit. It's sherry and chocolate for breakfast, and a smattering of presents under the tree to be unwrapped in the one-by-one way he insists upon. He opens from her a boxed set of *The Vigil*; a series he'd said he thought was *okay* three years ago. *Thoughtful*, he says, with no trace of sarcasm to suggest he knows she ordered it online in a last-minute panic, paying extra for delivery. He suggests she open hers in private but she doesn't take him seriously. It's flat and wide, clearly a picture. Probably something awful and eco from the village gallery. So despite his warning she opens it in front of the cheery roomful. It is a digital montage of photos of her dead brother. Her brother waving at her through the long years since his ashes were scattered on the top of Truleigh Hill. Her brother as a boy. Her brother with his arm around her at a family gathering. Some of these photos she has never seen before. Bastard, she thinks. Tears.

How did you do this? she asks.

It took a while to put together, he says. *I found a company online that prints onto canvas.*

She doesn't mean the practicalities. She means the looking straight into her heart to find what would touch her. Too much, as it happens. She has to leave the room. It means more to her than anything he has ever given her.

She has put herself back together by the time the roast is served; mascara reapplied, the blurred smudges of her cried-away first coat removed with a lotion that has trespassed into her eyes and is making them sting. In her absence, Finlay has roped in Frank and Phil as his minions; Phil has carved the turkey with professional precision and Frank might well have arranged the carrot batons with the help of a set square. Finlay has applied the care he usually reserves for his reports to the timing of vegetables and trimmings; alarms keep chirping as another perfectly judged item is decanted into warmed china dishes and brought to the table.

The table is chaos; Sue and Pat have done their best, but their best is a mishmash of three-star restaurant and roadside café. The best crockery, to be sure, but the second-best cutlery, and, folded into uneven rectangles, some God-awful napkins from Finlay's aunt that Jules has been meaning to ship to the charity shop. She sits at her usual place and feels her stomach tightening. But then Finlay gives her a shoulder squeeze as he passes with a bowl of sprouts and she decides on the instant that she doesn't care. She tops up the gin in her tonic, swigs, waggles a Christmas cracker at Sue like some half-hearted handshake. Sue wins the prize, of course. Jules is left with the smell of its small explosion and a fistful of paper. She pulls with Frank and, again, he gets the joke, the hat, the useless key-ring compass that only guesses true North, and then changes its mind. Her stomach begins to tighten again, even against the gin, the whine of *nothing works out for me*, but Finlay says, *You'll win this one*, and she does.

A ring falls out of it. The weight of it. No cracker ring, but a circle of white gold, encrusted with small red stones that Frank swears, even from a distance, are rubies.

I might have doctored it, admits Logan. *The cracker.*

She stares at him. Stares at the ring.

It's an eternity ring, he says. *Doesn't mean you have to stay with me for an eternity, though. You can swap it for something else if you like.*

Okay, she says.

Can I see? asks Sue.

Passed across, into the perfectly manicured hands. Then to the wiggling fingers of Pat.

Oh my, says Pat. *Finlay, I had no idea you were such a romantic.*

Yes, you do, says Phil. *You've seen the rose on his buttock.*

You have a rose on your buttock? asks Sue, who wasn't there in the beginning.

Jules feels herself watching this, as though she is watching a play. Is it a farce? The ring comes back to her.

Put it on! says Sue.

But she doesn't put it on. She makes a crêpe paper nest for it and puts it in front of her, so she can look at it. She feels

better for being a little drunk. The guests take turns reading
out cracker jokes.

What do you call Santa's little helpers? Subordinate Clauses.

*What is the best Christmas present in the world? A broken
drum, you just can't beat it.*

Around her, these friends of theirs giggle, clink glasses;
temporary kings and queens in their paper crowns. Finlay is
watching her quietly.

Later, when all six of them have walked Achilles into and out
of the forest, and the obligatory board game has been played,
and she has made her excuse to retire to bed early, Finlay follows her up the stairs. The ring, which he had pocketed without
comment when the table was cleared, he deposits, again without
comment, into her jewellery box. He sits on the edge of the bed,
watching her remove her make-up.

I'm sorry if the present made you sad, he says. *I meant well.*

I know, she says, tears reappearing in her eyes. Perhaps
because of the blurring, she puts a little too much lotion on
the cotton wool ball. *I feel like I don't know you*, she says. *I
don't know who you are.* He is looking at her in the mirror.
She cannot read his face. *And if I trust you, if I go with this
version of you, what's to say you won't hurt me, what's to say
you won't disappear again?*

His eyes are still steadily upon her.

It would be an act of faith, he says. *I understand. But you
don't really have to make it.*

How come? she asks.

*Just take it day by day. Day by day, if you find you are happy
in my presence, stay. And over time, you will learn that I am still
here. Trust won't be necessary. And in any case –* he stands, and
peels off his shirt – *not trusting doesn't protect you from hurt.
If we broke up now, even with you holding yourself apart from
me, it would hurt, would it not?*

She nods.

He puts a hand on her shoulder.

My good wife. You are such a good wife. You have put up with so much and I have hurt you so badly.

She twists on the stool and rests her wet face on his belly. Feels the warmth of his hand on her skull. Replaying his words, *I have hurt you so badly*, provokes another tide of tears to break over the barrier of her lower eyelids and run down towards the waistband of his trousers, their course saying, *Yes, you have, you have.* Finally she, too, submits to his strange chromatography: all her ugly feelings drawn up to the surface by his clarity, separated out into their individual colours: fear, and anger, and guilt.

For now she is too much like a child for their retreat beneath the covers to end in anything other than her clinging, naked, to his nakedness, crying until she feels empty. But in the morning she feels moved to kiss him, and he responds with tenderness.

April

Dr Logan sits with April for an hour. He says nothing. He arrived, he turned the chair at the window to face into the room, he smiled at her, and he closed his eyes. Now he is just sitting there. She can see he is breathing, but he is very still. His palms are open, upturned, on his knees, as though he expects to receive a present. Two months ago he was here getting upset with her, a week after they discussed whether death was the end, and now he is sitting in her room as though she doesn't exist. Maybe he is here to do nothing. Tick a box on a form. She likes the peace. He is emptying the room. Or is he filling it? For a while, she breathes with his breathing. They are breathing together, like lovers. Then something arises in her mind. The pool's blue surface, on a late summer evening. Still, still, not a sound, not a screech of laughter, not a thump of bass. An evening without a party. The only living presence a bat, sweeping the air for midges. Dr Logan takes in a deeper, fuller breath, surprisingly loud in the silence, and lets it out slowly.

Dr Logan, she says. *Have you ever had something happen to you? Something terrible?*

Logan opens his eyes. April looks infantilized in her regulation gown. A child of the madhouse. But her eyes are steady and sane. He re-engages that part of his brain that processes language and lets her question echo in his head. *Did something terrible happen to you?*

My daughter died, he says.

The words fall out of him so easily that they surprise him. How painless it is to say words unattached to resistance. *My daughter died*. Now he knows: for the first time, this is accepted fact. *My daughter died*. He has never said them this way. Painlessly. He watches them land with April, who receives them with the grace of an experienced fielder.

How did it happen? she asks.

He is going to see if he can do it again.

A plane jump, for charity. Her parachute failed.

Again, the words simply appear. They appear and vanish, and he is the same. They are no longer full of knives and treachery. There is no sense of them dragging him bodily into some dreadful abyss.

That's rough, says April. He can see she means it. And that there is something more. He knows that she asked him to make this ladder towards her so that she can cross it to him. She keeps her eyes on him and says, *Something terrible happened to me, too.*

April is amazed at herself. There! It is out. The cage door opened, the bird flown. Dr Logan lets it flap right past him. He doesn't try to lasso it with questions. He doesn't repeat it back to her like he used to; like kids do when they're being cruel to each other. Gratitude washes over her. Now she can reach for the other words, words she has never said and could never say, for fear they would razor her throat as she spoke them. Now, as they rise to her mouth, they are small and smooth as pebbles.

I was gang-raped, she says. *At a party.*

Oh, there are still tears. Tears for the sixteen-year-old girl who loved Jesus. Who believed she was saved, even as she drank the spiked punch. Who had to endure her Lord's name as a bass-line for their bestial act. And as she'd matched her breathing to Dr Logan's, he matches her tears with his own: even now, they are making their way down his cheeks.

I hated those Godless boys, she says.

Logan looks at the blinking red light on the eye of the camera. All of this has been recorded. Is still being recorded.

Because he wondered if this might happen, he has, in his pocket, a sock. His career could be ruined by what he is about to do, but it is the only human response. He crosses the room and places the sock over the camera. The judge and jury will want an explanation. In this dark moment, anything could happen.

What happens is love. Not the reportable physical sort, though the sock leaves that possibility open. He is in April's hands, having removed himself from legal protection. But she has been through the process and he trusts she is washed free of malice. He sits beside her on the bed and puts his arms around her, as he would his own daughter, and holds her as she cries, silently, into his shoulder. She cries for some time. When the knock comes, he removes the sock and opens the door. He explains that *Everything is fine* and even though the nurse frowns, he looks so peaceful, so definite, that she feels unable to override him, and disappears. The interruption has, in any case, roused April out of her crying.

Are you ready to explain what happened? To the camera?

Nodding.

Logan sits down and April explains to him and, through the camera, to the court gathered in her future, how she turned to God because there was no one else. She had always believed in God, from a little girl, because she had to believe there was someone who loved her, and if it wasn't her mother or father, or anyone she could see, then it had to be God. And after the rape, she had no one to tell but God. Who would believe her? There were four of them and one of her. They were respectable boys from wealthy families, long-established in the area; her mother was a single parent, a known drunk. And *she'd* been drunk; blood tests would have proved it. Her raised blood alcohol level would have comprised the only evidence: semen, skin cells, hairs, were slooshed out of her, washed off her, by the dunking in the pool. All this she had added up, the next morning, and known: she could tell no one. Least of all the mother who already figured her some kind of beast.

So she wrote to God. Asked God to help.

Now she admits that maybe what wrote back wasn't God at all. Maybe it was some buried, smouldering part of her, the angry voice so far from her pain and dismay that she didn't recognize it as her own. But it sounded like the God of the Old Testament. She thought she recognized it. An eye-for-an-eye kind of God. The kind of God that would ask a good man to murder his son. The kind of God that smites sinners; wants the faithful to smite sinners. And suddenly almost everyone she knew was a sinner.

At first, she was only smiting them in her diary: killing them with words. But when she went up to uni, when the administrators of the student accommodation department mixed her in with the sharp-brained scoffers of radical atheism, she saw this gift God had given her: science. Why else was she so good at it?

So the plan arrived like a bolt of divine inspiration. A holy mission, even. Yes, at the time, she was sure it was God's plan, and she didn't question it. She was taking instruction from the Lord. She knows now, she was mistaken. In a way, anyway.

Logan hesitates. The next question, the obvious question, sounds like it might lead her somewhere dangerous. But he has to ask it. There is a *what will be, will be* about all of this.

In what way weren't you mistaken?

The Kingdom of God lies within, Dr Logan. Whatever we do,
we are doing God's bidding. And the outcome is always good.

Even when the outcome is death?

Hardly anyone sees the good in death, Dr Logan, I understand
that. But how can we appreciate joy if we don't know sorrow?
And think of the good done in the name of those who die early.
The charities and foundations that people set up. The vows they
make to themselves. And if bereavement takes you to the edge
of something, Dr Logan, maybe that's somewhere you needed
to go, for your own sake, to forge a happier or more purposeful
life. I don't know, Dr Logan, you tell me. Has your daughter's
death changed you for the better?

Meditation

Since he lodged his report on April, his days have more hours
in them. He slips into meditation as a newly built vessel slips
from its launch into the water. Not deliberately: not by plumping
a cushion in a hushed room, lighting a candle, selecting – so
beloved of Rachel at the time of Flora's conception – ambi-
ent music sprinkled with Himalayan bells. But accidentally,
several times a day, he finds he has dissolved into a state of
simply being.

At his desk, he comes to a standstill, his hands rested on the
laptop's keyboard like a pianist waiting for the crowd to hush.
He falls into stillness, a limitless ocean of nothing: no land, no
weather. Sometimes, in the quiet, an idea will arise like some
great leviathan, coming up from the depths, and he knows it
is not a thing he thought into being but rather something that
inhabits those depths, making itself known. The resonant flesh
and slippery skin and unblinking eye of it only turn into words
as it breaks the surface. What unpeels first is language.

He takes his journal from behind the row of Jung and writes:

*Words have genuine power. We curse and bless ourselves
with the words we use. My father, whose mantra was 'I
can't stand'... busybody neighbours, January, chuggers,
tomatoes, the council, clothes with logos, multi-storey
car parks... gave out at the knees. Was in a wheelchair at
fifty-two. Never understood why he was hobbled while
his boss was ten years older and still playing squash.
Now it seems obvious. He cursed himself. Said, 'I can't
stand', until it was true. Committed, on himself, a slow
but powerful magic.*

*Unconsciously, we are casting spells on ourselves.
My father didn't know that he'd done so, because such
spells work slowly. And because he thinks knees are just
physical things, that their cartilage degrades from use,
and not because they're listening to what we say. Yet,
why shouldn't our bodies respond to our thoughts? The
placebo effect is well enough known that every pharmaceutical trial must subtract its power from their figures.
If a belief can make us better, it can make us worse. And
if you say to yourself, 'I can't stand, I can't stand, I can't
stand', does that not, to the body, sound like a belief it
should obediently render into truth?*

*It was there in my training. The psychology of author-
ity. A doctor's prognosis can be fatal. A parent's too. The
child, told he is evil, will become so. Isn't this just what
happened to April? Programmed to feel worthless. Her
mother's loathing explained by the child to herself as 'I
must be loathsome', and this signal transmitted to the
boys who responded with such contempt. Does it make
it her fault she was raped? Or her mother's? No. For all
of this is unconscious. We transmit our damage to others
unconsciously. Repeat it to ourselves unconsciously. You
could no more condemn April for her rape than condemn
her for her nightmares. We are a species asleep. A race of
powerful magicians who turn ourselves and each other*

*into frogs and toads, unaware of our power, believing we
are victims of circumstance.*

There is pleasure in ordinary things: in the thoughtless sensu-
ousness of the washing up, which he prefers now to loading
the dishwasher, though Jules despairs. Doesn't understand
*why you would want to do that, when we have a perfectly good
dishwasher.* Another symptom of his new strangeness; another
reason not to trust. She doesn't understand how he could love
it, this thing she has labelled a *chore*. And he excuses her from
understanding; doesn't try to explain something she can't imagine. But he loves it at night, especially, when the window over the
sink shows a ghost of him blending into their corner of the forest,
gloved hands in warm water, fishing things from the depths.

*Language is how we create the reality we live in. What
we label a chore feels burdensome. Tom called me an
arsehole so many times that, in his presence, that was
all I could be. Words are spells we are casting. Bless you.
Damn you. We should be more careful. The language is
full of clues to its own power. Even the Bible is explicit
on this; the creative power of language. In the beginning
was the word.*

Then there are the long walks with Achilles that he, too, once
considered a chore. Now he welcomes the quiet hour that recon-
nects him with the forest. Since his experience of singularity,
he knows himself as a locus of consciousness moving through,
touched and caressed by, the vast web of energy that makes up
the solid trunks of trees, the shush of the leaves, the flit of birds,
the warmth and light of the sun, the scent of wild garlic. The
knowledge of that connection is his anchor; he walks with a
different awareness, knowing that what he touches, touches him
back. The routes are recognizable now, every tree as distinctive
as a human relative, and he no longer fears being lost. He walks

through the forest with confidence, Achilles joined to him by an invisible lead, while his phone vibrates a lonely dance across the kitchen table. Under the canopy of new leaves, his breath falls into the beat of his steps. His mind slips out of its harness and his body carries on without him, whether for minutes or miles. Only when he is required to talk does he seem to fall back into himself.

And such a moment is here, on the path just in front of him.

An older woman in a brown dirndl skirt and a hunting jacket is standing over something, poking it with a long stick. Her black Labrador is sniffing at it. She turns to Logan as he approaches.

What a thing, she says.

He comes closer, until he can see the *thing* himself: a large bird, most probably a heron, he thinks, and freshly dead. Its neck is at an unnatural angle and there is something lodged in its throat; the head of which is visible just inside the bird's open beak. A toad?

How do you imagine such a thing happens? the woman asks Logan, as though mistaking him for the local naturalist. *Just greed, do you think?*

The bird looks like a youngster, he says, falling into the role. *Inexperienced, perhaps. Achilles!*

The dog flinches and backs off.

Leave it, Lucy, says the woman, and the Labrador turns its curiosity to Achilles and makes a nose-to-tail circle.

What a thing, the woman says again. *I suppose you never know what you'll find when you're out walking.*

I suppose not, he says. He is joining in her game, though he doesn't know where it's going.

And then she turns very pale blue eyes upon him and says, *Do you believe in God?*

What a question! He looks at her and just for a moment a tiny sliver of paranoia rises up in him, an ancient fossil of a thought that her sharp gaze has chipped out of the little-boy part of him, and he shushes and soothes it, *No, no, she means no harm.*

Because he hasn't answered her, she says, *I don't any more. How can you, when you see something like this? It makes no sense. It's just so random, isn't it? Nature.*

I don't know, he says. *I didn't believe in God, but now—*

And all those children. All those children dying on the news. It doesn't make sense.

He doesn't know to what news she's referring. He has stayed away from news for a long time for the very reason that there are *always* children dying on the news. He looks at the bird, the toad a lump in its throat, like emotion it failed to express, something it was trying to say.

I just think we've got the wrong idea about it all.

No intelligent person can imagine there's a God, she says.

If you mean some grey-bearded chap on a cloud, I'm with you, he says. *But as a shorthand for something else—*

Like what? she says, and again her eyes are so sharp, so inquisitive, that for a second or two he's afraid to answer. He breathes; he listens to the peace of the forest.

I can imagine this as the answer to somebody's prayer, he says.

She laughs. *Who exactly?*

A fox with cubs.

With the stick, she turns the bird's head over on its loose neck, this way, that way, as though it is saying, *No, no, no.*

Foxes don't pray, she says.

He nods. *I bet they wish for things, though. Edible things especially.*

She laughs and throws the stick into the brambles, the better to cross her arms and confront him. *Okay. But if they did, and wishing was the same as praying, and prayers worked, wouldn't we have enormous birds with frogs in their throats falling out of the sky all the time?* Head cocked on one side. Achilles, sitting beside her, takes up the same pose.

You can look at it many ways, Logan says.

What ways?

Maybe it's for the fox. Maybe it's for a local man who is breeding prize koi and needs one less predator in order to fulfil a dream. Maybe it's for the suicidal toad. Maybe it's just for you and me to have this conversation.

Maybe it's meaningless, she says.

I don't think it's meaningless now that we've talked about it. Do you?

Yes, she says. *It makes no more sense to me now than it did before.* Offers him a smile she has forced together, constructed from its constituent parts: a Lego smile.

Later, he runs the conversation through his mind. There are no words for this that are comfortable. Say you believe in God to an atheist and you'll meet with scorn. Some people you speak to will mentally drop your IQ by fifty points. Some will instantly cease to respect you. There is a prevalent belief that faith is delusional, and if someone believes that, there is no persuading them otherwise. Their belief in No God is not, to their minds, a belief, but a rational fact. They have reached their conclusion by reason. He has reached his by breakdown. His position is logically indefensible. He can only say, *This is what I know. This is what I have experienced*. And that is not enough.

God itself is such a troubling word. He knows God is the ancient word for this thing he is experiencing, that it has become grafted to religion and stupidity and killing, but he could no more say he didn't believe in it than he could say he didn't believe in his own hand.

He looks at his hand, reaching now for the tin in which Jules keeps the tea bags. He abandons his forest conversation and slips into presence: the cool smoothness of the tin in his palm and, as he pulls it open, the satisfying release of the lid. He handles it tenderly, grateful for the tea bag whose genius simplicity does away with the business of pots and strainers, the irritation of a stray tea leaf in the throat. He feels the weight of the kettle and is grateful for the engineering of his elbow. Pours the freshly boiled water, marvelling at its clearness – how extraordinary, the complexity of human endeavours that have brought beings from tramping down to rivers and wells to a time when clean drinking water is available from numerous points in his home at the turn of a tap. He is in love with it all: with the taps, with the water, with the kettle, with the cup, with the tea bag, with the tea-bag tin, with the musical tinkling of the teaspoon; so grateful to be alive at a time of these miraculous simplicities; so joyful to be suddenly conscious they are miracles, instead of running them flat with habituated ingratitude. In love, yes, and this is how God feels when it runs through him; a powerful and inclusive love. He stands completely still, the better to feel the joy of it flowing through him. A clock is ticking. He turns around. It is the kitchen clock. More than eight months they have lived there and not once has he noticed its gentle, patient tick. Love, love, love.

Now he can hear Jules shifting out of the sitting room and coming towards the kitchen, as if called by name.

Oh, good, she says, sweeping past him, *you made me a tea. I was just going to make one myself.*

She takes the right-hand mug and is on her way back to the sitting room when he asks, *You want to sit with me for a bit? I thought we might have tea together.*

I'm in the middle of something, she says. She studies his face. *Okay, sure, why not?*

They sit side by side at the table, staring through the window at the garden. That way she can comment on what the birds are doing on the bird table. *Look at that one with the peanut! What a greedy thing.* Always helpful to fill any awkward gaps. He rests his hand on her forearm.

I saw a huge bird in the forest today. A heron, I think. It had choked on a toad or something.

Dead, you mean?

Yes. I bumped into a woman; I think she's from the village. Black Lab.

Evelyn? Runs the choir?

I don't know. We had a conversation about God.

Jules goes silent.

I didn't start it, he adds.

The clock ticks. Jules is fixed on the outside.

Oh my goodness, look at that blackbird, that's very naughty. Shoo, you horrible thing!

Revelations

God is now between them like a bolster. At night they spoon and he kisses her neck, mornings they do the crossword together and exchange puns. They are even feeding each other lines, risking jokes they've never been safe to make before.

But mention anything spiritual and the conversation ends. She is afraid he will turn into some terrifying evangelist; some impossible-to-respect Bible thumper or worse, some hands-on mystical healer, communing with the dead. She doesn't want to encourage him, or even acknowledge that their renewed intimacy, the kindnesses she is finally receiving, have been caused by his bizarre intimacy with the Divine.

Yet it is hard for Logan not to share with her this unfolding origami of knowledge. He hears her cursing herself, creating misery out of her own mouth. *I'm so worried about Tom. You know that girl, Mei Mei, finished with him? He's not replied to any of my messages. He's not answering his phone. What if something's happened to him? What if he's done something drastic?*

You must stop thinking about it, he says. *Worry isn't taking you anywhere good. You're using your imagination to create something you don't want.*

And she looks at him like he's a crazy person.

Worry doesn't make bad things happen, she says. *If anything, it stops bad things happening.*

That's superstition, Jules.

What's yours, then?

He can't answer her. But he knows now that words have power; even the silent words in people's heads.

I'm sure Tom's fine, he says.

If he's fine, why didn't he come home for Christmas? she says.

He didn't fancy the full house. Look, I'm sure he's okay, Jules. That drug he's on just makes him forgetful.

The dog – who these days sits habitually at Logan's feet, rather than at his wife's – looks from Logan to Jules with childlike eyes.

Jules says, *What if it makes him forget – I don't know – to look when he's crossing the road?*

Logan feels himself beginning to worry too.

It's really important you focus on what you want, not what you don't want, he says. *Imagine him safe and protected.*

Then I would be deluding myself, says Jules. *It's not an easy world out there, and Tom's particularly vulnerable. Anything could happen.*

How does one begin the conversation? Whatever these processes are – the processes by which our thoughts transmute into our realities – even he is comparing them to magic, and after the age of nine or ten, everyone knows that magic is only, and always, illusion. Jules is unable to hear him, so the page is his confidant. Logan must keep this secret: the rational view is the illusion. The view that humans are accidents of random mutation, victims of circumstance, meaningless collections of cells – that consciousness is an accidental side-effect of brain function – *that* is the laughable nonsense. He has known himself part of a connected whole and has felt through the interconnected parts of this larger self into limitlessness. This interconnectedness is behind everything. When it raises its head from time to time, it's dismissed as coincidence. But there is no coincidence. How can one express such a thing and not sound like a loon? What is the science?

He e-mails Gabrielle Salmon with this question. *What is the mechanism by which thoughts become reality?* Before the end of the day she responds. Something about collapsing quantum waves of probability into a particular outcome, but he doesn't get it. And in any case, it's just a theory; nobody knows.

He would love to knock the thought about with Jules, but he can't talk to her about it. There she is, sitting across from him, reading *The Life of Pi*, and he knows they are like the boy and the tiger in their separate vessels, tethered together – he on the sturdier boat, she on the raft, terrified he might leap across and eat her with his God talk, his physics nonsense. No ground for his feet for many miles, so he wants to stay close to her. If he so much as starts telling her that thoughts and words have consequences, she pushes them apart with a long pole. Because it matters so much, he is undone by enthusiasm; by the flaming of light in his eye, his voice's lift of volume and pitch as though he might burst into song. Enthuse, from the Greek *en theos*, in God. She sees in him the terrifying passion of an evangelist.

So he cannot tell her. And surely with his regular drifting into a meditative state, he is more waveform than particle, more connected, therefore more influential, than a woman who worries, collapsing better futures as she goes? He decides to believe his thoughts have more clout than Jules's. He decides to decide that Tom is perfectly safe.

Consequences continue to unfold. Day after day, wave after wave, come these revelations. His body receives them with goose-bumps, responds with tears. His distaste for organized religion remains, but lines of scripture drift to him unbidden across the decades, transmitted from Mrs Holinshead's lovely young lips to his middle-aged ears, no longer opaque and meaningless, but sonorous with truth. *Ask and it shall be given you. Seek, and ye shall find.* A perfect description of what would be so if one's focus collapsed waveforms into reality. And more words, words that have carried their meanings undetected for years; he hears them now. He writes them down:

> *I realized.*
> *I made real.*

He takes new routes through the forest. Out of the trees and across the open heaths where small groups of cattle and ponies cluster and wander. His dreams are lucid; he has developed the sense of touch inside them; can run his hand over the fur of a peach, finds spinach in his teeth with his tongue. He knows he is dreaming; controls his direction. In one dream he's flying through a tunnel of branches and catches some thorns in his thumb. The pain of each thorn, embedded, is sharp and real. He says in his dream, *This is an illusion, just as pain when I am awake is an illusion*, and plucks out the thorns, understanding each one is a slight, an insult, a negative word.

One night he dreams he is at the Life After Death group in Southwark. He is present and Simon Merriweather is there too, but Simon doesn't recognize him, as if he inhabits someone else's body. Simon is crying. He says he needs to know if there really is life after death, because he needs to know Sam is still with him, and that he will join her when he dies.

But how can there be life after death without God, and how can there be a God if He'd let Sam die like that when both of us were doing good things? Just doing good things?

And Logan is crying too. He puts his hand to his face and it's wet. He wants to hold Simon and hug him and tell him everything is okay, but he is afraid if he does that Simon will recognize him, and will think he is insincere. When he wakes up, he is still crying.

All through the day, he thinks about Simon. Simon's pattern of loss: first Jules, then Sam. Had the one led to the other? Was Logan the root cause, triggering a fear of loss that created the crash? Or had Simon suffered some deeper, earlier loss that he, Logan, had somehow hooked into, obediently donning the mask, playing the part, stealing the lover? And had he not taken the role, would some other man have picked up the costume and done just the same? Had he simply responded to the signal emitted, an agent of universal forces, ensuring that what the poor man most feared, and unconsciously focused upon, collapsed into its final, particular state?

However he cuts it, he feels responsible. Each of them played their own blind game, propelled by their history. But undoubtedly Logan had caused suffering. And from the dream – which was vividly real – the man was still suffering. Walking Achilles across the heathland that evening, Logan watches the growing dark and considers his part in this pattern of destruction. If Jules had stayed with Simon, would Sam have died? Surely Sam was collapsing her own lines of probability, and to some higher purpose that none could yet understand? Was Simon meant to reforge himself through this tragedy? To discover, like Logan, that he was not alone, but eternally entwined in a miraculous whole? Had his pilot died to guide him?

Are you looking after him, Sam? he whispers aloud. *Are you leading him somewhere? Will you guide him to peace?*

Four hundred yards away, a single car is crossing the common. It flashes its headlights.

Flash. Flash. Flash.

And then turns off, north and away. He stops dead and stares after it. It is an answer. It is nothing to do with the driver. It is Sam, telling him yes.

Headaches

Jules is seeing the doctor. Headaches. Right-eye, right-temple monsters that sting in the light, rattle with movement, bang if she stoops to pick up a sock. Or those that thunk like a baseball bat to the back of the skull. Her doctor, whom she has never seen, is off with stress. So she gets the locum, a man name of Dr O'Connell. He has a lanky sixth-former-ness about him: a volunteer for any useful expedition. He looks at her over the top of half-rim glasses that seem considerably too old for him.

Out of nowhere, she says. *What can it mean?*

The locum doesn't know. He is sure it's not a tumour. But how can he be sure? She isn't sure of anything.

When did they start? he asks.

When my husband— She doesn't know how to continue. What are the right words? She shuffles several combinations through her mind, wondering which one to pick. *When he started being weird*, she says, wondering immediately why that one.

In what way weird? asks the doctor, who is surely too young to be a doctor. Is it not ridiculous that she should find herself going, for advice, to someone who looks so much like he's doing his A levels? Shouldn't their roles be reversed?

Not himself, she says.

The locum shifts forward in his chair.

Could you be more specific?

For example, she says, and she's not sure why she's going to use this example, but she hasn't stopped thinking about it for three days, *for example, he thinks that he's responsible for the death of my ex-boyfriend's fiancée.*

And is he responsible?

No! He just thinks— She pauses. Is she really going to tell him this? It sounds ridiculous. But she has started now. *He thinks because he tempted me to leave Simon for him, he set up a pattern of loss that made the death of Simon's fiancée inevitable.* There. It sounds even more ridiculous now she's said it out loud.

We often feel guilty when a friend dies, says the locum, but she cuts his platitude off at the waist. *No!* she says. *She wasn't a friend. He didn't even know her. I mean, it's ridiculous, isn't it? And he keeps going on about words. That words have power. It's like. The way he explains it, it's like when you say to a toddler on a wall, be careful not to fall, and all they hear is the word fall, and they start thinking about it, and the next thing you know they do fall, because you put the thought in their head.*

Well, that's possible, says the locum.

Yes, but he makes it bigger than that. He says — you, for example, doctors — that you kill your patients with a prognosis. That telling someone they have six weeks to live is no different from witch-doctoring. It's a voodoo curse.

The locum stares at the wall, which is covered in information charts with pastel-coloured boxes. He is thinking of something.

I just think he's going a bit crazy, she says.

The locum comes back to her.

You think he needs to be assessed?

Oh no, no… but she is hesitant. Does he?

Does your husband suffer from depression?

Yes, she says, *he does. Well, he did. I mean, he's not seemed depressed the last couple of months, but before that, yes, very.*

Is he under medical supervision?

Oh no! she laughs. *He's terrified of doctors. He is one, you know. Not a GP. A psychologist.*

The locum is looking at her very carefully, as if he is palpating her with his eyes.

But recently, he's been better?

Better, as in not depressed, yet. But he's weird.

Manic?

No. I don't think so.

You don't think he'd come in?

He doesn't think there's anything wrong with him. Maybe there isn't anything wrong with him. This is going nowhere. And the doctor seems more interested in her husband than in her.

So what about my headaches? Can't you just give me something?
A pill or something?

Later, with another headache coming on despite her new
prescription – do these young doctors even know what they are
doing? – she finds her husband making dinner. She can't get
used to him making dinner. And he is so slow with it, as though
every ingredient needs special consideration, and isn't just an
onion, or a carrot, or a lump of tenderloin, but a personal friend.
Today he is – again! – making something vegetarian, not that
they have to convert, he says, but he feels more comfortable
handling foodstuffs *of a slower consciousness*. He has told her
that everything is conscious – everything! Even stones. I mean,
plants, fair enough, even she remembers reading somewhere
about plants hooked up to electrodes reacting violently to
someone who has just mowed the lawn. But stones? Perhaps
she should have mentioned that to the doctor.

She's so cross about eating pulses again, and so ratty with
the oncoming headache (which the doctor has hinted is probably
her husband's fault), that she decides to have it out with him.

You explain to me, she says with a large glass of Pinot in her
hand, *you explain to me how child abuse victims have created
their own reality. Are you telling me on some level they want
to be abused? That they are asking for it?*

He is stirring his damn pulses.

And what about all the people that died in that recent tsu-
nami? Men, women, children, how many, a hundred thousand?
You're telling me a hundred thousand people all created that
reality for themselves? You think they're all sitting there, thou-
sands of miles apart, unconsciously working together to create
a natural disaster?

These are different questions—

They're the same fucking question! Different scale of mag-
nitude, but the same question. The way you have it, all these
people created their own deaths. Even the children. Even the
babies, for God's sake.

He is pouring the slop into two wide-brimmed bowls from the best set, like it was cordon bleu or something.

When you see death only as a tragedy—

It is a fucking tragedy. You're telling me Flora's death wasn't a tragedy?

The words are out of her mouth before she can stop them. He pauses. The saucepan is frozen at an angle in his hand. Then the wooden spoon moves again, and the serving is complete.

We just don't have the full picture, he says, placing the pan on the trivet, bringing over the bowls. *Say we're all in a play, and Flora has a part for a while, but then she moves on to another production. I can't see her any more, and I miss her, but she's just somewhere else. And when I'm done in this play, I'll see her again.* He goes to the cupboard, gets out two glasses, fills them from the filter. *Maybe the tsunami is like – every theatre in Asia simultaneously closing down. But not everyone dies, do they, in these disasters. You get survivors. And you get people who would have been there, but something stopped them. We call these things miracles and flukes, but maybe they're just in line with what the person was creating for themselves, unconsciously.* He places one glass by her wine, puts his hand on her forehead and holds it there for a moment. *Your head is hurting*, he says. *You should have some water.*

She looks at him. She knows he is a good man. And however much she doesn't understand what has happened to him, and she doesn't agree with him, isn't this better than before?

You know you sound like a nutter, she says.

Only to you, he says.

Only to me and half the country.

Half the country can think what they like, he says. He raises his water to her wine. *And so can you.*

Ghost

The perfect place to find Jules's birthday gift, he decides, is in Chase and Munroe's. He drifts through the departments, waiting for something to speak to him. Inspiration, he has learned, is a quiet voice; the voice of his gut or his heart, not the voice of his mind. So he drifts and he fingers, he wanders and he feels, and maybe it's here, and maybe it isn't. He lingers at the pens, just for their beauty, but Jules doesn't write any more. Even her lists, she makes on her laptop or her phone. Flora was punished once, he remembers, for submitting a piece of school homework handwritten. She had made a toy theatre, decorated it beautifully, and accompanied it with boiled-down scripts, carefully inked in a cursive hand... and just as he thinks this, he smells – yes, it is – Devotion. Like she's there with him, sharing the memory.

Flora, he says in his head, *is that you? Are you there?* And the scent rallies stronger as if to say, *Yes, Dad, it's me*. He looks about. There is no one there. Truly no one; not one human neck that might sport such a scent. He supposes there must be a perfume department – there usually is – but when he locates it, there are just two assistants, quietly chatting. Yet the scent, the scent is still with him, drawing him down to the counter where Jules's scent of the moment – Eau d'Ouverture – dominates the display. No sign, that he can see, of Devotion. *This for Jules?* he asks in his head, and his gut whispers, *Yes*. His gut, or his daughter, it's hard to be sure.

Even outside, on the street, the sense of her lingers. He feels like she's on his right shoulder. Leaning on him, the way she did the last couple of years of her life, once or twice, when they went out for lunch, and wandered out tipsy, bantering, making some joke out of words or the locals. He feels her so strongly there are tears in his eyes, not of sadness, but joy. She is with him, with him! *I love you*, he says in his head, and he hears, *I love you, you bugger*.

¤   ¤   ¤

That night, he rehearses in silence, measures the moment, detects *not now*. Keeps to light conversation. But as they're undressing, he says to Jules, *She was with me today. Flora.*

Jules carries on like he's told her that Argos is having a sale.

What do you mean? she says, putting her tights in the laundry.

I was thinking about her, and smelt her scent, Devotion.

Someone else was wearing it, then. Undoing her blouse.

There was no one about.

Where were you?

In Chase and Munroe's.

What were you doing in Chase and Munroe's?

It's a secret.

Ah, birthday, she says, and smiles. *Not so much a secret.*

But the place was empty. No women around me at all.

You must have been gutted, she says. *No women, you say. I'm surprised that you stayed there two minutes.*

I've changed, he says.

No kidding. Undoing her bra. *So you smelt Devotion, you say. The perfume department?*

I was nowhere near, he says. *I went there, of course.*

And what did you see?

Not a soul.

No one spraying testers?

No one spraying testers, he says. *It was Flora, I swear.*

Swear all you like, she says, *you know it's a turn-on.*

You bugger, he says, and then stops. *Hey, that's what she called me!*

She spoke to you?

Yes. Well, it felt like it. Just in my head.

Ah, voices, she says, coming round to his side of the bed. *Hearing voices now, are we? Let me examine you…*

No! He laughs. I'm *the doctor.*

I'm *Spartacus. Lie on the bed.* She pushes him onto his back. Resistance is futile.

Alert

As the train snakes along the house-backs, Logan stares down into the gardens: narrow pockets of territory, crammed with garden furniture and an extraordinary number of circular, safety-netted trampolines, some of them so large (and the gardens so small) that they almost stretch fence to fence. Sweet, he thinks, how many parents are prepared to give up their only patch of sky to their children. This is family territory: other gardens are littered with the debris of bright plastic toys abandoned mid-play. One has an above-ground pool: a deep and greened-over well of last summer's memory, full of hope for the summer to come. The gardens testify to lives of hard work and minimal contemplation. But they have resulted, nonetheless, in a welcome dose of wildness in these densely populated folds of London's skirts. Only a handful are manicured: a handkerchief of emerald lawn, a tidy shed; symptoms of the daily what-next of retirement.

Logan's head floods with wonder. How, in the blink of the planet's eye, we humans have expanded from caves and dirt floors to this sprawl of sophisticated dwellings, plumbed into running water and electric light, connected to global consciousness by television and broadband. We are oblivious to our miraculous lives. This journey, which a few hundred years ago was a six-day walk, is now a ninety-minute sit, with tea (from the other side of the world!) brought to his table. And the woman behind him is complaining to her friend that the train was five minutes late. Logan's uncontrollable smile provokes the man serving his tea to say, *Won the lottery, sir?*

Something like that, he says. Because in that moment, Logan feels with conviction, anyone with a life has won the lottery.

As the train approaches the centre of London, the untidy gardens of suburbia give way to tall buildings. Logan gazes on the landscape he has moved through so blindly, for years, awed by the spectacle. The more beauty and wonder he looks for, the more he sees. A train leaving the capital passes at speed, and in the flickering gaps between carriages, he sees the steel-girder framework of a half-built block of apartments behind it, and between those gaps, reflected in the windows of the passing train, the fully built block on the opposite side of the track. A show, just for him: the magical illusion of a building in both states, built and unbuilt, a flickering X-ray of a building being shattered, through the gaps, to its bones.

At Waterloo, Logan realizes he has inadvertently arrived during the evening rush hour. Armed police stand in pairs at the barriers, their semi-automatics slung across vis-vested chests. He spots the *Metro* in someone's fist, shouting: *RED ALERT!* The headline is always fear or scandal. On fear days, like today, commuters are perceptibly tighter, grimmer, weaving more quickly through these major transport hubs where a sudden explosive death is more likely. Yet Logan feels blessed. There is no reason for him to die today. No atrocity will befall him. He breathes deeply and strolls through this crowded urban meadow, judging his pace and direction so as not to cause anyone annoyance, slowing or stepping aside where necessary, and observing the inward-focused faces of those who pass him with the deepest compassion. Everyone is so closed, as contained in the shells of themselves as if their clothes were their cars, and no one need consider that anyone around them also has dreams and disappointments, longings and losses.

The underground is heaving and yet Logan easily finds a seat and appreciates the soft pressure against the small of his back, the stability when the tube train rattles at speed. Here we are, he thinks, a quarter of a mile underground, efficiently slicing beneath the traffic of the capital with minimal effort when, not six generations ago, all most of us had to get about on were our feet. Half the passengers are standing. And yet, he notices, there are smiles. A man animated in conversation with a friend, full of joy in his telling. A young man reading, not his phone, but a book: a huge hardback with a black and yellow cover, which he must hold with both hands, and cannot look away from even though he must plant his feet for balance, because something in the words is amusing him so greatly. A woman smiling for no other reason than she has seen Logan's smile, and they are in this full carriage together. And though it is a Wednesday at half past five, and though they are pressed together like livestock, and though they are told that strangers may kill them, this singular carriage is full of delight and amusement, as though they are friends on their way to a party.

When he surfaces, the street lights are sparklers: emitting their light as glittering particles. It's something that happens when he's connected. It will be good to remain connected tomorrow, he thinks, as he enters the lobby of the Temple Court Hotel.

Court

Their court is number six, in the new building. So Justice is off to one side, and no steps to stand on and be photographed. But still, the Old Bailey weighs heavy, its presence momentous. The bewigged and begowned float about like a separate species. The car park sign is in gothic font.

April looks like someone's daughter. Tiny white hands on the rail; intense green eyes. She could be at college in a fascinating lecture; she is listening intently. She is learning. He can't imagine a murderer looking more innocent. She floats him half a smile and he wishes she hadn't. What if a juror noticed? People who've killed other people's children must never be seen to smile. He returns it all the same. She is his client, yes. She murdered a bus-load of students, certainly. But she and he know – as no one else in the room likely knows – that they are two parts of the same grand animal, as individual polyps are to coral; as grains of sand are to a beach. They are only playing at separation.

From his vantage point in the witness box, he scans the public gallery for April's mother. She is easy to find. She is wearing a headscarf, like his mother used to wear, to cover the hair loss of chemotherapy.

He stays very calm when he's cross-examined. Without fear, what comes out is the truth. The process, the sock; he explains them, and does not apologize. *To get her to talk was the object*, he says. *To understand*. For when someone or something has killed your child, isn't that what matters? If there's only one word you can speak, it is *Why*. So this is why. And does it make April insane?

The jury, in a couple of weeks, will agree it does not. Today, he will leave with an intuition of that verdict. What he hasn't foreseen remains sixteen months down the line – and the inkling of that will come fractionally ahead, in a dream. He will wake up and find it strange that he dreamed about April. That they kissed by a swimming pool. Not a kiss, but a snog. Inappropriate enough to make it memorable, cutting through the fog of his early-morning head until long after breakfast. Inappropriate enough that when he hears on the news that April has been stabbed – by a fellow inmate with a sharpened comb – he'll know, before he's told, that she bled to death. That she kissed him in his dream to say goodbye.

Achilles

There is a light wind coming in off the sea, sweeping across the field like a soft broom, removing the fugginess of the previous evening. Logan and Jules walk hand in hand, despite the narrowness of the path: Logan in front and Jules behind, but their fingers nevertheless entwined. It is, thinks Logan, as if he were towing a secret; for anyone standing directly in their path would see only him, yet behind him is his wife, whose devotion has been rewarded. Achilles runs ahead of them, scouting. Ruffled by the wind, she breaks into small barks of excitement. She finds a stone, snuffling it up from the mud, and drops it hopefully at Logan's feet. He throws it a few yards ahead of them on the path, and, in only two seconds, the dog is back blocking him. The second time, he lobs it across the deep drainage ditch that runs along the edge of the field. Achilles leaps joyfully into the gully and bounds through water which comes up to her belly, threading through reeds and resurfacing some yards ahead of them with the stone. Logan bends down and throws it again, ker-sploosh. Again, Achilles comes back with it, wet and wagging. Once more. The sploosh of the stone is followed by a larger splash as the spaniel vanishes over the edge of the field. When the dog emerges, her muzzle is completely black with mud.

You foolish creature, says Jules.

The dog's an idiot, says Logan.

Devoted, says Jules.

To a stone, he replies. *I rest my case.*

To you, Jules laughs. *You threw it, and she didn't want to let you down.*

She just likes mud, says Logan. *Especially bad-smelling mud. Dogs like nothing more than smelling bad.*

Bad to you, delicious to her, says Jules.

It was true enough. He grips his wife's hand and kisses her.

I love that we have a stupid dog, he says. *One needs to feel superior to something.*

The path bends around to the left, and soon enough they are crossing the quiet road and are on the beach.

We'll have to get her in the water, says Jules, picking up a large pebble. *She might go for this.* She lobs the stone into the sea, but the dog isn't as foolish as all that. The waves are up, and she's wary of the breakers.

They separate for beachcombing. Jules finds a spray of seaweed, not unlike the rag-rope toys one buys at pet shops. Achilles is there in an instant: bark, bark. But refuses to follow it into the waves. Logan finds a small stalk of cow parsley, but it is so light that, as he throws it, the wind grabs the thing and blows it further up the beach.

Here! says Jules, dragging a long piece of newish-looking wood from some abandoned project.

Perfect, says Logan. As soon as he lifts it into the air, the dog is all wag and bark and jump. Big wood, big wood. As Jules had done before, but without the commentary, Logan wobbles it over the dog's head, pretends to throw it twice, before lobbing it into the waves. Achilles follows without a thought, leaping through the surf like a launching battle craft until she reaches the smoother water beyond the breakers. She snatches it and turns around slowly, her tail an ineffective rudder. Her face is still black all the way to her eyes.

She's not ducking her face, giggles Jules.

If there was something that would sink a bit, says Logan. *Try again!*

And so they do, cracking up at each failure, the sun ducking in and out of clouds. The two of them, and the dog between them, are enough to feel like a family. It is Logan, Jules and Achilles, the three of them, and nothing is wrong.

Again and again, Logan lobs the half-plank into the water. Like an athlete, he thinks, in the most primitive Olympics, before the hammer and the javelin, when there was only whatever hunk of wood a person could find. If the prize is a clean dog, he will never reach the podium. The dog is grinning and uncleanable. It is the dog, trotting back out of the waves time and again with the same black nose, that has Jules bent double with laughter.

He sees once more how beautiful she is. Not only outwardly, but in her age-worn love for him; love softened like old wood, so you're no longer likely to catch a splinter in your finger when you touch it. A love that has developed a patina through use and usefulness, a depth through care and polishing, possessing the warmth of something familiar and real. A love that is still there when you wake up in the morning, and solid enough for you to rest your weight on, knowing it will not collapse or melt away. She knows him as intimately as one knows the route from bedroom to bathroom; she can navigate him even in the dark. She has stood by him, remained faithful, even when he has tested her to both of their limits. He feels such a surge of love for her that he has to march across the pebbles, hold her face between his hands and kiss her as though they are brand-new lovers.

Let's give up, she says quietly, when he has released her. *With the dog!* she adds when she sees his face. *We'll hose her down at Warbler's.*

They walk along the shore for a while, Jules's arm linked through his elbow. She steers them into the copse that leads back to the Ilex grove and the sound of the breakers behind them begins to fade.

It was kind of you to do the dishes first thing, he says.

No problem, she says. *It's nicer to get up in the morning and not have to face the crap from last night.*

But I'm still here, he says.

Aw, don't speak of yourself that way, she says. *You're my crap from ten years ago.*

He jabs her in the ribs.

Wait! she tells Achilles, and the dog vibrates at the kerb.

That's a bit harsh, he says.

Come on, you fed me the line. Over!

Sun is flickering through the silver birch trees. Straggling bluebells have pushed through the leaf mould. There's a smell of wild garlic in the air.

You think we could invite Gabrielle Salmon for the week-end? he asks.

What weekend?

Any weekend. She's an interesting person. I think you might like her.

She got a husband or boyfriend or something?

No idea. I'll ask.

Jules is kicking the leaves.

You didn't ever—

No! God, no.

His wife is amused.

God, no? Come on, she's hardly hideous.

No, he says, *but—*

JESUS!

Jules smacks her right hand to her heart as if to make sure she's still there, she's still breathing. The car has already vanished.

Did you see that coming? I didn't see that coming. She drops to her knees to pet the dog. *God, I can't get used to silent cars. It's unnatural.*

Nothing bad was going to happen, says Logan. *I think we're too happy to create an accident.*

And in that moment, the realization falls on him. Flora's accident.

He can already name the ingredients. The terrible words that spilt from his wine-fuelled mouth. Her shock that she arose not from love, but from error. His monumental fear that he would lose her. The story about herself she couldn't live with.

Daddy's girl. What a dutiful daughter she was. He told her she was an accident and she became one.

Jules is saying something about *voodoo* and *naturally, when one is a powerful shaman*, but she sees his eyes and trails off.

Fin, are you okay?

He cannot see. Her face and the dog are blurring. There are only two words in his mouth.

Oh God.

EPILOGUE

Opening

Dusk is falling. Inside the building, lights are coming on automatically in occupied rooms. As Logan walks through the Alterman complex, tonguing the twinge of his wisdom tooth, the corridors light up ahead of his footsteps like a pinball's high-score totalizer. Whether he is illuminating them, or they him, he isn't sure. Nor is he sure where he might walk that would be roomy enough to lay out his thinking; away from Dr Salmon it feels tangled and chaotic. Preoccupied with unravelling pros from cons, he allows his unconscious mind to dictate his direction at junctions: left or right, straight on or turn. Now, directly in his path, a wall of glass, a glass door. Behind the glass is darkness: an internal oasis of shadow he can only make out dimly in the failing light. A ghostly reflection: half him, half darkness, one overlaying the other.

Pass through the glass or let himself be deflected? To go forward, he will have to walk through himself; push himself out of the way and enter the darkness. It will surely be cold. And who knows what's in there?

To his right, a corridor that seems to have life at the end of it: the bright illuminations of an eatery, people murmuring anonymous conversation. But he wants to be alone.

This isn't the choice he needs to make. It doesn't matter either way.

ACKNOWLEDGEMENTS

The Alterman Centre is a fictional conflation of the Institute of Noetic Sciences (noetic.org) and the Sackler Centre for Consciousness Science (sussex.ac.uk/sackler). The consequences of daily EFT ('that tapping bollocks') inspired Salmon's fictional 'process'. The book Logan reads is *Science and the Near-Death Experience: How Consciousness Survives Death* by Chris Carter. Credit for the radio analogy must go to Bruce Lipton, author of *The Biology of Belief*. 'Then a miracle occurs' is a cartoon by Sidney Harris. 'A fascinating study of baseball players' refers to Abel, E. L., & Kruger, M. L. (2010), 'Smile intensity in photographs predicts longevity', *Psychological Science*, 21, 542-544.

Seeing no reason why the dead shouldn't be acknowledged along with the living, my thanks are due first to Professor John Maynard-Smith, who ignited my lifelong passion for the biological sciences and planted some of the questions which provoked this novel. I am deeply grateful for the underpinning encouragement of my agent Rupert Heath, the sensitive editing of Ros Porter and Tamsin Shelton, and the enthusiastic support of everyone at Oneworld. Thanks are due to David Hill for the ovation and to Catherine Smith for front-line support. But the deepest gratitude is due to my husband Paul, who has made all this possible, and who loved this book from the start.